EAGLE

ASCENDING

DAN WHITFIELD

Relax. Read. Repeat.

EAGLE ASCENDING
By Dan Whitfield
Published by TouchPoint Press
Brookland, AR 72417
www.touchpointpress.com

ISBN-13: 978-1-952816-51-2

Editor: Kimberly Coghlan
Cover Design: David Ter-Avanesyan, Ter33Design

Connect with Dan Whitfield

@danwhitfield82 @DanJWhitfield @danjw82

First Edition

Printed in the United States of America.

To Michael and Jennifer Whitfield, who started it all.

IT'S HARD TO CONCENTRATE when the guy next to you is playing with a gun.

Sighing, Joe Krueger turned to his partner, his eyes narrowing in frustration. "You gotta do that, Sammy?" he asked.

"Relax," Sam O'Brian replied. "Pressure getting to you, honey? You want me to turn on the AC, hmmm?" O'Brian chuckled to himself as he settled back into the seat of his Chevy. A former boxer, he was the tallest detective in New York City, almost seven feet, and Krueger was usually happy to partner with him, except when he got the fidgets on a stakeout—especially on a stakeout so fraught with risk.

O'Brian holstered his Sig Sauer and ran his fingers through his curly brown locks. "It's been two hours," he said, thumbing the smart, sunlit sidewalk opposite. "I think the buyer got cold feet."

Krueger shook his head. Across the street, Krueger saw the man whose photo he had been staring at for the last eight months, during long winter nights and lonely weekends, trying desperately to get inside his head.

"It's going down," Krueger said. "Transit Police identified Lucas using the subway this morning. He only comes into the city if it's for a big score."

Grimacing, Krueger opened the window, closing his eyes as the faint breeze kissed his troubled brow. The smell of hotdogs wafted in the air.

As he tried to keep his breathing even, Krueger opened his eyes and looked across the street once more. Past the crowds, shaded by the red awning of Gimbels department store, he saw the man he eagerly wanted to see in handcuffs: Marty Lucas, a hood from upstate who had started selling his meth on the streets of Krueger's hometown.

Dressed in a blue blazer and spectacles, Lucas was the kind of guy you'd pass a thousand times in the city and never look back. But the poison he was selling had already killed three people.

Possessed with a low cunning to match his short stature, Lucas had gotten his homebrew meth onto the streets last year, and powerful people were demanding that Krueger personally put a stop to it.

Of course, dime store meth dealers like Lucas rarely won the attention of the Narcotics Division of the Organized Crime Control Bureau, but that was before the daughter of the Mayor's golfing buddy had been found strung out on Lucas' poison.

Priorities had shifted soon after, and Krueger's captain, Mac Hassler, had ordered him to shut down Lucas' operation.

The radio inside O'Brian's car crackled into life.

"Krueger, this is Lieutenant Holloway, you copy?"

"I copy, Lieutenant," Krueger replied. Holloway and his SWAT team were hidden in the plain white van idling behind the Chevy.

"Still no sign of the buyer?"

"Negative," Krueger replied, growing more frustrated. The radio hissed, and Krueger imagined Holloway and his boys at the end of the line, cramped in the dark, sweating in their Kevlar, as the sunshine beat down on the asphalt.

"They want the order to stand down," O'Brian said.

"I know!" Krueger barked in response.

Krueger got the breakthrough on the case five weeks ago. Patrols in the Bronx, Queens, and Brooklyn hadn't turned up a thing. The low-level dealers knew nothing either.

But then came the DeGroot robbery. Two professionals had

busted into a Manhattan jewelry store in the early morning and made off with several hundred thousand dollars' worth of stones. Reviewing the tape from the day of the robbery, one of Krueger's colleagues had spotted Lucas loitering outside the store and handing over odd-looking packages to passersby in exchange for cash.

Lucas hadn't been part of the robbery, but the video was all Krueger needed to break the case open. Krueger and O'Brian began checking the security footage from similar high-end retailers, and it proved how the pale-faced amateur from Oswego had outsmarted the police for over a year.

Lucas didn't risk selling his wares in dark alleys late at night, like so many of the toughs hawking drugs. He was doing it on the busiest, most exclusive streets of the city, dressed like a white-collar worker. Heck, he'd even instructed his buyers to come dressed like the cream of New York's society.

Cops rarely bothered men dressed in suspenders for fear they were donors to the Mayor's election campaign.

"Here we go," O'Brian said, his voice cut to a whisper, "this looks like it." The Irishman's eyes grew hard, and he pointed to a thin man shuffling along the street. He wore a silver double-breasted suit, but the evil red blotches on his skin revealed the truth: he wasn't a stockbroker; he was an addict.

"Stand ready," Krueger spoke into the radio, as a bead of sweat rolled down his flushed cheeks. He was parked on Madison Avenue, and dozens of tourists strolled past Lucas as he waited for the buyer, oblivious to the firepower in the white van parked on the opposite side of the street.

Having cracked Lucas' distribution route, the next challenge had swiftly confronted Krueger: how to apprehend him without harming civilians. Lucas and his sellers always used carefully selected pick-up points, places that were very popular with tourists. Krueger knew that if anyone was hurt, particularly anyone important, Hassler wouldn't hesitate to heap all the blame on his shoulders.

"We're ready to roll," Holloway replied, in a high, strained voice, which proved to Krueger that he was becoming too excited for the job.

"Be careful," Krueger said icily. "You don't fire unless they pose a clear threat."

"We got this!" Holloway yelled, angered by the implication he didn't know what he was doing.

The addict stumbled onward, following the orders he'd received from Lucas. He paused outside a clothing boutique, admiring the expensively-tailored suits in the window. Finally, he moved on, as if enjoying a casual stroll, until he faced Lucas.

The addict slowly handed the short dealer a bundle of cash wrapped in paper.

Lucas, in turn, picked up his leather briefcase from the sidewalk and handed it to the buyer. It was all the proof Krueger needed and the signal for the bust to start.

"Go! Go! Go!" he shouted into the radio, before he and O'Brian leapt out of the car. Together, they ran onto the street, heedless of the oncoming traffic, laser-focused on the drug pusher in front of them.

Behind him, Krueger heard the heavy thud of boots, as Holloway's SWAT team disgorged onto the street and spread out, ready to foil Lucas' escape.

A female shopper, admiring her purchase from Gimbels, gave a cry of surprise when she saw the black-clad men approaching the store, and the sound alerted Lucas to the danger he faced. He'd been in the Coast Guard before turning to drugs and was as lithe as a sprinter. Ignoring the stupefied addict in front of him, Lucas picked up the case and ran northwards, toward Grand Central Station, where the crowds of summer tourists provided ample chance to escape.

Lucas was quick, but Krueger was quicker. Three tours in Afghanistan and two more in Iraq had left him with the body of a well-drilled athlete, and he mounted the curb with ease, breezing past the stunned pedestrians. Holloway and the SWAT team, weighed down by Kevlar, helmets, and AR-15 rifles, couldn't hope to match the detective's speed, and instead pounced on the dazed addict.

Drawing huge gulps of air, Krueger surged forward. Lucas faltered in front of him, his lungs starting to burn, his arms flying in panic and desperation. From the corner of his eye, Krueger saw O'Brian beside him, but his pace was beginning to slacken. Krueger had expected as much. The Irishman was handy with his fists but too big for running.

Lucas darted past the wide-eyed shoppers, his blazer flapping wildly, ignoring their curses and cries. He blundered onto 41st Street, shouldering past a young family and the taxi they were hailing. Behind him, Krueger grew closer. Timing his breathing, feeling the steady weight of the Sig Sauer in his hand, Krueger saw glimpses into the future: Lucas cuffed and sweaty in the back of an NYPD Crown Victoria, while O'Brian shook his hand, promising him that the crook would soon be headed to Riker's Island.

But then the sound of a freakish explosion tore across the New York sky, and it shattered Krueger's reverie along with the windows of Gimbels.

The force of the blast was enough to lift Krueger off of his feet and slam him into the side of a parked taxi. The wind was wrenched from his lungs, and he crumpled to the ground, defeated by the brutal force of the shockwave. In front of him, it appeared as if the whole of 41st was being eaten by the flame and ash of Hell itself.

The sound subsided, and for a precious moment, an unnatural silence fell over the street, before being replaced by a cacophony of screams.

Krueger held out a feeble hand and grabbed the cab's broken side mirror. He used it to pull himself up onto unsteady legs in time to see plumes of smoke, black and acrid, rising swiftly into the air.

Krueger closed his eyes. The blast had taken him back in time, back to a dark time he'd tried hard to forget. He was no longer in New York, with its sweaty August haze. He was in Fallujah once more—that hellscape of torn buildings, bodies, and hopes.

Krueger knew what the blast meant: he would soon draw his M4 rifle and begin dealing death to those fanatics who'd threatened his platoon. He'd done it many times before.

But then Krueger opened his eyes, and the city in crisis was not a desert rat-hole; it was *his* city, the best city, and it needed him.

The blast had come from the opposite side of 41st Street. The plain grey building that had stood there moments before was now a smoking ruin.

Lucas, hidden amongst the other bodies flung to the street by the blast, rose and stood with his limbs trembling. His blazer had been reduced to rags, which smoked and flapped at his sides. No longer the target of the cops behind him, Lucas sped away, his escape hidden by the crowds which raced from the explosion.

Krueger tried to shake the ringing from his wounded ears. Blood ran from his head, painting a red ribbon down the side of his face.

"Museum's hit!" Holloway shouted over the radio, which soon erupted in a tinny chorus of yelled orders and exclamations. "Corner of Madison and 41st!" The lieutenant and his company of SWAT soon caught up to Krueger, grim and eager to help.

"Get your team down there," Krueger ordered, pointing toward the blast site in front of him. He was summoning the courage that had seen him graduate both the Army Ranger School and the New York Police Academy with distinction. "O'Brian and I will meet you there; we'll head through Gimbels and rendezvous at the store's exit on 41st."

Holloway nodded, understanding Krueger's grim logic. Terrorists often planted secondary bombs timed to explode a few minutes after the first, with the hope of killing first responders the moment they arrived. By taking two different routes to the explosion, Krueger and his team reduced the odds that they'd all be hit by a second blast.

Holloway led his men forward, leaving Krueger and his partner to force themselves through the swelling crowds of shoppers emptying onto the streets. Trembling, tattered, and grey, they fled from the scene, fear swelling in their eyes. They looked like the victims of other terror attacks, which had struck the Big Apple too many times, and hurt too many people. Krueger felt anger kindle in his heart.

Gimbels was filled with an oily, hazy smoke, and Krueger's lungs soon raged in protest. Coughing, he pulled a wad of tissues from his back pocket and held them to his mouth. O'Brian yanked a pricey sequined shirt from its hanger and covered his face.

The screams in the store were terrifying, but Krueger knew they were the sounds of the shocked, not the sounds of the sick or dying. He learned the difference long ago. Darting through the smoke, patrons and staff headed to the doors that Krueger had just used, desperate to escape from whatever evil had struck. Outside, the wail of police sirens rose in the air, but the sound provided small comfort to the men and women whose lives had just been irrevocably altered.

Running past once-clean rails of expensive clothing, Krueger and O'Brian soon arrived at the 41st Street entrance to Gimbels. The doors were smoldering ruins, metal deformities lying on the ground next to the broken glass and debris from the road outside.

Surveying the scene, Krueger knew it must have been an enormous blast. Smoke obscured the worst of the damage opposite, but the blood splattered like paint on the sidewalk gave enough of a hint of the horrors inside. Krueger wiped tears from his eyes, brought on by the smoke, and as he did so, the first fire truck bounded into view. The guys inside were already on the sidewalk before the vehicle had come to a stop.

Krueger and O'Brian slowly descended the broken steps of Gimbels onto 41st Street. Another fire truck and an ambulance pulled up, as uniformed officers began pulling the wailing survivors from the carnage. Clenching his massive jaw, Krueger dismissed his own injuries, nodded to O'Brian, and plunged into the chaos before him. He was one of New York's best cops, and he was going to prove it. The people he'd sworn to protect were hurting and were depending on him.

"Jesus," one paramedic said to another as they pulled a gurney from their ambulance. "What is this place? Apartment building?"

"Nah," replied his partner. "This is some Jewish Museum. Well, it *was* a museum."

IT WAS ONE WEEK since the bombing, and New York was still reeling.

Although no terrorist group, foreign or domestic, had admitted responsibility for the blast, the FBI had quickly discovered that a nitromethane bomb had been responsible for the devastation. Their experts, working alongside agents from the ATF, had combed the blast site and discovered the remnants of a detonator inside the ground floor restrooms along with a can containing nitromethane residue. ATF agents were openly theorizing that tovex had been used too, an explosive that Krueger knew was safer to manufacture and less toxic than dynamite. Because of that, it was popular in mines, oil wells, and quarries across the country, and thus easier to steal. Even more troubling for the investigators was that fact it was made in dozens of factories across the globe, from Canada to Croatia.

"This looks just like the Oklahoma City bombing," O'Brian had said through gritted teeth when he discovered what the analysis proved.

Ninety-six people had died in the explosion, which had utterly destroyed the Meyer Cultural Center, and another three were still in intensive care. The media ran stories about the victims, blaring their names and their catastrophic injuries from every TV station in the country. They told of the dead security guard, a single mother from Brooklyn, whose youngest daughter was sick with kidney failure. They told of a toddler who lost a leg and a missing janitor whose fiancé had recently arrived from El Salvador in anticipation of their wedding.

The stories never stopped. There was always some new heartbreak, some new outrage.

And Krueger saw it all. He didn't turn away from the bloody carnage or try to close his mind to the enormity of the attack. Long tours in Iraq and other warzones had taught him that you needed to keep your eyes open to catch the killers, even if it meant looking at horror that would turn lesser men insane. It had to be done.

But looking at the obscenity that was the bombing came at a steep price for the forty-one-year-old. Krueger found himself having three drinks at night instead of his usual one. He'd taken up smoking again too, an addiction he'd quit the same time as his marriage.

There was no room for Krueger on the investigation, however. NYPD's Intelligence Division & Counter-Terrorism Bureau was working alongside the suits from Washington law enforcement agencies, who'd arrived armed with a casual disregard for the New York cops whose resources they were commandeering. The NSA had also descended on New York too, and their agents came with angry orders from the President still ringing in their ears.

"You did choose Narcotics," Krueger said to himself one morning, seated at his desk as he watched a fresh collection of officers, led by a man wearing a navy FBI jacket, depart for the FBI Field Office in Federal Plaza, where the investigation was being overseen. And he was right; years spent in the Middle East had left Krueger sick of the bombs, the rage, and the incessant hatred of America. He figured busting drug dealers was preferable to fighting demented totalitarians.

Krueger and the Narcotics team shared a cavernous, wooden-beamed bullpen on the seventh floor of Police HQ, and the sunshine was already flooding through the windows onto the scuffed vinyl flooring. On the far side of the room was Mac Hassler's office, and as the officers left he came tumbling out while fixing the collar of his grubby shirt.

The captain was functioning thanks only to coffee and brightly-colored energy drinks. He stumbled up to the newcomers and offered his hand. He was a big ball of a man, all belly and shoulders, but in his eyes there was a keen, grasping intelligence.

"Good luck guys," Hassler said, in a voice that was as ingratiating as it was insincere.

Knowing he'd never be called on to join the team tasked with finding the killers, Krueger turned to his computer and grimaced at the sight. Marty Lucas, free and grinning, haunted the screen with his pale, pinched face.

"He's gone, brother," Krueger said, "get used to it." Krueger nodded in grim certainty. Lucas would never show his face again in New York, not since he now knew how closely he was being watched. A trip upstate might shake a few leads free, but Lucas had friends there, and he was smart enough to stay hidden.

Hassler watched the officers depart. As head of the Narcotics division, he would not be part of the investigative team either, but that didn't mean Hassler wasn't trying to make friends with the powerful strangers arriving in the city. "So still no leads?" he asked the man wearing the FBI jacket.

The man shook his head as he walked past Krueger. "Lotta chatter online," he replied absently. "Folks in the Middle East celebrating. They cheer when Americans die and when Jews die, so when *American Jews* die . . . well, you can imagine how they get."

"Damned foreigners," Hassler muttered.

"And tovex is mass produced in Pakistan," the man said, ignoring the remark. "From there it would be easy to get it into the hands of any assortment of scum-bags, provided you had the cash for bribes and transport."

Hassler nodded, feigning understanding. A traffic cop who'd taken a job in internal affairs before grabbing a promotion at Police Plaza, he'd never taken a trip outside the country in his life. His knowledge of the outside world came exclusively from talk radio and tabloids. "I see," Hassler replied, trying to sound more important than he was.

Suddenly, a young man in a vest and impeccably knotted tie came running from the corridor and nearly crashed into Hassler and the FBI agent. He was breathless.

The agent grabbed hold of his shoulder. "Calm down, son," he said. "What you got?"

The young man whispered into his ear. The bullpen fell silent. They could see in the boy's face that he had important news about the only case any of them gave a damn about any more.

"Get me the radio!" yelled the FBI agent, as his calm, indifferent exterior shattered.

Hassler nodded and led the team to the Comms room nearest the bullpen. Krueger could smell his sweat as they passed.

Sam O'Brian crossed Hassler as he barged into the bullpen. He wore an expression of fury beneath his curls.

"What's up?" Krueger yelled to his partner over the commotion. O'Brian looked down and noticed the deep lines under Krueger's slate-grey eyes. His dark hair was mussed and the stubble on his unnaturally large jaw was a least a week old.

"They've got a suspect," O'Brian replied, finally. "Bastard's image is being handed out now."

Hearing this, several other cops bolted from their desks and headed toward the Comms room.

But O'Brian grabbed Krueger's lapel and stopped him from following. "I never trusted the wisdom of crowds," he said, before shoving a large piece of greasy fax paper into Krueger's unsure hands. "I got a heads up from a buddy of mine over at the Feds' building. He just sent over the image they got. Wanna see the sicko who did this?"

Joe Krueger looked down at the photo O'Brian had put into his hands, and the moment he did so, his mouth fell open in confusion and black despair.

The shot was taken from a convenience store security camera. It was grainy, and the ink had smudged. But still Krueger recognized the piercing eyes, the aquiline nose, and the aristocratic smirk.

"Oh, God," he muttered in a voice that did not sound like his own.

O'Brian could see the horror in his partner's eyes, and he protectively brought a huge hand to his shoulder. "You know this guy?" he asked.

Krueger's guts turned to ice as he saw, disbelieving, the face of the man who had done more to shape his life than any other—the man who'd haunted his dreams and the dark corners of his waking thoughts.

"Yes," Krueger said. "It's my dead grandfather."

2

"AW, HELL! WOULD YOU move, buddy?" Krueger yelled from behind the wheel.

Slamming his foot on the accelerator, he threaded his Ford Maverick Grabber past the snarl of idle traffic around 62nd Street and headed to his apartment in Queens. O'Brian was in the passenger seat, worried both about his partner's driving and his state of mind.

"Take it easy, pal," he whispered, but Krueger shook his head in defiance. His stomach was turning summersaults as his mind tried to comprehend the incomprehensible.

The moment Krueger had seen the picture of his dead grandfather, he'd run toward the parking lot beneath police HQ with O'Brian dashing behind him, bewildered. Five minutes later, they were speeding through busy New York streets.

"It can't be," Krueger said. His knuckles were white as they gripped the cracked leather steering wheel.

The Grabber was a wreck, but with half his paycheck going to the ex and her stockbroker boyfriend, it was all he could afford. Krueger ignored the belching and protesting coming from the car's engine, sped over the Throgs Neck Bridge, and descended into the warren of busy streets around Murray Hill, which he now called home.

Krueger left the car idling in the street and ran into his apartment building, a Victorian red-brick mansion. O'Brian whistled as he saw the place, wondering how Krueger could afford such a nice apartment. He didn't know that the owner had given Krueger a steep discount on the rent as thanks for busting his daughter's abusive boyfriend.

Once inside, Krueger didn't stop to call the elevator. He launched himself up five flights of stairs, ignoring O'Brian's cursing and wheezing behind him. Still clutching the photo O'Brian had given him at Police Plaza, Krueger fought through the burn that started to kindle in his legs as his sprinted up the stairs. Tired limbs didn't matter; all that mattered was the picture of his grandfather—the picture beneath his bed that would prove Krueger was wrong—that he was not going crazy.

Krueger shouldered his door open, pushed past the shabby furniture, and dived under the bed, ignoring the glass that had held last night's whiskey as it smashed on the floor. Swatting aside the assorted mementos of his service as a Ranger, he grabbed a battered manila folder. Krueger pulled it into the sunlight just as O'Brian emerged, sweating, in the doorway.

"This is all I have on my grandfather," Krueger said, opening the folder with fear and apprehension. Behind him, O'Brian could see yellowed newspaper clippings within, mostly written in German.

And then they saw it together—a large grainy photo, crumpled and blurry. But the face of the man in the picture was easily recognizable. His eyes were light blue. His nose was aquiline. His grey hair was slicked back. And, according to the investigators at the FBI, he was responsible for the Meyer Center bombing.

Krueger placed the image O'Brian had given him next to the older photograph for comparison. "Oh God," O'Brian said as he saw them lying together, wondering if God, indeed, heard him.

"This is General Wolfgang Andreas Krueger," Krueger said wearily. "General of the Third Reich, recipient of two Iron Crosses, and my late grandfather."

"You gotta be kidding me!" O'Brian exclaimed.

"I wish," Krueger replied, sitting heavily on his bed and speaking slowly. "This guy saw action across Europe during the war. Froze his butt off at Stalingrad. Hitler showered him with medals for that. He then had him lead a Panzer Army against our boys during the Battle of the Bulge. But after the attack failed, German resistance crumbled and grandpa here put his wife and daughter—my mom—on a Danish ship headed to neutral Sweden. Three months later they arrived in New York and never looked back."

"How . . . how do you know?" O'Brian asked, feeling as though he were intruding on a man's grief.

"Mom told me the story right before I headed to college. Told me everything. Most kids grow up seeing their grandparents as old cuddly retirees. Me? I saw my grandfather as the monster he was."

"And now he's here, in New York?"

"He can't be!" Krueger yelled, rising from the bed and grabbing his pack of smokes. "He died of cancer in a German sanitarium in the early 50s! Look here!" Krueger turned to the back of the folder and picked up the last clipping. It was written in English and the headline read: *Wolfgang Krueger, German who terrorized US forces at the Bulge, dies aged 63.*

The report was dated November 3rd, 1951.

Krueger suddenly realized that his mouth had gone dry. The photographs in front of him, the one taken seven days ago and the one taken in the middle of the last century, showed exactly the same man.

"Science," O'Brian mumbled.

"What?" Krueger asked, crushing his smoke and grabbing another.

"Science," O'Brian repeated, as if it were a holy incantation to ward off ghosts lurking behind him. "There's obviously an explanation. Maybe a forgotten member of the family . . . maybe a doppelganger."

Krueger snorted with derision.

"Come on, man!" O'Brian yelled, grabbing Krueger roughly by the shoulder. "We're all exhausted after what happened last week. But think clearly! A man who died sixty-six years ago can't be walking the streets of New York."

Suddenly a light flickered behind O'Brian's eyes. An idea was kindling.

"Grab your stuff, Joey," O'Brian said. He used the name *Joey* whenever he felt his young partner needed some fatherly mentoring. "I know a guy who knows a guy."

"SO YOU'RE GEOFF DUBCHEK'S kid!" O'Brian bellowed, as he enveloped the timid man's dainty hand with both of his bear paws.

"I sure am," he replied, hesitantly. "My name's Colin."

"Well, we sure are pleased to meet you," O'Brian said. He and Krueger stood in the entrance to the FBI Field Office in Manhattan, O'Brian having insisted on driving Krueger's Grabber while his partner wrestled with his roiling confusion.

"Your old man sure was one of the best forensics guys I ever worked with," O'Brian said, as if we were sharing drunken remembrances in a bar, when in fact he was talking to a man he had only the flimsiest relationship with. He'd asked the receptionist to call Colin down.

"And now you've gone into police work yourself! Good for you, kiddo!"

"Actually, I work for the FBI," Colin said stiffly.

"Hell, we're all on the same team!" O'Brian replied.

"Look . . . Mr. O'Brian," Colin said, shifting restlessly on his feet. He may have followed in his father's footsteps by joining law enforcement, but he was pencil-thin and nervous. Wearing a t-shirt and cutoffs, he sure didn't look like a cop to Krueger.

"Oh, please call me Sam," the older detective replied.

"Well, it's good to meet you, Sam," Colin spluttered, "but I'm pretty slammed right now. They've got us working overtime here."

"Oh sure . . . sure," said O'Brian, raising his hands. Krueger waited next to him, gritting his teeth. "I just need a quick favor. Something stupid." O'Brian smiled, trying to pass off his request like it was a joke, when his heart was racing. "Could you use the computers you got here and tell me if the guys in two different photos are the same person?"

Colin bit his lip, wondering how best to refuse the request. "It's not really appropriate," he said. "Our kit is expensive, and it's not really to be used for jokes."

"It's for a case," Krueger said, cutting in with a low, angry voice.

"Which case?" Colin asked, not pretending to hide his disgust at Krueger's odd appearance.

"*The* case," Krueger replied, scorning the techie's stares, and he shoved the two photographs into his hand. Colin gawked at the images. He didn't stop gawking at them, even as he led O'Brian and Krueger past security and into the elevator.

Colin Dubchek may have been a small, stringy guy, but he was one of the smartest agents inside the FBI's Facial Analysis, Comparison, and Evaluation unit, cheekily dubbed F.A.C.E. He was the undisputed master of their Next Generation Identification database, which contained over 400 million photographs taken from everything from visas and driver's licenses to library cards. And though he hated to let these two New York cops enter what he considered his inner sanctum, he relished the challenge they presented. Since his arrival in New York, he'd been chasing one dead end after another, identifying people from security camera footage who turned out to be nothing but summer tourists. In one embarrassing case, he searched his enormous database for a suspicious-looking guy he found on a traffic cam and discovered he was an NYPD desk sergeant on his day off.

"Come," Colin said, sounding like a battlefield general now they were entering his area of expertise. His lab was a dark, air-conditioned room in the heart of the building, with ranks of humming computers along the wall.

Silently, Colin smoothed the image of General Krueger and placed it on a scanner. Moments later, the image flashed up on the nearest screen. Soon another image came up: the photograph taken of the terror suspect.

The room fell silent. Krueger only heard his own labored breathing and Colin clicking away at his keyboard.

Please tell me I'm wrong, Krueger thought. *For the love of God, please.*

Suddenly, a series of red dots blinked to life over the faces of the two identical men. A faint beeping came from Colin's computer, followed by a sharp intake of breath as the techie reviewed his data.

"Yes," he said solemnly. "I can say with 95% certainty that the two men in these photos are the same."

Krueger didn't hear what Colin said afterward. The world in front of his eyes melted, and he steadied himself on the table. He'd lost good men in Iraq, and chasing the guys who'd killed them had driven him to very edge of collapse. But this was different. This was so much worse.

"We need to take this higher," Krueger said finally, trying to forget the dark riddles racing through his mind.

"How high?" O'Brian asked.

"Right to the top," came the reply.

SPECIAL AGENT LUCILLE Hawtrey, head of the FBI's Counterterrorism Division, was wise enough to understand she wasn't being pranked. A waspy New Englander with twenty-five years of service in law enforcement, she knew that the three men before her were serious-minded professionals.

Nevertheless, their story was so ridiculous she was tempted to order them each to undergo a psychological evaluation.

"Enough!" she said, rising from her seat. Around her in the

bland conference room sat various officials from other agencies assisting with the investigation into the Meyer Center bombing, plus the two New York cops and the techie who had arrived with their tale of Nazi generals returning from the grave.

Hawtrey sighed loudly. As the woman who the President had personally tapped to head the investigation, she was managing the inflated egos and simmering stress of her team—and now, cockamamie ghost stories too.

"I know how it sounds," Krueger confessed. He felt the eyes of very important people staring at him, judging him and his ludicrous claims.

Krueger pretended to scratch his freakishly large chin, but was actually trying to hide it from those hard eyes peering from across the table. He'd been diagnosed with cherubism in high school, and the disease had left him with a bulbous jaw that people couldn't help but gawk at. He'd gotten it from his dad, a gambling addict who'd split for Florida when Krueger was still in diapers. It was, as Krueger's mother was so fond of saying, the only thing he'd ever gotten from him, and since his chin had begun to grow, since his cheeks had inflated like a hamster's, he'd heard every possible insult—some offered in jest by his classmates, others spat with venom by instructors at Ranger school. He'd heard them so often that even when they weren't spoken, they still rattled around his head, tearing his confidence like a ricocheting bullet.

They think I'm a freak, Krueger thought.

Krueger was lucky, his was a mild form of the disease. He'd read of other people who'd been left grotesquely disfigured by cherubism, which was caused by an abundance of fibrous tissue in the face. Nonetheless, his cheeks and his chin were enormous, and he felt secretly humiliated whenever strangers stared at him.

Mac Hassler, who was sitting across from him, sighed so loudly his breath could have reversed the tides. He'd somehow managed to get himself invited to the meeting in the Field Office, and his chorus of laughs and snorts during Krueger's presentation had done more to anger Hawtrey than anything else.

"I'll talk to him," Hassler said as he stood and approached Hawtrey, as if offering the FBI agent a favor.

A single shake of Hawtrey's head was all it took to silence the captain and return him to his seat. Hawtrey knew that this was the largest investigation of her career, and she was determined not to be railroaded by any of the ambitious men surrounding her.

"Dubchek," Hawtrey asked, trying to keep her voice calm, "have you run this picture against everything in the database?"

"Yes," came the swift, confident reply. "I got no other matches. At first, I thought these guys were pulling a joke, so unbeknownst to them I picked up additional photographs of Krueger and ran them through the system: one from Pathe footage taken in Berlin and another from his testimony at Nuremberg. They both match the shot we have of the suspect."

The room fell silent. Krueger knew the enormous stress the people around him were under. The families of the deceased and the honor of the nation were demanding they find the man who caused such carnage. He could see the strain in Hawtrey's eyes. She masked it well, as long years in the service had taught her the importance of projecting an aura of calm confidence during tough times. But she couldn't hide her weariness. Krueger had seen it in too many eyes during those five tours in the deserts of Iraq and Afghanistan.

"And when was the NGI database last audited?" Hawtrey asked.

"Er, last spring as I recall, ma'am," Colin replied.

"Time for another," she said. Hawtrey poured herself a glass of water as she eyeballed Krueger. Her face was as grey as her suit.

"I'll get right on it," Colin said, rising from his seat.

"No!" Hawtrey said. "You're not to enter that computer room or access the database until further notice. Is that clear?"

Judging by the look on Colin's face, it was all too clear to the young techie. "I didn't do anything wrong!" he protested. For a small guy, he had quite the pair of lungs.

"I know that," Hawtrey said, "but I need to know if there is an error with the technology you are using to make this incredible claim."

Hawtrey offered a glass of water to Colin, by way of apology, and beckoned another agent, the young man in the vest and impeccable tie Krueger had seen running into his office that morning.

"Munroe, call the head of FACE and tell him to send me his best agent. I want the software checked for bugs and malware," Hawtrey ordered.

"But . . . Colin Dubchek is the best, ma'am," Munroe said.

"Then get me the second best, dammit! I want someone who has perspective." Hawtrey replied.

"It'll be a waste of time," Colin grumbled. "The Brits helped imprison Krueger after the war. I asked them to run the same analysis I did this morning, and they drew the same conclusion. So did Interpol."

"You had no right to authorize such action!" Hawtrey said, slamming her glass on the table. *That's more potential leakers I need to watch*, she thought. Hawtrey grimaced. Journalists had been waving checkbooks and promises of fame in the faces of every person associated with the investigation ever since she'd arrived in the Big Apple. Keeping things secret was fast becoming her biggest challenge, and she knew it was only a matter of time before the suspect's face was projected on every TV screen in the country.

There was a crisp knock at the door, and a harried woman in a pencil skirt entered. She wore thick-framed glasses. "I have the information you requested ma'am," she said. "Wolfgang Krueger was born to aristocratic Prussian parents on June 14th, 1888. His father was—"

"The death, Jean," Hawtrey said, "the death is all I care about!"

"Oh," Jean replied, hurt that her hard work had been dismissed so casually. She flipped through the stack of pages in her arms. "It's true what Detective Krueger said. General Krueger died of throat cancer in a sanitarium attached to Spandau Prison in 1951 He was buried in his family's plot in a cemetery in Berlin." Jean flashed a photograph of the gravestone as if it were proof. "Spandau was demolished in the 80s, and all records transferred to the German Defense Ministry. But their *totenregister* proves Krueger died in 1951." Jean again flashed another print-out to the group, this one showing Wolfgang Krueger's death certificate.

Hawtrey finished her water. She desperately wanted to scream but knew her wearied agents were depending on her calm leadership. She would scream later to her husband when he called her that evening from their Maryland home.

"Okay," she said, no longer willing or able to confront the mystery surrounding the suspect. "Let's take a look at the other side of the investigation. Munroe, tell these two detectives what we know so far about the attack. And if any of what Agent Munroe reports is leaked to the media, I will personally destroy the career of the person responsible."

With Hawtrey's threat hanging in the air, Munroe stepped forward. He casually flung photographs taken from various New York CCTV cameras onto the table as he spoke. "At 11:34 hours a 2004 black Lincoln town car pulled up outside the Meyer Cultural Center on 41st Street. The suspect exited from the front passenger seat with a large black haversack. This haversack contained the bomb."

"Who was driving the car?" Krueger asked.

"This fella," Munroe answered, holding up an image of a man behind the wheel. He wore a grey roll-neck sweater, a woolen cap pulled down low over his ears, large sunglasses, and an obviously fake beard.

"Slow down," O'Brian said, raising his hand. "Why did they go to such trouble hiding this guy's appearance, but let Krueger . . . I mean the suspect . . . walk in without a disguise."

"Maybe he was disguised to look like Krueger?" Munroe asked.

"Impossible," Dubchek protested, but the rage inside him was shrinking into a small ball of greasy disappointment. Hawtrey, Munroe, and the others clearly had no respect for his labors. "I know my tech, and it knows how to spot everything from a disguise to a doppelgänger."

"Carry on Munroe," Hawtrey said, ignoring Dubchek.

The younger agent nodded and flipped through his photographs.

"While the car circled the block the suspect deposited the bomb in the ground-floor men's restroom before returning outside and getting back into the Lincoln at 11:42 hours."

"That old guy, the suspect, he carried the bomb?" asked Krueger, being careful to keep his voice neutral. "How heavy was that bag?"

"With the amount of tovex sausages and nitromethane needed for a blast of such size," said a nearby ATF agent, "we estimate the bomb weighed a little under three hundred pounds."

Krueger chewed his lip. His grandfather, if it was him, was carrying the haversack as if it contained nothing more than cotton candy.

"So not only a ghost, but a ghost with super-human powers," O'Brian whispered.

"And where is this car now?" Krueger asked, eager to change the subject.

"We found it in a parking lot near Gramercy Park," Munroe answered. "The way we figure it, they drove to the lot, exited the Lincoln and left using another vehicle."

"Damn it," O'Brian muttered.

"There must be something in the car," Krueger said. He remembered a militia cell in Iraq had tried a similar trick in Fallujah when he'd first arrived in the city. But the driver had left a crushed napkin under his seat, which was all the evidence Krueger had needed to collar him.

"Not a thing," Hawtrey said. "That car looks like it just rolled off the assembly line. It was reported stolen three weeks ago from a retirement home in Harlem. Apparently, it is in better shape now than the day it was taken."

"Mysteries everywhere," O'Brian whispered to Krueger.

Krueger nodded in agreement and was amazed to find himself ashamed as the conversation continued. His grandfather, his own blood, was responsible for all the pained, tired looks he saw around the table.

"So now you know what we know," said Hawtrey, reassuming command of the room. "Which amounts to a hill of beans. Even worse, we will soon be under the clock, people: FBI Director Cullingworth has decided to release the suspect's image to the press this afternoon, and when he does, we'll start getting a thousand tip-offs an hour from people convinced they know the suspect."

You can't do that! Krueger's mind screamed. He pictured his mother, frail but defiant, crushed by the news. And he knew it'd only be a matter of time before some basement-dwelling sleuth made the connection between the suspect and his disgraced grandfather.

O'Brian had the same idea. "You sure that's wise, ma'am?" he asked. "Some World War II nut might find the link between Krueger and the suspect and post it online . . . and then we'll be a laughing-stock."

Hawtrey pursed her lips. The idea had crossed her mind, but with so few tangible leads, she needed help, even if it meant a few unfavorable headlines in the New York press.

"Okay, can we move on from this zombie shit?" the ATF agent asked, throwing his hands up to reveal ugly sweat patches on his suit jacket. "Finding this dead Nazi is just one thread in the investigation, and with all due respect, it's a thread I don't think will lead anywhere. The bomb is much more promising. We need to investigate every sale of tovex and nitromethane from the last year at least, maybe more, and that will mean a lot of valuable man hours."

"And thefts must be checked, too," Hawtrey added. "Nitromethane can be used as an expensive fuel in various motorsports, and a few of those motorbike and drag racer fans prefer to steal it from dealerships rather than pay. All the reported thefts will have to be followed up as well."

"Chalk that up as item 7,001 on our *to do* list," Munroe said.

"It sure is," Hawtrey said, "and each of those items needs to be checked off. Now Munroe, make sure the NGI database is audited just like I asked. Jean, keep in contact with the German authorities. Hassler, if you want to make yourself useful, then find me some volunteers ready to help go through all the public's tip-offs. Most of them will likely be garbage, but they've got to be checked nonetheless."

Hawtrey rolled off her list of instructions, giving each person in the room a task to complete. But she ignored Krueger and O'Brian.

When the meeting broke and her subordinates flew off in different directions, she approached the two cops. "We are sending a team to speak with your mother," Hawtrey said calmly.

"I understand," Krueger replied. "When do we leave?"

A single, swift frown revealed that Krueger was not part of Hawtrey's plans. "You'll be staying in New York, detective. I'm ordering you to report to my team so that we can analyze your family history. I want a full accounting of whatever you know. This suspect could, after all, be some long-lost cousin you don't know about."

"The Hell I am staying here!" Krueger roared. "That's my mother!"

"You know as well as I do," Hawtrey said, taking Krueger's arm gently in her hand, "that law enforcement never interviews their own damned family. Not even for informational interviews. Your mother might clam up."

Krueger opened his mouth to speak, but a small shake of O'Brian's head told him to hold his tongue. *Wait till we're out of the room*, he appeared to be saying.

"Get him back to Police Plaza," Hawtrey said to O'Brian, "and get him a coffee. My agents will be waiting when you get there."

25

O'Brian grunted, which Hawtrey took as an affirmation, and led his young partner out of the conference room.

An hour later, Krueger was still steaming. And so was the coffee which O'Brian served him in a chipped mug. "I gotta see my ma," Krueger said. "I gotta warn her."

"Sure you do, kid," O'Brian said. They were conspiring together in the break room, watching the buttoned-down FBI agents standing impatiently by Krueger's desk. "But let's do it right. Let's figure out how I can distract these Washington pukes while you head to the parking lot."

Krueger smiled. For a man who so proudly and regularly broke police procedure, it was amazing O'Brian still had a job on the force.

"Can you go make small talk with 'em?" Krueger asked hopefully. "Show them the ol' Irish charm while I sneak out?"

O'Brian chuckled. "That might work on a rookie cop, Joey," he said, "but these guys are Quantico-trained hard asses. They'll see through it."

Krueger drained his coffee cup, thinking about how best to get past the agents waiting for him outside. But just as he did so, he heard a loud scream coming from the bullpen.

His distraction had arrived.

3

"WHAT THE HELL IS going on?" Krueger yelled, drawing closer to O'Brian and looking into the bullpen. From the window, he could see half the narcotics team swarming around Captain Hassler's office door.

"It don't matter, kid," O'Brian replied, pointing to the FBI agents as they both headed toward the commotion. "This is your chance. Get to your car!"

O'Brian slowly opened the door, and Krueger darted out. He walked softly, but also with speed and purpose, like a ballet dancer. Within seconds, Krueger was obscured by the shadows in the stairwell next to the break room.

"Call you later," he said, before disappearing.

Alone, O'Brian lumbered up to Hassler's office, picking up the raised voices as he drew closer.

"Now, ma'am, if you just remain ca—" someone said in a smooth voice, before being cut off by a loud and distraught woman.

"Damn you!" she cried.

O'Brian barged past the crowd to discover an incredible scene: an old woman, crooked with age and grief, jabbed her thin, claw-like fingers into the toned, tanned chest of a man who looked to O'Brian to be a surfer. Next to him was a pimpled youth wearing glasses too big for his porcine nose.

"You!" the women cried, stabbing another tobacco-stained talon into the tall man's chest. "You are responsible! It was you who put the Center's name in all the tabloids. You may as well have put on target on my husband's back!"

The last words sounded as though they had been wrenched from her tormented soul, and the woman collapsed into a female officer's waiting arms, her wails piercing even the hardened hearts of the veteran cops surrounding her.

"Who is this?" O'Brian whispered to the nearest cop, who was watching the altercation.

"It's Sara Simovich," the cop replied. "Her husband died in the blast. She's got it into her head that Dennilson's responsible."

"Dennilson?" Sam asked.

"Curt Dennilson," the cop said, nodding toward the man who looked like a surfer. "You telling me you've never heard of the world's seventh richest man? He's the founder of Gemini.com, the first combined online retailer and bank. Imagine Walmart and Bank of America joined together and set up a website. That's what Dennilson's got. And it's made him a fortune."

O'Brian looked at the surfer with new-found respect. He had the tan of a native Californian and wore what was the undisputed uniform of the Silicon Valley magnates: open-collared shirt, casual pants, and sneakers.

"What the heck has he got to do with the bombing?"

"It's his money that funded the Meyer Center's latest exhibit: *Antiquities from the Time of the Torah*," the cop replied, before sauntering back to his office. With the outburst over, the rest of the crowd slowly returned to the work waiting on their desks.

But Dennilson was not left alone. Mac Hassler, acting as though he could smell the fame and fortune on his body, came bounding up to him with his hand outstretched.

"Mr. Dennilson," he said, beaming. Dennilson returned the smile, revealing two rows of brilliantly white teeth, which contrasted with his dark tan. "I'm so sorry to disturb your vital work, captain," the magnate said in a deep voice, which sounded as though it had been marinated in rum.

Hassler, of course, assured him that he was making no such disturbance, and attempted to hustle him into his office.

But Sam O'Brian stopped him. A forty-year veteran with no family, he'd made police work his life. And he'd developed a healthy distrust of people intruding on cop work.

"You're that internet guy," O'Brian said, feigning surprise, as he approached Dennilson. O'Brian saw that Dennilson's brown eyes were wide and shone with an easy charm. Only the eyebrows, which reared like furry caterpillars, revealed the calculating intelligence that bubbled beneath.

"Well, yes, I suppose I am," Dennilson replied, smiling broadly, before introducing himself. "This is my Vice President of Imagination, Preston Gates," Dennilson said, introducing the bespectacled youth. He, too, was wearing an open-necked shirt, as if mimicking his boss, but the similarities ended there. Gates was wan, and his lips, filmed with spittle, were twisting into a poisonous scowl.

"I sure don't have a clue what that means," O'Brian said, only half joking, "but it sounds important." He dismissed Hassler's fierce look of annoyance with a wink.

"I am a futurist," Gates replied huffily. His auburn hair was receding and greasy. "Curt and I dream about what the future should look like, and then we build it."

O'Brian smiled and casually put his arm against Hassler's office door, preventing anyone from entering.

"If you don't mind, dete—"

"So what's a pair of futurists doing in our dingy office?" O'Brian asked, interrupting his captain. Hassler had never worked the streets, never been close enough to a thug to feel their hot, threatening breath on his collar. O'Brian knew he didn't have the guts to challenge him in front of people he was desperate to turn into friends.

"Well," said Dennilson, hiding his embarrassment at O'Brian's brazenness with fake laughter. "I know you fellows are doing such stellar work in very difficult conditions, and I wanted to make it known that we, the citizens of the nation, are deeply grateful for your efforts. I bought along donuts as a small token of my deepest respect."

Dennilson pointed to the stacked boxes on a nearby melamine flip-top table. The donuts had come from the boutique bakery near Riverside Park, the one where a cup of coffee costs you half your paycheck. *Of course they'd come from there*, O'Brian thought.

O'Brian said nothing as he turned back to face Dennilson. The silence soon became oppressive, and the tall Californian planted his hands on his slender hips in frustration. Back in San Francisco, his employees recognized this pose and had learned to dread it. It was the sign that he was, like a viper, about to strike.

"There's another reason too," Dennilson said. "But it's of a more personal nature."

"Which means it's none of your damn business," Gates added.

But O'Brian didn't move.

Finally, the young kid sighed and drew closer to the cop. O'Brian noticed that behind his ridiculously oversized glasses were a pair of dark eyes that burned hot with anger.

"Curt made a substantial investment in the Meyer Cultural Center before the bombing," he said. "Since the launch of Gemini, Curt has made it his mission to save the history of the ancient Middle East, which is being ravaged by the various terrorist cadres rampaging through those lands as we speak. At enormous cost, and quite some personal risk, Curt and the team he employs have retrieved countless artifacts from war zones and brought them to the United States for safekeeping. Pottery, jewels, papyrus, religious totems, the list is endless. Many of these items were on display at the Meyer Center, and . . ."

". . . and we'd like them back," Dennilson said, dropping his friendly façade. "Those that survived the blast, that is."

"Even the remnants of those pieces lost in the blast would still hold considerable value," Gates added.

"Lemme get this straight," O'Brian said, lumbering toward Dennilson. "You saw the numbers killed, the families torn apart by this outrage, and you think you can come here and ask for ya finger paintings back?" O'Brian raised his voice, not caring who heard him. Having investigated murders, robberies, and rapes, practically every act of depravity the human mind could conceive of, there was little that could stir him to genuine anger any longer. But callousness masquerading as concern was one of them.

"Those antiquities are quite literally priceless," Gates said, his voice dropping to a threatening hiss.

"And those lives snuffed out by a madman aren't?" O'Brian replied. "What the hell are you doing here, anyway? Why aren't you throwing your sugary bribes around at the FBI building?" O'Brian caught the look in Dennilson's eye, the look which answered his question. "Ahh," O'Brian said, chuckling, "you've tried that already, haven't you? And Hawtrey told you to get bent. So you thought you'd try your false charm on us blue-collar schlubs."

"That's enough," said Hassler icily, as if he'd just rediscovered his courage.

"It sure is," O'Brian said, departing with a look of rage. "If this is what you futurists do, valuing old art over young lives, then count me out. Oh, and you suck at choosing donuts."

That last line tickled O'Brian, and he smiled as he left the three bewildered men standing by the office door. But his smile died the moment he turned and saw the two FBI agents standing with their arms crossed next to Joe Krueger's desk.

"Okay joker," one of them said, "what the Hell did you do with your partner?"

DETECTIVE JOE KRUEGER slammed his foot on the accelerator, as if trying to escape the misery that surrounded him.

He drove his old Grabber through Forgeham, the place his mother, Trudy, had moved to when Bill Clinton was re-elected President. The economy was booming, and Trudy, full of the vim that defined America's immigrants, was going to set up a small farm out in the country, having seen her only son head off to college.

But this particular scrap of Pennsylvania was not a place where the dreams of people like Trudy Krueger took flight. It was where they crashed into the grey, barren earth. Flying past Krueger in a miserable haze were the scars of a town in decline. Shops were boarded up, and those that remained offered either drugs or booze. The drug Trudy Krueger relied on, religion, was provided by a bare Catholic church just up the road, about where the thunderclouds were presently menacing, as if God intended to wash the filth from the streets.

Over fifteen years ago, Joe Krueger had dropped out of a Dartmouth MBA program and joined the Army on the promise that he would keep his country from harm. That solemn pledge had sustained him during those long months overseas, where the sundry threats and miseries combined to form a blanket of pain, which wrapped close around his body. That pledge, spoken only to himself, drove him to fight, even as his friends were felled by bullets, grenades, IEDs, and later, addiction, too.

"And this is what I fought for," Krueger muttered as he shook his head, turning his car right onto a dirt road. The house on the corner was a nineteenth-century mansion, which in years gone by would have housed a proud, rich family. But now the windows were all smashed, revealing a dusty blackness within. The roof was yawning open like a crooked smile. Shingles were scattered on the overgrown land close by.

"Nice neighbors, Ma," Krueger said to himself.

Half a mile down the road was Trudy Krueger's attempt at a farm. She owned a single-story house with a well-tended front porch. Richly-colored drapes hung from every window. But her son knew that outside appearances could be deceiving. Trudy had not entertained guests in years, and the home inside was cold and spare.

Swallowing hard, Krueger pulled onto the driveway and was greeted by three loud dogs, his mother's sole friends and companions. They escorted him to the doorway, tails wagging, where his wiry, rawboned mother stood waiting.

"Joseph," she said, kissing his cheek absently. There was a dullness to her grey eyes, which Krueger could not recall having seen before.

"Good to see you, Ma," he said, embracing his sole family member. *She's getting thin*, Krueger thought. "You eating, Ma?" Krueger asked, but his mother ignored the question as she brought both her hands to his enormous chin to stroke it.

She'd performed the same tender rite ever since Krueger had received his diagnosis, as if she was trying to smooth away the tissue that had inflated her son's cheeks and robbed him of his handsomeness.

No parent wants to be reminded of their child's imperfection— and of their mortality. Perhaps they fear it reflects badly on them or reminds them that one day, their progeny will all be spent. Either way, since the cold tragic day when Trudy Krueger was told her son would grow into manhood disfigured, she had always been overly and annoyingly protective of him. Perhaps, Krueger figured, that was why she'd protested so vigorously when he'd joined first the army, and then the police.

Trudy invited Krueger into her house. It was poorly lit and humid. The air conditioner was either broken or switched off to save money. Each was as likely as the other. Slowly, Trudy led her son down the corridor and into the kitchen, her slippers making *shwooshing* sounds on the bare floorboards as she did so. There were no pictures of family on her plain walls, just old portraits, ghostly and threatening, of the patron saints of Germany: Saint Ansgar, Saint Boniface, and a half dozen other long-dead men with long-forgotten names.

"You don't call, anymore," Trudy said as she puttered into the kitchen.

"That not true," Krueger replied, knowing that it was, in fact, perfectly accurate. "I ask you to come visit me and you never do."

This was the pantomime Krueger and his mother practiced every couple of months to prove that theirs was a healthy relationship: he would invite her to New York knowing she would never accept, and she would promise to consider it knowing she never would.

"I called ahead, didn't I?" Krueger asked as his mother poured coffee into broken, mismatched cups. He sighed through his teeth when he heard no answer. "How's Damien?" he asked finally, hating the silence that had covered the house like a grimy shroud.

"Awful," Trudy answered. "I should have eaten him years ago." Damien was a garrulous sheep, the last surviving member of Trudy's hoped-for farm. "So what brings you here?" Trudy asked, smoothing her hands out onto the Formica table top. "I thought a big cop like you would be busy hunting those terrorists." Trudy spat the words *big cop* like they were rancid candies.

"Well, I'm kinda working on that case," Krueger said.

Trudy eyed him suspiciously. They had begun growing distant the moment he had put on a uniform after 9/11. For this elderly German refugee, uniforms only ever meant bloodshed and chaos.

"Yet you found time to come visit," Trudy said.

"Ma," Krueger replied, cutting to the chase, "have you watched TV lately?"

"Oh no," Trudy answered, waving her hand dismissively, "it's all potty mouths and violence! The only news you need is the good news delivered by Father Bell at Mass."

Krueger suddenly put down his cup and took hold of his mother's hands. He knew he should have been a better son; should have respected his mother's contempt for the military and addressed her fears with tenderness rather than mocking indifference. And because he accepted the mistakes in his past, Krueger also knew that he was bound by duty to help his mother through the terrors of the present. He was going to break the news to Trudy and take her back to memories she had tried very hard to forget.

It would not be easy. But he would be there for her.

"Ma, the bombing in New York, they've got a suspect," he whispered, and the suspicion in his mother's eyes turned to dark apprehension. "I've got a photo here, and I'm going to show it to you. But . . . brace yourself, okay? It's going to be upsetting."

"I . . . I don't understand," was all Trudy could say, before Krueger delicately pulled a photograph from his pocket and showed it to his mother.

Trudy saw the blue eyes, the aquiline nose, and the slicked back grey hair.

For many moments, there was silence in the room, as if Krueger's mother was consciously deciding which emotion best fit the moment. He saw traces of each on her face: anxiety, trepidation, even fear. But then she settled on anger and launched herself from her chair and away from her son.

"You are lying!" she screamed. "Why would you do this?"

Krueger raised his hands, as if trying to shield himself from his mother's wrath.

"What kind of son are you? What kind of son terrorizes his own poor mother?"

"Ma, it's the truth," Krueger said quietly.

"How can it be the truth?" Trudy replied. Her three dogs, who understood Krueger's mother better than he did himself, departed the kitchen. "He died so long ago! You think a ghost did it? A zombie?"

"Of course not!"

"Then how do you think your dead grandfather got to New York?"

Krueger noticed that his mother had begun speaking in a German accent, which, like her memories of the past, she had spent many years trying to escape.

"I don't know," Krueger said, and found that his own anger had

35

been ignited. "I don't know anything, goddammit! And that's why I came to you. You know... my boss is sending a team to come visit this place? They want to interview you. I came here to warn you."

Trudy suddenly had visions of men (they were always men) busting through her door, striding arrogantly around the property wearing boots and guns.

It was more than her frail heart could take, and she collapsed back into her kitchen chair. When Krueger held her hands, she did not resist.

"I know it's not easy. I know it doesn't make any sense. But it's the truth. Your father, my grandfather, was photographed in New York City planting the bomb."

Trudy murmured, as if her imperishable soul was being called to confront something it did not want to face. "It cannot be," she whispered, as Krueger wiped the tears from her eyes, "he died so long ago."

"I know," Krueger replied, "so let's figure this out together. General Krueger passed away in 1951, right? In Spandau prison? Due to throat cancer?"

"Yes, yes," Trudy replied. "The damned Allies let so many of the officers walk free after the war: von Rundstedt, Guderian, Skorzeny. They all died free men. But Papa! They kept him locked away from his family. Even when he started coughing up blood, Papa was denied his liberty."

Krueger had never heard his mother refer to General Krueger as *papa* before. Her eyes shone with anger, and Krueger wondered to whom that anger was directed. Was it to her father, the black-clad wager of war? Or was it to those who forbade her from seeing him? Handing his mother a tissue, Krueger guessed that Trudy was angry at the world that had denied her the kind, caring father all girls need.

"Why did they keep him locked away?" Krueger asked.

"Because they hated him," Trudy shot back instantly. But Krueger's suspicion was roused, and he narrowed his eyes.

"Ma, the Americans would not have locked the general away just because they didn't like him. Was he involved in the Holocaust?"

Trudy turned and faced her son with dismay written on her face. "Never!" she replied. "Papa was a Christian. From the moment he could talk, he kept a burning faith in his breast. And he would never had involved himself in such cowardly slaughter, even if that man had ordered him to." Trudy had never had the courage to refer to Hitler by name, preferring to call him 'that man' on the rare occasions she deigned to discuss him at all.

"Then why was this Christian locked away when other officers were being let go?"

"He was locked up because of his Christian faith, not in spite of it."

Krueger took a step back, confusion roiling his already overladen mind. "Ma, you're not making any sense!" he cried. "Did your father have some secrets from his time on the Eastern Front? From the Bulge?"

Outside, the clouds overhead finally burst, and fat drops of rain rattled the window. They were so loud Krueger couldn't hear his mother as she sighed. It was time at last for her confession.

"Papa never served in Europe," she said.

Krueger felt his entrails run cold. Without knowing it, he cocked his head like a dog who'd just heard a strange noise. "But . . . but the stories you told me . . ." he said, "those newspaper clippings . . ."

"They were all lies," Trudy mumbled, and her tears fell again with renewed vigor. "I needed to tell you a story . . . to keep the truth from your young ears."

"Wha—" Krueger's voice trailed off. He staggered away from his mother and the enormity of her deceit.

"It was for you!" Trudy protested. "It was all for you!"

"I don't want to hear it, Ma!" Krueger cried. "Just tell me who the Hell my grandfather really was!"

Trudy's old, cracked lips pursed, as they wrestled with the truth trying to break free. "He was in Africa during the war," she said finally. "Serving on that man's direct orders. He was sent because of his love of Christ. He was sent because the Fuhrer wanted immortality ... he wanted the *lignum crucis* ... the True Cross!"

4

JOE AND TRUDY KRUEGER sat on the kitchen floor, listening to the rhythmic fall of the rain outside. Their anger was spent, and they were repairing their relationship over a bottle of bourbon and Joe's pack of Marlboros.

"It was his knowledge of the Holy Land that saved him," Trudy said softly. Two dozen photographs, newspaper clippings, and letters were spread out over the floor, which Trudy had retrieved from a carefully preserved box next to her bed. "The Fuhrer sent the cream of his military into the Soviet Union after the invasion, even after it became a charnel house. Papa would have gone too, but he was too important."

"He was a scholar?" Krueger asked hopefully.

Trudy snorted in derision. "He was a soldier," she replied, in a tone that suggested she believed soldiers to be incapable of intellectual study, "but a soldier with a keen understanding of religion, and the myths which nourish it. He'd toured British Palestine and French Syria during the 20s, actually became an expert on the imperial administrations there. He was teaching at the Prussian Military Academy when the Nazis seized power, and that's when Papa caught the eye of . . . *him*."

Trudy produced a sepia-toned image of her father, Krueger's forebear, shaking the hand of the leader of Nazi Germany. He shivered, as those ghosts of the bloody past haunted his mother's small Pennsylvania kitchen. *They should have no place here*, he thought. And yet, their faces, their schemes of decades past, were weighing on his shoulders.

"The Fuhrer always had a tortured relationship with Christ," Trudy said. "His father burned with hatred toward the church, but his mother was a good Catholic. I suppose that's why he made a fetish of Christian icons. And of course, if he suspected that any of them could enhance his worldly power, he wanted them.

"Before the war, that man created the Ahnenerbe, a group of researchers tasked with finding Christian relics. Papa was its first director. It was he who seized the Spear of Destiny from Vienna when Austria was forced into the Nazi Empire."

Trudy picked out another picture. General Krueger was stood alert in the desert, next to a smaller, wiry officer.

"That's Rommel," Trudy said, "the Desert Fox, who commanded Nazi Forces in the Mediterranean. The Fuhrer ordered the Ahnenerbe into North Africa when the fighting broke out there. He thought it a great opportunity to plunder the ancient world. And the one thing he wanted more than anything was the True Cross."

"The cross on which Jesus himself was crucified," Krueger said in hushed tones. He swallowed the last of his bourbon and immediately poured himself another generous glass.

"Exactly," Trudy said. "The True Cross taken by Saladin during the Crusades to Damascus, and never seen again. Papa got it into his head that he knew where it was."

"And that's why the Americans kept him prisoner after they released all the other German officers?" Krueger asked. "They wanted it for themselves."

"Yes," his mother said. "They suspected Papa knew the location of the True Cross and refused to release him until he confessed what he knew."

"Shame he took those secrets to the grave," Krueger said, before remembering that his grandfather was last seen walking the streets of New York days ago.

"Maybe not," Trudy said, rising to her feet. "It is said that whoever holds the True Cross possesses incredible power. The power, perhaps, to rise from the grave."

"Ma, there are churches across Europe that claim to have parts of the True Cross. If Hitler wanted them that badly, he could have ordered his Stormtroopers to take them."

"They are forgeries, for the most part," Trudy said, "and the Fuhrer didn't want to start a collection. No, he wanted the *real* cross, the cross upon which God's son was crucified, on which his blood was spilled. The one lost hundreds of years ago in the deserts of the Holy Land."

Krueger wanted so desperately to laugh. He lived in a world where bad guys used bullets and bombs, not old relics. And yet, with the black of night closing in, with his mother's face haunted by anguish, and with the grave faces of patron saints staring at him from the poorly-lit walls, he didn't feel like laughing at all.

He felt, in fact, very much afraid.

Suddenly, Krueger heard tires crushing the gravel of his mother's drive, and the hallway flooded with the golden glow of headlights. He turned to ask his mother if she was expecting visitors, but her suspicious glance gave him all the answer he needed.

"Ma," he said, gathering the photographs and newspapers from the floor, "I've got to go. Those agents who are coming to see you—"

"Will be told nothing but lies," Trudy said, interrupting her son. "I . . . I love you, my boy. I was saddened by the choices you made in your life, but I never stopped believing in you."

Krueger smiled broadly, despite his rising dread.

The headlights switched off.

"Don't forget this," Trudy said, picking up the last of the items on the floor. It was a blank piece of paper, yellowed with age. "This was the last letter your grandmother ever received from Papa."

"But it's blank," Krueger said.

"I know," Trudy replied, "but mother received it in the mail two weeks before Papa died. I've always thought it might mean something, but I'm not sure what. Now . . . I'm not sure I want to know."

There was a crisp knock at the door. Krueger heard the mumbled voices of two men. Shaking off the bourbon-infused fog that had fallen across his mind, Krueger silently leapt up the stairs, hoping to reach his mother's bedroom, which faced out onto the porch.

'Take 'em out back, Ma," Krueger whispered. "I'll get to my car using your bedroom window."

"Be safe," Trudy said. There were no more tears now. She was renewed and heart-whole, and her love for her son, so long dormant, was beginning to flourish once more.

"I'll take care of these mementos," he promised, as he vanished into the upstairs darkness.

"Do whatever you want with them," Trudy said in a voice too quiet for her son to hear. "I am finished being a prisoner to the past."

From his mother's bedroom, Krueger heard his mother open the front door and invite the two gentlemen inside. He was too far away to understand their small talk, but one of the men suddenly cut in with a barking order. "Take us to your son, please."

"Of course!" Trudy replied with such excitement that even Krueger would not have known it was fake. "He's just tending to Damien. Would you like to see him? Have you ever owned farm animals?" Trudy's questions trailed off as she led the agents away from her son, toward the large fallow fields out back.

With the voices gone, Krueger opened his mother's large bedroom window, wincing as the wood creaked. FBI agents were not fools, Krueger knew, and Trudy could not deceive them for long.

Outside, the rain had banished the evening's bone-wearying heat, and Krueger shivered as he shimmied outside. The parting clouds revealed a full silver moon, and his shadow stretched long on the ground beneath.

With a sure step, Krueger landed onto the porch roof, and then, holding the drains for balance, he dropped onto the sodden earth. Controlling his breathing, Krueger rolled away from the door, feeling the moisture seep into his shirt, and sprung to his feet expecting agents to be surrounding him.

But he was alone.

The FBI agents had parked their Chevy Tahoe behind Krueger's Grabber, but not close enough that he couldn't reverse out of the drive and back onto the dirt road. And as he sped away, he guessed that his mother must have done a masterful job fooling the agents, for he never saw them reappear.

But the success of Krueger's escape did nothing to still his racing heart. He'd come to Pennsylvania for answers . . . but was leaving with even more questions. Even worse, those questions were leading him to mysteries he would have preferred to leave in the past. Krueger had never found God to be a source of comfort and inspiration the way his mother had, but he had a fierce respect for the Church and understood, in a hazy, unthinking sort of way, that it still held terrifying power, even in a world as rundown and cynical as the one he worked in.

Making sure to use the back roads, the ones that even the best satellite navigation systems knew little about, Krueger departed Forgeham, unsure of his next play. A few cars passed him, and whenever they did, he gripped the wheel so tightly that his fingers turned white in the harsh glare of the headlights. He began to feel the eyes of federal agents eyeing him from every darkened field.

Thirty minutes into his ride, Krueger realized he hadn't a clue where he was headed. Cursing, he massaged his forehead, wishing he'd brought the bottle of bourbon along when he made his escape. Busting jihadist scum in Iraq and drug-dealing scum in New York had taught Krueger the importance of precision planning, concentration, and daring. But as he pondered each piece of the mystery, as he ran them through his not inconsiderable mind, he was left thinking this was a case beyond his skill.

With a sweaty hand, Krueger reached for his cell.

"What you find?" Sam O'Brian asked. His voice was thick with worry.

"Nothing good," Krueger answered. He was sailing past another abandoned burg, and the streets were dark and empty. The traffic lights were busted. "It appears my grandfather was on some archeological mission during the war. Top secret stuff. Got the Americans all worked up. They made him pay for it once he was caught."

"And does this help us here in New York?" O'Brian asked.

"I'm not sure that it does," Krueger replied. He fell silent, not knowing what else to say. Krueger wondered if he should simply drop the investigation into his family's past and let Hawtrey and her team do their job. But with a defiant jerking motion, Krueger shook his head. It was his grandfather who stood at the heart of the riddle, and his family's honor was at stake. His mother, so long the carrier of a terrible secret, was owed an explanation.

"Sam, I may need you to cover for me," Krueger said, hesitantly.

"Sure thing, Joey," O'Brian replied without hesitation. The Irishman had an almost psychic ability to distinguish between the good guys and the bad, and ever since they'd first worked on a crack cocaine case down by Wallabout Bay four years ago, he'd known Joe Krueger was a man of valor. And when a man of valor asked for help, O'Brian knew you gave it to him without hesitation.

"I'm heading out of town," Krueger said, "and I need you to keep Hassler off my back."

"It might be tough," O'Brian said, his voice sounding faraway and thin through the cell phone. "And to be honest with you buddy, he's not the worst of your problems. You still owe Hawtrey's minions an interview."

"I know," Krueger said, remembering the hard tone in the

agent's voice back at Trudy's house. "But I got bigger problems. It looks like people aren't taking the connection between my grandfather and the bombing seriously. And to be honest, I don't know if they *should* take it seriously. It's like a nightmare that makes no sense, and you don't know why you should be afraid, but everything sure feels scary."

"I know it is," O'Brian agreed, as he turned his eyes mournfully to the newspaper on his desk. The front page had a picture of the latest victim of the bombing: a seventy-three-year-old vacationer from Idaho who had died while undergoing surgery at New York Presbyterian. "So where you headed?" O'Brian asked, expecting his partner to confess he was going to retreat to a bolt hole in New England, which is why his mouth hung open when he heard the reply.

"I'm going to Berlin," Krueger said.

5

THE 747 DESCENDED toward the shrouded grey city, and Joe Krueger awoke from his shallow, fitful sleep.

A trained soldier and survivor, Krueger always traveled with a passport and one thousand dollars in cash. He'd picked up the habit after his exfiltration team had gotten an Iraqi translator out from Baghdad the day his neighbors discovered he was working with their enemy. A firefight followed, and ever since, Krueger had figured it was best to have a few key possessions handy if you ever needed to leave the country in haste.

But he never, not even in his wildest nightmares, thought he'd ever have to use them. And yet, the same night he'd visited his mother, he found himself at Philadelphia International Airport, looking over his shoulders as he bought a ticket for Berlin. He'd been lucky and gotten a Lufthansa flight that very evening, albeit one with a long and unwelcome layover in London.

Krueger gratefully took the coffee offered him by the auburn-haired flight attendant and chased it down with a handful of the candies he'd bought at the airport. He knew he'd pay for such a poor breakfast later, but he needed the sugar and the energy. He was running on little sleep, and he'd taken too many samples from the bar in the airport while waiting for his plane.

Sighing, Krueger took the results of the previous night's work out from his coat pocket and examined it. He'd grabbed some paper in Philadelphia along with the candies, and using a translation app on his phone had spent the long hours hurtling over the Atlantic trying to translate his grandfather's papers.

With little knowledge of German, beyond what he'd learned at his mother's knee, and a mind full of wondering thoughts, the task had not been either pleasant or easy. At first, he was paralyzed with indecision, unsure which document to translate first, and his anger upon discovering that he'd spent thirty minutes deciphering a love note or an old lecture brought him to the edge of misery.

"Working hard?" The flight attendant had cheerily asked him.

"I must be the only person in economy who isn't eager for the flight to land," Krueger dryly replied.

Nonetheless, Krueger's mind, sharpened by years of study and the hard experience of merciless warzones, had served him well, and his evening's labors had resulted in a baker's dozen of fully translated papers.

It was all he had, his only window into the world of General Wolfgang Krueger. And while it was a small and grimy window, Joe Krueger was still eagerly looking through, hungry for clues:

January 2ⁿᵈ, 1941

My Dear Elsa,

It is all agreed.

General Rommel, recently returned from his string of victories in France, has been ordered to North Africa in support of our Italian allies. A large army follows with him.

I'm afraid I have been ordered to accompany him, too. Those orders come from our Fuhrer himself, and cannot be ignored or put off. This means yet another forced parting; another season when I will not see our baby daughter grow. And yet, my dismay at being torn from you is tempered by the excitement of facing the challenge set before me.

He wants it, Elsa, he wants the True Cross, on which our Prince of Glory died, and I am the one he has chosen to retrieve it. Just imagine! If we succeed, the power we will hold in our hands will be incalculable. You know as well as I do that the Byzantine Historians all tell the same tale: Empress Helena discovered the Cross and proved its provenance by laying it against a mortally sick woman who subsequently recovered. Even more astounding is the fact that upon her return to Rome, Helena, already an aged women, lived for many years in perfect health . . . remarkably far beyond the normal span of years for a human female.

Can you imagine what wonders the power of the True Cross could work in this modern world of ours!

Though I am far from you and Trudy, please don't waste your days worrying about me. French Syria is ruled by the Vichy government now, and I have friends at all levels of the local bureaucracy. With Mr. Churchill and the English cowering under the bombs of our Luftwaffe, I've little doubt I will be interrupted in my search.

I leave Berlin tomorrow, headed for Damascus. The housekeeper Frau Fischer has been provided wages enough to last her till the end of the summer, by which time I shall have returned.

Returned, I hope, in glory.

Yours,

Wolfgang

"Arrogant bastard," Krueger muttered, and flipped through to another hastily-made translation. He paused, wondering if the words before him were lies, lies like those his mother had told him for years before the terrorist bombing had forced her to admit the truth.

April 14th, 1941

General Krueger:

Reichsführer Himmler was happy to learn that his man arrived safely in Damascus late last night. His presence should remind you that the Fuhrer is growing impatient, and you and your team are expected to extend Colonel Klopf every courtesy. Klopf, of course, will be in regular communication with my office, and will notify me of any failures on your part, of which I suspect there have been many already.

Chief among them, General, is your refusal to respond to my telegram dated March 31ˢᵗ, in which I asked for a translation of the mathematician's monograph. If it is, as you claim, crucial to the locating of the Cross, we must have a copy here in Berlin!

Should you and the colonel work together, as Reichsführer Himmler expects, I've little doubt that this expedition will soon draw to a successful close, and the greater glory of the Fatherland shall be assured. Anything less will be noted with dismay here in Berlin, and may cause some to question your commitment to the cause of National Socialism.

Cordially,

Herr Doctor Würst

Adjutant to Reichsführer Heinrich Himmler

The muffled voice of the captain, purring in a soft German accent, erupted over the speaker system, informing the passengers that they were minutes from landing.

Krueger massaged the bridge of his nose, and flipped through the photos which had been hidden amongst the papers his mother had given him.

One showed General Krueger wearing a pith helmet as he stood next to a dig site somewhere in the desert. In German, the words "a great mistake" where scrawled in a thin spidery script in the dog-eared corner.

June 22ⁿᵈ, 1941

My Beloved Elsa,

It is both a disaster and a relief. The Allies have defeated the Vichy French in Syria and we have been forced into a retreat. I write this while onboard an aircraft heading for General Rommel's headquarters somewhere in North Africa. I leave behind a job unfinished, for the True Cross is still lost.

Mere words cannot capture the enormity of this failure. The Fuhrer is enraged, and promising retribution upon my return to Berlin. SS men are looking at me like a traitor, and I half expect poison in my rations or a knife in my back before I make the journey home.

And yet I cannot lie, my love. I feel relief. I will reveal more when next I gaze upon your face, but as we both wait for that tender moment, you deserve a few words of explanation.

Himmler dispatched an underling to Syria when he grew impatient with my work. This man was too fond of the brandy, and in his nightly exuberances confessed that there are those in Berlin who were seeking the True Cross not to bring our fallen race closer to God, but to simply to seize the power it undoubtedly contains.

I fear I may be talking in riddles, my love, but fear not, you shall have a full account of my time away from you the moment we meet again.

Until then I remain faithfully yours,
Wolfgang

Krueger put the papers back in his pocket, pausing briefly to examine the last item Trudy has given her son: the blank piece of paper. Krueger rubbed its worn edge, and held it up against the light streaming from the windows, but still couldn't understand its purpose. No text was written upon it, not even in code, and yet it was, according to Joe's mother, the last letter the family ever received from the General.

Krueger was torn from his reverie by the jolt of the aircraft's wheels touching the runway at Berlin Tegel Airport. Closing his ears to the excited murmurings of the other passengers, who had plans for business meetings and vacations, he retrieved his small notebook and pencil. He chewed the pink eraser thoughtfully before writing on the first page of the book:

IS MY GRANDFATHER STILL ALIVE?

Five words. One enormous question. And little time to find the answer to it. Hawtrey would by now be searching for him, along with Hassler, and there was no telling when the attackers in New York would strike again.

Once inside the airport, Krueger hired a Volkswagen Jetta and drove to a fusty hostel near the Oberbaum Bridge where he booked lodgings. His small room, filled with dated furnishings and the smell of stale smoke, nonetheless boasted a good view of the river and the imposing red bridge that crossed it.

But Joe Krueger wasn't there for a leisurely sojourn. He ignored the pleasant view and the sound of the river, and focused instead on the papers fanned out on his plywood desk.

Joe looked at his watch and saw that it was approaching 2pm. He pulled out his notebook, and next to the question he'd written earlier, he added four locations:

Krueger's grave

Prussian Military Academy

Spandau Prison

Federal Ministry of Defense

Grumbling, Joe scratched out Spandau. It has been demolished after its last inmate, Rudolf Hess, had committed suicide in 1981. Any records kept there would likely have been moved the Ministry. He then drew a question mark next to Krueger's grave, as he asked himself what benefit he would draw from visiting it.

"It's not like I can exhume the body," he said, before reaching for his cell and dialing a familiar number. Back in the United States, Sam O'Brian, walking beneath the early morning sun, answered after the first ring.

"Guten tag," he said. "How's the sauerkraut?"

"Am I missed?" Krueger asked, smiling.

"Sure are," O'Brian answered, "I told 'em you needed to take a break and were holed up in a cabin in Vermont. Hassler looks like he's one bad day away from a heart attack, but at least he bought it. But Hawtrey could smell the bullshit. She has an agent posted outside your apartment, and one tailing your ma. Don't bother checking your emails, by the way. There are sure to be a lot of threats and curses amongst 'em."

"That's about what I expected," Krueger said. "Listen, I need a favor. Hawtrey's secretary-"

"Executive Assistant," O'Brian said, cutting in.

"Whatever. Jean's her name. Jean Dupree. Go find out who her contact is in the German Defense Ministry. I'm about to go pay a visit, and I need to know who to talk to."

"You got it buddy," O'Brian said, "I'll text you the name the moment I have it."

Krueger hung up and showered. The water refreshed him and helped beat back some of the exhaustion that was fogging his mind. He then pressed his shirt and slacks, and exited the hotel looking like just another American professional headed to a convention or seminar.

As he drove across the bridge, above the grey-green waters of the Spree River, Krueger received a text from O'Brian. It contained only two words, the name of Jean's contact in the ministry: *Jürgen Bonheim*. Appreciating the debt he owed his partner, Krueger smiled as he put the phone back in his lap, but the smile died on his lips when he looked through his rearview mirror. A black Tiguan with tinted windows was fast approaching.

"Hawtrey must really miss me," Krueger said to himself as he squeezed the accelerator with his foot, but even as the words left his mouth he doubted the driver of the SUV was from law enforcement. FBI agents, and police across the world, were taught that high speed pursuits should only to be attempted when the target was a dangerous criminal, and Krueger hadn't yet reached that exalted standard. Besides, there was something about way the Tiguan was approaching, with callous disregard for the other cars and pedestrians on the road, which suggested that the people inside were not afraid to kill innocents.

Krueger was reaching the end of the bridge and the traffic in front was growing thicker. He turned off the radio with a single jerking motion of his hands. His breathing slowed, and he recalled the long tortuous drives he'd taken in a Humvee in some of the Iraq's deadliest cities.

He'd tried so hard to forget those hellscapes. Now, he was trying hard to remember how he survived them.

Krueger suddenly swerved into the outside lane, heedless of the blaring horns. Easing his sedan between two compact cars, he took an off ramp which plunged into a confection of riverside hotels and bistros. Behind him, Krueger heard the angry revving of the Tiguan, and knew that his pursuers were still behind him.

Krueger gripped the wheel as he pushed the car above sixty, and soon was going so fast he could no longer make out the looks of shock and rage worn by the patrons enjoying their afternoon tea. Having had their weekday routines disturbed, these Berliners watched in alarm as the little Jetta and the Tiguan raced along their hushed, handsome street.

The Tiguan drew closer, and Krueger had to try to control his breathing. Panic, he knew, would be a far worse enemy than whoever was sat in the car behind him. As the Jetta reached 80kph and swiftly surpassed it, Krueger turned his car down a little warren of a street. The tires screeched in annoyance, and burned rubber was left hanging in the air like cobwebs.

The Tiguan breezed past those cobwebs, drawing ever closer to its quarry.

In dismay, Krueger realized the street he had chosen led to a well-tended park called Rudolfplatz, and there were crowds of tourists on either side of the street. A ball of greasy worry began to summersault in his stomach, as he knew he'd placed these people in danger.

Kruger needed to slow the chase, even if it meant risking his own life. He nudged the brake, and took the car down to fifty. The Tiguan behind, sensing an opportunity, drew closer until it finally rammed the rear of Krueger's car.

The New York cop was catapulted out of his seat. His knees slammed into the dashboard and his shoulders screamed in pain as Krueger fought to keep control of his car. The loud thud caused by the collision caused the tourists on either side to look on with concern. One girl, too young to understand what was happening in front of her, dropped her ice cream cone.

The Tiguan struck a second time, but Krueger was prepared now, and he gripped the wheel tightly with his mighty, sweat-stained hands.

By chance, a gap opened amongst the pedestrians, and Krueger spotted a narrow alleyway in between two groups. It was an opportunity he simply had to take, and Krueger mounted the curb, banging his head as he did so. Blood was soon trickling onto his pressed shirt.

Krueger ignored the shrieks of shock around him, and he was soon down the alleyway, a cobblestone street lined with artisan traders. To his dismay, he saw the Tiguan behind him still, but the way was narrow, and the bigger car's doors were soon being dragged alongside centuries-old frontages. Orange sparks flew into the summer air. Another swift left turn took Kruger onto a larger, more modern street, and he realized he was heading back toward the bridge.

This ain't working, he thought to himself as he gunned the engine. Krueger had the smaller of the two vehicles and could not possibly hope to outrun his pursuers. Even the narrow alley had not deterred those who were clearly so eager to get hold of him. Even worse, it was likely the murderous driver of the SUV knew Berlin well, while Kruger had all the knowledge of an ignorant tourist. He chewed his lip as he sailed past a large soccer stadium, pondering his dwindling options.

Then, a large sign caught his eye, and the word written on it was a word he'd highlighted in the glossy map of the city he'd bought at the airport:

Alexanderplatz, the sign read.

"That's my best shot," Krueger yelled to his reflection in the rear-view mirror, and drove his sedan east, following the river.

Alexanderplatz was the main public square and transport hub of Berlin; and Krueger knew that meant the roads leading to it were choked with taxis, buses, and trams. Kruger didn't know Berlin, but he sure knew chaos. He knew how to use it to his advantage.

And he knew there'd be crowds sprawling through Alexanderplatz.

Pushing the Jetta past ninety, Krueger felt his heartbeat in his throat. The blood was running freely from his head wound now, dark claret staining his shirt and filling the air with the smell of iron. But it wasn't his own blood Krueger was worried about, but those dozens lining the streets. He could sense that that whoever was driving the Tiguan would be happy to see their blood spilled if it meant they could capture their quarry.

The sound of sirens began to fill the air, rising above the roar of the engines. Krueger narrowed his eyes, focusing his attention on the busy road ahead. "Come on!" he whispered to himself, desperate to reach the plaza.

Finally, he saw another sign hanging in the distance pointing rightward toward Alexanderplatz. Krueger spun the wheel with both hands, leaving behind a trail of smoke and bewildered drivers fearfully swerving away from him. The SUV barreled past them, shunting cars and trucks, heedless of the damage.

A moment later, Krueger was heading down another narrow street, which soon opened onto a wide, concreted plaza. He mounted the curb and opened the door before the car had come to a stop. Then he was running, running toward the tall glass buildings above him and the throngs of people eager to catch a ride by taxi or tram.

Raised voices prompted Kruger to look behind. The Tiguan was stopped and its passengers tumbled out: one tall and clad in black, the other pot-bellied and sweaty. They saw him and pounced, chasing after him, pausing only once while the tall man punched into unconsciousness a man angered by their reckless driving.

Krueger was smart, healthy, and well trained, but truthfully it was luck that saved him. By chance, a slim dark-haired man, wearing roughly the same color shirt, was ambling toward the massive, silver Fernsehturm tower in the middle of the plaza. Hoping for a decoy, Krueger ducked between two groups of tourists before leaping behind a circular world clock, standing in the middle of the plaza. And there, shaded by the orrery at the top of the clock, Krueger crouched down and hid.

Pretending to admire the craftsmanship of the clock, Krueger took out his smartphone. Using the camera feature, he stretched out his arm and his screen caught the moment when his pursuers feel into his trap. They grabbed the collar of the man and shoved him to the ground. But just as they realized their mistake a Berlin cop walked past, clad in white and dark green, and began peppering them with pointed and angry questions as he tended to the fallen man. Krueger slunk away as he did so, taking one of the smaller side roads. He had finally escaped Alexanderplatz and his pursuers.

KRUEGER STAGGERED through the magisterial doors of the ministry, which occupied the same offices once used by Hitler's infamous navy. *What evil men once walked these very floors,* Krueger thought, as he entered the cavernous hallway.

The sounds of Krueger's steady footfalls echoed off the pristine walls, and a rumpled security guard noticed the stranger and instinctively and brought a hand to his pistol. But Krueger flashed a smile and approached casually. He'd bought a new shirt on the way to the ministry, discarding the one bloodied in the pursuit, and had bandaged his head. Flashing his NYPD badge was enough to convince the guard to let him pass, and he pointed Krueger in the direction of the archives.

"Totenregister that way," the guard said in broken English, pointing to a flight of stairs.

Krueger descended two flights of stairs, feeling the air grow hotter as he did so. He was soon lost in the bowels of the building, and the musty smell and bare brick walls convinced him that this was the place bureaucrats had hidden Germany's secrets. A place where they could die without being disturbed.

Walking a long, poorly lit corridor, Krueger came upon a wooden door with frosted glass and the word *archive* written in big black lettering. He rapped on the glass and entered.

The smell of time struck Kruger in his nose, a smell of decay and rot. In front of him was a small counter, behind which stood serried alcoves, lining up like old troopers, stuffed with bundles of yellowing paper and tied with string.

Krueger tapped the bell on the counter, and almost immediately an ancient groan, full of pain and dismay, echoed far out beyond the alcoves. Shuffling into the half-light was a man wearing a corduroy jacket and frayed checked shirt.

Jürgen Bonheim looked like he was entering his seventh decade of life, but in fact was just 52. Having afflicted himself with a job he loathed, his body had crumpled over the years, and now he looked like a college professor at a third-rate school.

"Yes," he asked in German. Krueger replied in English and hoped for the best.

"I'm detective Joe Krueger of New York," he said. "You've been working with a colleague of mine helping to provide information on the life of General Wolfgang Krueger, who died in 1951 at Spandau Prison. We needed the information for a case we are working on."

"Identification?" the bored bureaucrat asked. Krueger promptly handed over his badge, used to the casual contempt of low-level government functionaries. Whether it was in the government offices of Baghdad or New York, it seemed all government workers had developed the same hatred for their work.

Bonheim threw the badge back to Krueger as he yawned loudly.

"We are deeply grateful for your assistance thus far," Krueger said, hoping that if he slathered on enough false praise Bonheim might even smile, "and I've been sent to personally examine the totenregister kept at Spandau from that time."

Bonheim sighed, aggrieved to have been torn from whatever he did by himself in the darkness when not disturbed by guests.

"We're just trying to tie up a few loose ends," Krueger said.

Shaking he head, Bonheim shuffled into the nearest alcove. Soon all that remained of him was his echoing complaints.

"Jeez" Krueger said, believing he was alone. The only company he had was a house spider waiting ponderously in his web high above the countertop. But as he shook his head, Krueger caught sight of a figure standing next to him and he spun on his heels, reflexively bringing up his hands as he did so.

Appraising the figure, Krueger realized he had nothing to fear. It was a woman: slender, blonde, and keen-eyed, and her oval face was a sea of big brown freckles. She did not, to Krueger's surprise and relief, flinch when she saw his massive, malformed chin. Instead, she looked into his eyes and shrugged, as if to say that she too was not pleased to be spending her day lining up for dusty files.

Feeling embarrassed, Krueger averted his gaze as he put his badge back into his pants pocket. But when he straightened up, Kruger found that the women had silently disappeared. He was, once again, alone in the room.

But the disappearing stranger had left something for Krueger: a crumpled note on the countertop. *Ask for the Volcker-Blum files*, it read in a clear, confident script.

Krueger turned, shaking his head in disbelief, and stared at the door through which, presumably, the women had just left. But through its glass he could see no silhouette beyond. Krueger bounded forward and flung open the door, but the corridor was empty.

She's good, he thought to himself. *She's damned good.*

Nodding, Krueger realized that whoever the woman was, she was tough. She hadn't flinched or even grimaced when Krueger faced her with his hands raised. A typical civilian would have at least backed way, but the blonde, freckly woman had stood her ground with a smile still on her lips.

And she was quick on her feet too. It had taken perhaps less than ten seconds for her to enter, drop her note, and leave, but she'd done it with such speed and surety that Krueger's head felt like he was riding a rollercoaster without a seat belt.

Was she the one who had me followed? Krueger asked himself, before quickly dismissing the question. No one would have driven that recklessly through crowded streets merely to drop off a cryptic note.

Bonheim returned, wheezing and miserable. He placed a decayed folder onto the counter and the string that bound it.

"Wolfgang Krueger," he said. "Died in Spandau. 1951. If you need any other files pertaining to Krueger, you'll need to go to the main archive in Bonn. That's 300 miles away." Bonheim smiled as he mentioned the last part.

"Anything else?" the bureaucrat asked impatiently. He was strumming his fingers loudly on the table as Krueger took a photo of the death certificate of his grandfather using his phone. To avoid Bonheim's wrath he chose not to use the flash.

"Ye . . . yes," Krueger said hesitantly. "I'd like to see the Volcker-Blum files."

Bonheim's mouth opened, and then, to Krueger's surprise, curved into a dismissive smile. He chuckled and muttered something in German, which Krueger suspected was an insult, before shuffling away into his dark alcoves.

The bureaucrat's response both surprised and dismayed Krueger. If the files were going to help expose a conspiracy, as he hoped they would, why would he laugh at Krueger's request to see them?

It took Bonheim twenty minutes to find the files, and they were coated with a grey layer of dust so thick Krueger guessed they had not been touched in decades.

"You crazy Americans," Bonheim snorted, "this kind of stuff ist garbage!"

"And I can review these?" Krueger asked, nervously taking hold of the folder.

"Yes," Bonheim answered, as if he'd just been asked if the sun would rise in the morning.

Without waiting for Bonheim to change his mind, Krueger gathered up the grimy papers and took a seat at a desk near the door. He fanned out the papers, and to his delight, found that some of them were written in English. Krueger took hold of the topmost paper, which looked like a telegram, and read:

My dear Professor Blum! Sacha, I am delighted that we have procured the necessary space for our new facility, and that our Fuhrer has expressed interest in our work. I depart from Southampton tomorrow by ferry and hope to be in Berlin four days hence. God willing, we will be able to begin screening the first applicants soon after my arrival. Thank you for organizing my accommodation; I'm sure my humble needs will be met most satisfactorily. Give my warmest regards to dear Rebekah. Your friend, Gunther.

The next few pages looked like lab reports, each written in an indecipherable German script, but Krueger nonetheless photographed each one. He found the next page written in English was a hastily composed letter, written in a faltering hand. The page was torn and grubby.

Sacha, I am so deeply sorry about your predicament. I've thought about your request; thought and prayed, in fact, but I've decided it would be impossible for me to shelter you. I'm sure you'll understand my reasons. Our work is so close to completion, and I would hate for our facility to be closed by the Fuhrer's Stormtroopers because I offered aide to a Jew and his wife. My heart breaks for what has been done to you, but humanity needs our work! Needless to say, I wish you a swift and speedy escape from Germany. In time, the Fatherland will come to recognize the debt he owes to your brilliance. Godspeed, Gunther.

Krueger shuffled through the next few papers and found that the language used to write them shifted from German to Russian. Nazi letterhead was replaced with an image of the Soviet hammer and sickle.

Then, a single phrase leapt from the page and into the half-light of the room and struck Krueger on his face with the force of steam train.

CRYOGENIC FREEZING.

A sudden, terrible idea blossomed in Krueger's mind, and he flipped through the pages faster and faster, as if trying to overtake the nightmares that were swiftly curdling in his mind.

Then he found it. A list of names. The names of Professor Volcker and Professor Blum's test subjects. Written in a black scratch were two words that sent Krueger's already precocious hold on reality into a tailspin.

Krueger, Walter.

6

THE TASTE OF INSTANT COFFEE always reminded Krueger of late nights and danger, but he needed the caffeine. Gulping down the last dregs in his Styrofoam cup, Krueger shuffled toward the dark, tumbledown factory in front of him.

From his flimsy knowledge of German and the files he'd read at the ministry, Krueger was beginning to draw a picture of the man who was his grandfather. He clearly wasn't a Christian, that's for sure. After all, what Christian would pay the small fortune Volcker had charged for his groundbreaking cryogenic freezing, when glorious paradise waited for them in Heaven?

No, Krueger thought, *General Krueger was a fraud*. He'd taken the job at Hitler's Ahnenerbe to find the True Cross, not because of his love for Jesus, but because of his love for himself. He wanted immortality. And when he failed to find the Cross in the deserts of the Middle East, he turned to science to realize his ghastly dream.

Krueger crushed his cup and tossed it into a sad-looking trash can. Not that littering would have made the place look any worse. Krueger was stood on a darkened sidewalk in a dark part of the city, lined with the husks of old factories slouching on the cracked concrete. The sun was setting, and red light winked on the jagged broken windows, like teeth steeped in blood.

Of all the parts of Berlin destroyed by Allied explosives, of all the buildings torn down and blown up, this slum had somehow survived. And deep in its belly was the former headquarters of Volker-Blum Engineering.

It was not bombs that had deformed this part of Berlin, but rather misguided city planners. The tall brick factories, once the pride of Nazi Germany, had had grim brutalist wings grafted onto them, robbing them of their majesty and setting them on their downward path to dereliction.

A simple online search had revealed the fate of the two visionary scientists who had brought Krueger to this slum: Blum and his wife were killed at Bergen-Belsen concentration camp; Volcker, the coward, died in 1972, having grown rich, even in communist East Berlin, from the labor of his dead associate. The company died alongside Volcker, and his wretched factory, and the machinery inside, were left to rot.

Krueger pulled up the collar of his black shearling jacket and exhaled. There were no birds here, no children playing, no cars rushing past. There was only silence—the silence of a place best forgotten.

"Did my grandfather die here?" Krueger asked himself as he gingerly walked forward toward the factories.

Fire had gutted the first building, and inside, Krueger only found rotted furniture nested with rats. The second, a low and surly office, had once been an accountancy firm but was now a place where graffiti artists demonstrated their skill.

The third, taller but no less austere, had a sign hanging from above its main entryway, which a single rusted nail kept from falling onto the trash-strewn porch below. All that remained were the last three letters, soiled and faded, that read: lum.

It was the home of whatever remained of Volcker-Blum Engineering.

Krueger entered, wishing he had a weapon.

The door opened with a sharp *creak*, which sounded as loud as a tiger's roar in Krueger's alert ears. He raised his flashlight, a wind-up he'd bought before arriving, and played the light over the tumbledown drywall in front of him. *This was obviously the reception room,* Krueger thought. A large desk lay on its side in the corner, alongside a high-backed chair with garish orange upholstery. Krueger imagined Professor Volcker sat on the chair, wearing wide lapels and sideburns, charming old retirees out of their meager pensions. Did he ever have a moment of guilt, Krueger wondered, at having abandoned his friend and partner to the thugs of the Third Reich?

Krueger shuffled past the desk and left the reception room. The door this time moved freely and without sound, and he stood in a long, low-ceilinged room, thick with the smell of decay.

"So this is where the magic happened," Krueger muttered, before shivering. *If it was magic,* he thought, *it was definitely black magic.*

Fat wires hung from the creaking ceiling, torn and black like a witch's hair. On the far side of the windowless room, beneath these cobwebs of busted technology, were banks of smashed computers, fat beige boxes stained with measureless grime. To the old and sick, to Volcker's desperate clientele, these computers would once have looked like a life-saving invention, a gift from God to keep His people from joining Him before they were ready. Now they were as dead as the people they had been charged with keeping alive in a frozen, timeless void.

Lining the other side of the room, like coffins from some distant and unwelcome future, were the cryo pods into which Volcker placed his customers after they died. They were all smashed open now, the metal lids hanging off their hinges, the seats torn and moldering within.

And the bodies which had once occupied them were all gone.

It was just like Krueger had figured: he knew that the bodies would have been transferred after the company's collapse. After all, the city, the government, and the families were not going to let Volcker's hapless customers rot once the electricity was cut.

Krueger was here to find out where those bodies had been taken.

Walking down the long room, Krueger saw a recess in between the computer banks. There was a door there, and he tried it.

"Dammit," he whispered, when he realized he'd just found the restroom. A rat popped its gnarled face out of the toilet bowl as if to welcome him.

He'd been in the factory for twenty minutes now, and though he could not see outside, Krueger knew the sun had completely set. Remembering this, he suddenly found the urge to hurry his search, and when he left the restroom and continued down the room, he walked faster.

The next recess was on the opposite side of the room, between two of the ugly, stinking pods. Krueger darted between them, opened the door, and found a small office. Two metal filing cabinets stood erect next to a wooden desk, withered by remorseless time.

The stench was worse here, much worse. Gone was the offensive scent of burnt wiring and rust; this was the green smell of putrefying flesh.

Breathing hard in spite of the stench, Krueger set to work and began emptying the drawers in the metal filing cabinets, ignoring the nasty scraping sound as they pulled free. He then took the files and shoved them into his haversack for inspection back at the hotel. After all, Krueger did not want to spend his hours poring over dusty old papers in a place haunted by the futile dreams of the soon-to-die.

Dusty.

Krueger stood erect. The word had shot into his head without warning. Dusty.

"Something's not right," he said. He'd passed something that should have warned him. But with his head filled with images of ghosts and nameless corpses, he'd missed the clue.

Krueger played the light over the room, over the disintegrating desk and the filing cabinets, over the grimy walls, over the scuffed vinyl flooring growing black with mold.

Dusty.

Krueger saw his footprints in the dust on the floor, leading from the door to the middle of the room. But then he saw a second, and third set of footprints.

And they were fresh.

Krueger turned his hands into fists and swallowed hard. He wasn't alone.

Using his flashlight, Krueger saw that the footprints led to the chintzy yellow rug. He pulled it aside, exposing a scurrying cockroach and a large access panel. The lock was broken.

Thinking quickly, Krueger crouched low and brought his ear to the metal panel. Beneath him was the definite humming of machinery . . . but no voices.

'That's a plus, I guess," he said as he unshouldered his haversack and set it beside the crumpled rug. Krueger ran a trembling hand through his hair and looked around the room one final time to be sure he wasn't being watched. And then he grabbed the unlocked door, pulled hard, and entered the secret room below.

Beneath the access panel was a long flight of steps, brightly lit and clean. He descended slowly, his sneakers masking the sound of his footfalls. Making certain to close the door silently, Krueger soon reached the bottommost step.

All around him was Volcker's dream transplanted into the 21st century.

On the one side of the room he saw banks of computers, just like in the ruined room upstairs. But these weren't busted relics of the embarrassing past, these were state-of-the-art black behemoths, larger than refrigerators. Bars of blue light streamed from their smooth sides, and the Chinese symbols, written in gold lettering, suggested to Krueger that they were Petaflop Sunway TaihuLights, some of the most advanced computers in the world. He'd once shared a drink with an NSA buddy, a friend he had made in Iraq, when the Chinese had first announced their manufacture, and could tell by his sour expression that the reds had developed a machine of extraordinary power.

Three of the beasts stood working hard in this deserted basement, at a cost which Krueger could not begin to imagine.

But on the opposite side of the room was technology greater still. Twelve pods stood next to the wall, wires like cobwebs connecting them to the wall. They didn't look like metal coffins, but rather giant eggs, fat and ponderous, with a confection of blinking multicolor lights flashing on their sides.

Krueger stepped forward, approaching the first of the eggs. They were, as far as he could see, spotless, without any hint of the decay upstairs. And the doors were not open, rusting on their hinges . . . they were sealed shut.

His mouth dry, his heart racing in morbid expectation, Krueger looked inside the first of the eggs. There, beneath the glass viewing window, was a girl no more than twelve-years-old.

With the bloom of youth still fresh on her face, the girl looked like she was taking a nap after a day in the park. But her skin was blue and waxy, and ice crystals gathered in her auburn hair.

A clipboard next to the egg gave the child's name as Elsa Griessel.

Krueger continued down the line, checking the clipboards for names and the windows for faces. Each egg had someone inside; each clipboard told a tragic tale. Brain tumors. Cancer. Stroke. The afflicted had retreated to these catacombs, retreated from diseases they could not beat, in the hope that they would return one day when medicine would help deliver them a victory.

Were they fools or visionaries? Krueger did not have the wisdom or the courage to say.

Krueger approached the back of the room, toward egg number twelve and found to his shock that the door was open. Cursing, Krueger found the seat inside empty, and the buttons, which on the other eggs had flashed and beeped, were black. He grabbed the clipboard dreading what name would be written on it. And his dread turned to raw, nauseating fear when he saw the name Krueger.

Walter Krueger had once been a prisoner inside that egg. But someone, something had freed him.

But before Krueger could investigate further, before he could give voice to his suffering and regret, the first of many bullets shattered the viewing window of the egg, and he was forced to run for cover.

7

JOE KRUEGER LEAPT BEHIND the egg, watching in shock as the bullets tore apart the door. Sundered wiring flapped uselessly; touch-screen panels cracked and fizzled into nothingness.

Leaning forward, Krueger saw the two men who had followed him earlier. The fat, grey-haired man was shooting at him, something which obviously displeased his taller black-clad associate, who yanked at his collar and shouted insults in German. He was clearly a professional, well trained in soldiering and surveillance. Krueger understood his anger: with the element of surprise, one carefully aimed shot could have ended his life; instead, the pudgy amateur had started firing the moment he caught site of his prey, and given Krueger the chance he needed.

Krueger crouched low. Wincing, he looked down into his empty hands, wishing they held a Sig Sauer.

The gunfire stopped, and Krueger suspected that his assailants were approaching. They might even be splitting up, which would sharply reduce his chances of escaping. Feeling feeble, he reached into his pocket and drew out his cellphone, hoping to reach the police. But far down in the basement, there was no signal to be had.

Beside the egg was a metal gurney, as sleek and as clean as the day it rolled off the factory floor. Thinking quickly, Krueger hunkered down, grabbed the gurney's bar, and darted across the room, toward the supercomputers. Two bullets greeted him as he came into the light, but Krueger was fast, and he was across the room before either of his foes could fire anymore.

These TaihuLights cost billions, Krueger thought, *and neither of these guys look like the mastermind of this operation. They'll be too scared to fire on these machines.*

And so it proved. The taller man whispered something that suggested his annoyance and exasperation; then the room fell silent.

Krueger leaned close to the machine, feeling the hum emanating from within, ignoring the sweat gathering on his brow.

Slowly, he grabbed the clipboard containing the information about his grandfather. He removed the paper and rolled it up tightly. It was something he'd learned in Ranger school after 9/11. His instructor had told him, in a soft Tennessee purr, that in close quarters combat, a rolled-up paper jabbed into the eyes can stun an armed opponent and give you the seconds you need.

Krueger had never had to use that advice. Until today.

Over the hum of the TaihuLight, he heard uncertain footfalls. Someone was drawing closer. If it was the tall pro, Krueger knew he would likely be killed. But if his luck held, and if it was the pudgy dilettante, then he might be able to make his escape.

Sure enough, Krueger caught site of the unkempt grey hair and the long black moustache, and before his opponent could react, he jabbed the rolled-up papers into his unprotected eyes.

The man screamed: a sound borne of his shock, surprise, and dismay. He dropped his gun, a DD44 Dostovei, and Krueger swooped and grabbed it, ramming the clipboard into the older man's crotch as he did so. The man fell to the floor howling, his vision blurred by tears as Krueger began sprinting for the stairway.

But Krueger paused in time to realize his error . . . and how close he was to death. The taller professional was still lurking among the computer banks, and if Krueger exposed himself by running the length of the room to get to the stairway, he'd be surely be killed. Cursing his stupidity, he dived behind a polished desk, next to the computer banks, just as a gunshot rang out. The bullet, meant for Krueger's skull, instead hit the handrail on the staircase.

Panting, Krueger checked his gun. Three bullets in the clip; one in the chamber. Would that be enough to stop his two enemies?

Suddenly, Krueger heard the squeal of metal. Somebody was opening the access panel above. Krueger hissed and shook his head, realizing that the two men had bought reinforcements with them.

"Outta luck. Outta options," he muttered to himself, as he heard loud footfalls on the steps. Biting his lip, Krueger tensed his legs, ready for the fight.

Lightning fast, Krueger leapt to his feet, emerging from behind the desk. He raised his Dostovei ready to kill whichever thug came running down the staircase.

But instead, he saw the slender woman he'd met fleetingly in the archives that morning. She looked as surprised as Krueger, and for a split-second, they stood, yards apart, staring at one another.

"What?" Krueger heard one of the men ask. He spun to find the shorter man pulling himself up from the floor, taking a pistol from a holster around his ankle as he did so. His eyes still watering, the man stared at the stranger he obviously had not expected to arrive. Then he saw Krueger, fully exposed, and realizing his opportunity raised the pistol. Krueger, however, was faster, and with a single pull of the trigger felled his enemy. He fell dead with a bullet in his heart, the blood pumping over the immaculate white floor tiles.

Hearing his comrade collapse, seeing his blood flow, the taller man finally emerged. Whether angered by the sudden arrival of the female stranger or the incompetence of his dead partner, Krueger could not guess, but the rage worked to his advantage. The tall man stepped forward a little too far, and Krueger fired another shot.

The bullet struck the computer against which the tall man was leaning, and a violent shower of blinding sparks which followed was the opportunity Krueger needed. He ran forward, gathered the woman up in his arms, ignoring her shrieks and protests, and launched himself up the stairwell. He and the woman were back in the moldering office above by the time the first shots rang out.

Krueger, his heart racing, began to think he had his enemy cornered, and feelings of joy and relief seeped into his mind. He tried to push those feelings way, knowing that they would make him sloppy and take away the edge he needed in combat.

Sure enough, two more shots exploded, both striking the edge of the access panel.

"He's coming!" the woman cried. She was too panicked to notice when a small black canister came flying through the air, landing with a small pop as it hit Krueger's haversack.

"Get down!" was all Krueger has time to say, before the flash grenade exploded, filling the black hole with blinding light and robbing Krueger of his most important senses. His ears filled with what sounded like rolling thunder, and the world around him was sheathed in a brilliant white light.

His heart galloping, as if trying to escape his chest, Krueger nonetheless paused, fighting the urge to panic. Without his hearing and his vision, he knew that the next few moments were crucial. *What I do next will determine if I make it out alive,* he thought.

Ignoring the muted wailing of the strange woman, Krueger stomped toward where he guessed the office door to be. Using his hands, he found it open, and threw his cell phone far into the hallway beyond. Then he quietly retreated back into the room and took the woman by her wrist, locating her thanks to her cries. He fixed his hand firmly over her mouth, and together they both hid behind a decayed bookshelf.

Seconds stretched into what felt like long, tortuous years. The screen of bright light before Krueger's eyes gradually melted into large blobs of white. And as his sight returned, Krueger noticed a bald head emerge from the access panel. His enemy climbed into the room and headed straight for the hallway, thinking the sound of Krueger's thrown cell phone was proof his quarry was retreating.

Krueger emerged from behind the bookshelf, aimed at the tall man partially eclipsed by the floating blobs, and emptied his gun into his body.

His heart pierced, the man spun and fell to the floor, his lifeless eyes staring in disbelief at the couple of strangers who had bested him.

A wearied sigh escaped Krueger's lips; finally, he was alone, alone with the woman who had, with her unexpected arrival, helped save him. But he did not feel safe.

Working with the swiftness and precision of a man who has looked down upon many dead bodies, Krueger patted the tall man's corpse, swiftly removing his wallet, phone, and weapons. He was sure to watch the woman carefully as he did so. When he was satisfied that the tall man was both dead and unarmed, he returned to the basement and performed the same rites on the shorter man.

His pockets heaving with their possessions, Krueger returned to the office and fixed his hard, uncaring gaze on the woman, whose face was lit by the green glow of her cell phone. He could see she was finally regaining both her site and her hearing, but by the look of horror on her face, Krueger guessed she would have preferred to remain blind to what surrounded her.

"Who the Hell are you?" Krueger asked, swiping away her cell phone.

"I'm Tessa Brandt," the woman confessed, tears of shock rolling down her high cheek bones. She struggled to catch her breath, and the words came out in whispered jags. "Dr. Brandt. I'm a professor at Humboldt University here in the city. A historian!"

Historian? No historian Krueger knew would wander by herself into a rotting factory under cover of darkness.

"Bullshit!" Krueger said. He grabbed Tessa's shoulder and slammed her into the drywall. Dust fell onto her jacket, and her tears of shock became tears of pain. "Give me the real story or you'll be as dead as those two creeps!"

"It is true!" Brandt protested, grabbing Krueger's wrist with a strength he didn't suspect she possessed. "I teach Nazi history. Search my name online if you need to."

"Wouldn't mean a thing!" Krueger snorted in derision. "Anyone can cook up garbage on the internet. So keep talking!" Krueger tightened his grip, just to make sure Dr. Brandt got the message.

"Damn you, I just helped save your life!" she said.

"And I saved yours!"

"Look," Brandt said, "my grandfather worked with the Americans. He was an investigator for the prosecution at Nuremburg and went on to teach what he'd learned at the university. I followed in his footsteps. I teach the German history others would prefer to forget . . . so our nation never again commits such sins."

"How did you hear about me? And why did you come here?"

"My friend in the archives told me people from America were asking about General Krueger. I knew he had always been of interest to you Americans because of his work in Syria. I discovered that the call came from New York, and I found your name on the NYPD website. I guessed you were his relative. But before I could contact you, you'd arrived in Berlin."

"And how did you know I was here?" Krueger asked in a voice that was higher in pitch that it should have been. *Jesus*, he thought, *if this academic could find me in a few hours, then Hawtrey and Hassler will have me in cuffs before the night is out.*

"Quite by chance," Brandt said, and Krueger allowed himself to relax a little. "While you were tearing up the streets of Berlin, your colleagues back in New York published General Krueger's face and labeled him as the prime suspect. When I saw his face, I rushed to the archives and saw you there. That's when I took my chance to warn you about the Volcker-Blum connection."

"Warn me?" Krueger shook his head. "You didn't warn me, lady! You just handed me a note and split! Those guys got the jump on me."

"I thought you were the advance man for a whole team of investigators!" Brandt answered, "And I knew that if I gave you anything more than an anonymous tip I'd be under interrogation by your famously unfriendly officers. That's why I handed you the note."

Krueger could see the terror growing in Brandt's eyes. He figured it was because of the shock of what had just happened. But he was wrong, for Brandt's terror was magnified by what she saw in Krueger's face. There was none of the fear or panic she expected to find in his eyes, rather a white-hot rage and ironclad determination. *Oh God*, she thought. *This is a man who lives for violence.*

"So you figured you'd toss me a scrap of paper and run away?" Krueger asked with his deadened eyes.

"How was I to know you'd be coming here alone like some kind of John Wayne character?" Brandt wailed. "Believe me, if I'd have known the lengths those . . . those bastards were prepared to silence you, I would have warned you to stay away from here."

Krueger lessened his grip and allowed Dr. Brandt to shake free. "If this place is so dangerous, why did you come here?" Brandt's eyes grew wide, as if she were suddenly excited to divulge a great and important secret.

"I've wanted to walk through these offices since I was a teenage girl," she whispered. "I thought by now you'd have ordered the place examined, and I came down to witness it. It's a good thing I did." Brandt allowed herself to look at the corpse by her feet and shuddered.

"So why didn't you come before?" Krueger asked.

Brandt snorted in derision. "Because this places crawls with Neo-Nazi gangs every night. Drugs, gunrunning, prostitution, they are all rampant round here. Every vice you can think of is catered to in this neighborhood." Brandt shook her head, believing that the thick-headed American would never understand. "We'd better call the police," she said.

"Not a chance," Krueger replied sternly, before pulling a card from his pocket. "This ID says baldy here is Thomas Weber, officer in the Grenzschutzgruppe neun der Bundespolizei. I may not know much German, but I know that that's the name for the toughest, meanest police outfit in Germany. And I know how tight those units are. If they hear we killed one of their comrades, they're not gonna look too kindly on us. And the guy down those stairs? According to his business card, he's the head of IT for a rubber molding firm. The cops are hardly likely to believe they attacked us."

"So you're going to leave them here, like a common killer?" Brandt cried.

"No, I'm going to confess everything. But I'm gonna do that back home, back in the USA, after I've found myself a damn fine lawyer who'll make sure I never have to set foot in Germany ever again."

Dr. Brandt shook her head in confusion and dismay.

"But first," Krueger said, "you and I are going to have a chat, and you can help explain why this shithole is so important."

Brandt was scared, but she still possessed the heart and sprit of teacher, which is why, despite the chaos around her, a small, excited smile crept across her face. "Of course," she said, "but not here. It's too dangerous. Come, I know a good café. The patisserie is better than anything you'll find in France."

KRUEGER FINISHED HIS third cup of coffee. On the table in front of him was a sticky, intricate pastry, completely untouched, next to the files he'd taken from Volcker-Blum and the personal effects of the dead men he'd left there. Their wallets suggested they both lived the lives of dull, middle-class men, aside from a business card for a Cairo hotel found in Weber's wallet.

Seated opposite, Dr. Brandt was busy reading with hungry eyes the letters Krueger had brought with him from Pennsylvania, his mother's last reminders of her father. Around them, the shop was bustling, the windows misted, and the air was filled with steam and happy conversation. Joe Krueger allowed himself to relax and absorb what Dr. Brandt was about to say.

"Your mother was right to tell you that General Krueger died in Spandau in 1951," she said. "He was serving a tough sentence, but I don't know why."

"The Americans wanted to know his secrets," Krueger answered. "Hitler appointed him the first director of his Ahnenerbe."

"Nazi zealots," Brandt said, nodding her head. "Tasked with looting the conquered lands of their treasures. You know, by the war's end, a fifth of all art in Europe and the Middle East had been stolen by Ahnenerbe troops and taken back to Germany, including the Holy Lance."

"Well Hitler wanted something else," Krueger said. "Something more powerful: The True Cross. He seemed to think it would grant him eternal life, and he sent gramps to find it. Somehow the Americans figured he knew where it was and wouldn't free him till he confessed." Krueger showed Brandt the rough translations he'd made on the flight to Berlin.

"Remarkable," Brandt said.

"And you don't know anything about this?" Krueger asked.

"Not much," Brandt said. "The Americans were always so keen to publicize how severely they were punishing Nazi leaders. It was all part of their plan to de-Nazify Germany. Heck, they broadcast the Nuremburg trials across the globe. But for some reason, they always kept General Krueger's incarceration a secret. This might explain it."

Brandt speared her pastry and watched as the flaky crust broke to reveal the milky custard inside. She chewed thoughtfully.

"The moment he died," she said between bites, "he must have been taken to those offices you just visited and placed inside one of the cryo-pods."

"Greedy bastard," Krueger muttered, "he paid Volcker for his voodoo because he was desperate for eternal life."

"Which," Brandt said, "is something he might have achieved, *if* your FBI is right."

"Impossible!" Krueger said. "I came here trying to find a rational way out of this mystery, and instead, I find myself heading deeper into the tunnel of a madhouse."

"Perhaps, but at least you're not alone now!" Brandt said, and she suddenly grabbed his hand. Smiling nervously, she looked back down at the table.

"So what happened to Volcker-Blum after Volcker died?" Krueger asked. He signaled the waitress, a grinning blonde in pigtails, for another coffee.

"The official line is that the German Democratic Republic took over the property, ended Volcker's heathen experiments, and returned the dead to their graves." Brandt rolled her eyes. "In truth, they pimped out those offices to the highest bidder. And after the Berlin Wall fell, all kinds of American companies started sniffing around government assets looking for a bargain. One of them was the Castor Group. They put the right kind of money into the hands of the right kind of people and got hold of those offices you saw about ten years ago. It was all legal."

"But if Castor owns the place, why did they let it rot?" Krueger asked, and Brandt raised a thin eyebrow.

"Did that basement look rotten to you? Because it looked to me like one of the most expensive labs in the world. No, detective, my guess is Castor deliberately let the exterior of the building fall into ruin, all the better to hide what they were doing inside."

"Which was?"

"Realizing Volcker's dream!" Brandt cried. "Resurrecting Nazis from the dead!"

Krueger rolled his eyes. It sounded like the stuff of 50s B-movie scripts. "Is that why you've been itching to go see the place?" Krueger asked.

"Local police know that Neo-Nazi gangs are fond of using that place as a meeting spot. The think it's a coincidence. But I've always suspected they were there under orders. They've been told to guard the place."

Krueger tried to laugh at the impossibility of it all. But the laugh died on his lips. "Those pods in the basement all had people inside," Krueger confessed as Brandt nodded along. "All except one . . . the one furthest from the door. The clipboard next to it said my grandfather was supposed to be inside it."

Brandt took a sharp intake of breath and cursed, which, in her German accent, Krueger found strangely comical.

"You're a detective," Brandt said finally. "As am I, in a strange sort of way. And so we both rely on evidence to draw conclusions. Well, let's take a look at what we know." Brandt paused, took a deep breath, and closed her eyes.

Krueger could sense that she was gathering her ideas, as if they would be her soldiers in a battle of wills.

"These letters from your mother," she said, pointing to the yellowing papers Krueger had shared, "prove that General Krueger was sent by Hitler to French Syria to find the Cross. We know that your grandfather believed whoever found the True Cross would be granted supernatural powers, perhaps even eternal life. We know he failed in his mission. We know that upon his return to Berlin, he contracted with Volcker-Blum and paid his way into one of the cryo-pods. Fast forward to today, and his pod is hanging wide open, while the world's media is reporting that a man who looks like him is responsible for bombing a Jewish museum!"

"So what are you saying?" Krueger asked.

Brandt's eyes fell to the table, as she let the question hang in the air unanswered. They both knew what Brandt wanted to say: Nazis, honest-to-goodness Nazis, were being resurrected.

Krueger pushed back from the table, spilling his coffee as he died so. The steaming black liquid started to stain the papers on the desk, and Brandt gathered them up with worried hands. But Krueger shrugged. Once again, his mind was wracked by the chill certainty that he was on the fringes of a vast conspiracy, and he wondered if he had the grit to find out more.

"Look what you've done!" Brandt hissed, and when she didn't receive an answer, she turned to find Krueger heading to the door. "Where are you going?" she demanded.

"To bed," Krueger answered truthfully.

"But you can't!" Brandt protested.

"Why not?" Krueger said. "There're too many questions that need answering, and I've had too little sleep to ponder them. I need shut-eye if I'm to carry on working on these Goddamned conundrums that don't seem to lead anyplace except places I don't want to go."

"Then stay with me!" Brandt said. "If they knew to look for your rental car, then they likely know your name and your apartment."

Krueger nodded slowly, accepting the truth of what Dr. Brandt said. Silent, weary, and grim, he allowed the young professor to lead him to her car. But before he did, he retrieved his phone and sent a text to his friend and partner, Sam O'Brian, back in New York.

Hey buddy. I need a favor. I know it sounds crazy, but can you research cryogenic freezing?

"SLEEP WELL?" TESSA Brandt asked as she came into her lounge. She wore a silk robe and carried a tea tray. Her apartment groaned under the weight of ancient books, monographs, and assorted dusty gimcracks, proving to Krueger that she not only taught history, but lived it too.

"Sure," Krueger lied, running his hand over his stubble. Brandt's couch was a vast leather dream, perfect for stretching out and enjoying a long and untroubled night. But Krueger had spent the evening lost in his own head. Questions which had no good answers kept swirling through his thoughts, taunting him and denying him the sleep he so badly needed.

Still, the night hadn't been a complete waste. While Brandt was in dreamland, Krueger spent his time checking up on his host. Several hours scrolling through his cell phone, which had survived being thrown in the Volcker-Blum factory, plus a surreptitious glance at the files she'd left in her lounge, proved Brandt was who she claimed. A PhD from the Free University of Berlin, followed by stints at the Sorbonne and the Smithsonian, had left the thirty-six-year-old with a reputation as a tenacious scholar, a fine teacher, and an implacable foe of Nazism.

She was also a Taekwondo enthusiast, and judging by the gaudy trophies gathering dust on her mantelpiece, an amateur champion of sorts.

Krueger grabbed the tea Brandt offered him with her muscular arm. "What now?" she asked.

Krueger shook his head. "A shower and a swift return to New York," he said, "where I'll confess everything I've done."

Brandt clicked her tongue but did not try to stop him as he rose. There was a hardness in Krueger's eyes that suggested he could not be argued out of his choice, and anyone who made the attempt would suffer.

"I'll need a cab," Krueger said.

"Sure," Brandt replied sullenly and pulled her cell phone from her pocket. But something flashed on the screen, and the doctor's expression turned suddenly dark. Despairing, she thrust the phone into Krueger's uncertain hands, and he read with tired eyes the text on the screen. His hands were trembling by the time he'd finished.

8

"HELLO?" THE EXHAUSTED voice answered.

"What time is it there, Sam?" Krueger asked.

"Stupid o'clock," O'Brian replied, "but it don't matter; none of us are getting any sleep tonight."

"Tell me what you know," Krueger said. He was still staring at Brandt's phone, with the Bild headline announcing the latest terror attack to hit the US.

"Berkowitz Gallery in Portland was hit yesterday afternoon," O'Brian said, massaging the bridge of his nose. Outside Police Plaza, New York was as still as that magnificent city ever gets. "Twelve confirmed dead, three times that still in the hospital."

"Linked to the New York blast?"

"Likely," O'Brian answered. "Either perpetrated by the same sickos or by a copycat. We've got no positive ID on the suspect, but ATF investigators working out of Seattle report that the bomb was made using the same homebrew recipe as the one that tore up the Meyer Center."

"Jeez," Krueger said, feeling guilty that he'd fled his homeland in a time of crisis.

"That's not all," O'Brian continued. "A movie mogul from LA financed the gallery, an Israeli citizen, which has got Hawtrey thinking this is an anti-Semitic thing."

Krueger cursed.

"What's up, Joey?" O'Brian asked. "You sound almost as tired as me."

"You remember I asked for information on cryogenic freezing?" Krueger asked, answering his partner's question with a question of his own.

"Sure do," O'Brian said, "but with this latest attack, you'll forgive me if I put your newfound hobby on the back burner."

"Sam," Krueger said, "I don't think this is a hobby no more. You need to know what I found out . . . and what I did . . . last night."

DAWN WAS BREAKING warm over New York by the time Krueger has finished his story. "I'm screwed, aren't I?" he asked his partner.

"Most likely," O'Brian confessed, grimacing as he took a swig of the coffee that had grown cold while Krueger was speaking. "You need to get on a plane back here, buddy. Those GSG-9 are bad hombres. Get back to New York and lawyer up. You'll most likely be extradited, but at least you'll have Uncle Sam on your side."

"I'll be out the country by the end of the day," Krueger said. "In the meantime, I need whatever you can find about cryogenic freezing. Is it . . . is at all possible that my grandfather could be walking the streets?"

"I'll see what I can find out, partner," O'Brian said. "I'll show you what I dig up when I see you tonight. That means you call me the second you land, capiche? I'll take you for a beer, then I'll take you to a lawyer. He's an expensive SOB, but he'll work day and night to make sure you never spend a day in German cell."

Cheered by his partner's promise of aid, Krueger hung up with a smile a face. For the first time in twenty-four hours, he felt hope that he'd get through this nightmare without losing his mind. He even allowed himself a bite of the cured meats Brandt has offered him for breakfast.

But no sooner had he swallowed the first mouthful than Brandt returned to the lounge, wearing an expression that told Krueger his good cheer was about to be banished.

"You ready for the second bad headline of the day?" she asked.

"Nope," Krueger answered, before taking Brandt's cell phone. The homepage of a local Berlin newspaper was up on the screen. It was a tabloid, judging by the lurid way they reported the deaths of Sergeant Thomas Webber, hero of GSG-9, and Herr Gunther Frick, Vice-President of Gummi Pro.

The article was in German, and with his tired eyes and numbed brain, Krueger was in no mood to translate. He handed the phone back to his host.

"We knew they'd find them sooner or later," he said, shrugging on his black shearling jacket.

"No!" Brandt said, "it's worse." She pulled up the article and began reading. "Both victims were found at dawn in the Neukölln district, close to the notorious derelict factories used as a meeting point by drug dealers and gangs. Early reports suggest that they were found stripped naked and hanging from a nearby tree, though police have refused to provide details on the deaths."

Krueger shivered despite his coat. He was well acquainted with death; he knew how quickly it could come, and how it showed no respect for youth, age, money, or power. He'd faced killers in foreign war zones and on the drug-clogged streets of New York and had grown wearily indifferent to their rage. But mutilating the dead, disturbing bodies without motive: these were not the signs of a simple killer, but of a madman.

The conspiracy Krueger was facing, if conspiracy it was, was far blacker than he thought.

"What do you make of it?" he asked Brandt, finishing the last drop of a glass of water he did not remember picking up. Krueger's mood was dark, but it grew darker still when Brandt began talking in what sounded like riddles:

"When someone is convicted of a crime punishable by death and is executed, you hang him on a tree, but his corpse must not remain all night upon the tree; you shall bury him that same day, for anyone hung on a tree and abandoned is under God's curse."

"Where did you dig up that nice little limerick?" Krueger asked.

"The book of Deuteronomy," Brandt replied, "in the Bible." The weight of that mighty two-syllable word seemed to bear down on Krueger, and his shoulders crumpled. He sat back on the couch, as if trying to escape its portent.

"So our two boys were discovered last night," he said. "Their pals found them, realized their failure and grew mad, and because they are zealots, they decided to hang them—"

"So they would forever be under God's curse," Brandt said, finishing Krueger's sentence. "What sort of people would do this?" she asked.

"The kind that are about to feel the long arm of American justice," Krueger said. Clenching his jaw, he rose to his feet and strode out of the room and into the hallway. "These guys are mixed up with the attacks back home," he said, "and they are mixed up with my goddamned family too!"

Krueger hands became fists, and he slammed his right paw into the wall. His face, already massive, looked like it had been carved in marble by angry, slashing hands and was terrifying to behold.

"And by God they will pay!" Krueger bundled his papers into his coat pockets. His first flush of despair had been burned away by a rage that was now roaring heartily in his chest. "Tessa," he said, "I'm heading home. Once I land, I'm getting my boys in NYPD to help clear this up. Soon there'll be American agents all over this city like a rash. Till then, you sit tight; don't go exploring that Volcker rat hole no more!"

Brandt, impressed by the older cop's passion, blushed. Her eyes grew wide in surprise and admiration, and she opened the door of her apartment. Krueger took a step into the hallway, but as he turned he caught site of two tall officers approaching, clad in the green and white uniforms of the Berlin Landespolizei.

Their eyes fell upon his, and the officers broke into a sprint. Krueger cursed and retreated into the apartment, locking the door behind him. "Goddammit Sam! I told you not to tell anyone!"

The footfalls outside came to sudden stop, replaced by loud banging on the door.

"Cops!" Krueger said to Brandt. "Either Sam's blabbed to someone or Hawtrey found me. Either way, we're screwed."

"But your partner didn't know you were staying in my apartment!" Brandt cried over the din behind the door. She lived in a smart apartment building near the Tiergarten, and already her neighbors were spilling into the hallway sharing worried glances as the police continued to batter the door.

"You're thinking these guys could be friends of Weber?" Krueger asked.

Brandt nodded her head and grabbed a large silver sculpture atop the hallway table. It looked like a sham Remington, depicting a cowboy riding a horse.

"Slow down," Krueger said, but events were moving too fast now. If the men behind the door were Weber's confederates, perhaps even the men who had hung his naked body, then he and Brandt needed to escape. But if they were here on the orders of Hawtrey, or had somehow linked them to the murders, then his career, and his liberty, depended on playing nice.

Krueger leaned his head against the door, watching his sweat drip onto the floor below. He felt like he was back in the Middle East, not knowing friend from foe. Everyone, it seemed, was hiding their names and intentions beneath a veil of lies. It was enough to drive even reasonable men to black despair.

"What do you want?" Krueger cried.

"You are wanted for questioning," the officer replied in English, "in connection to the murders last night in Neukölln district."

Krueger sighed. In times like this, it was all too easy to reach for a gun, and sure enough, Krueger patted his back to make sure the Dostovei was still tucked into his pants. It was empty, but no one knew that except him.

Looking at Brandt, Krueger shrugged and opened the door.

The two men leapt into the hallway and slammed the door behind them. Batons raised, they swiftly disarmed Brandt, who had not expected Krueger to let them in, and they slammed her against the wall. A picture hanging from a dusty alcove fell to the floor, spraying the carpet with glass.

Too violent, Krueger thought, backing away from the other officer who was approaching him. Gaunt and wiry, he wore a feral smile and a mud-stained jacket that was too big for him.

"Hey Neumann," Krueger yelled, reading the name tag on the front of the jacket. But the officer did not flinch. His lupine smile did not waver.

Krueger yelled the name again, but once more the man did not respond.

These aren't cops, Krueger slowly realized, as his meager breakfast turned summersaults in his belly. These were the men who had hung Weber and Frick from the tree. As if to confirm his suspicion, the man stepped into the light streaming from the lounge door, and Krueger saw that the stain on his jacket, which he had mistaken for mud, was something far worse.

It was blood.

Krueger roared, a sound guttural and fierce, and the phony cop took a step back in fright. His smile vanished completely when Krueger presented his gun, and he dropped the baton.

"Get back Fritz!" Krueger said, and the man did as he was told.

Seeing Krueger menace the man closest to him, Brandt raised her leg and struck the guy behind her in the crotch. He stumbled, but not as much as Brandt had hoped, and when she tried to seize the sculpture, his fist was there to stop her. The man grabbed Brandt's hair and yanked her violently, before using both his hands to hold the baton against her throat. He pulled hard, and as Brandt began to choke, her attacker turned to Krueger and grinned triumphantly.

"Get back!" He said in English, "or her neck is broken."

Krueger paused. The man holding Brandt had a tattoo on his neck, and the violet bags under his eyes suggested a drug addiction. Depending on what garbage was coursing through his veins, he could kill the doctor before Krueger took another step further.

"Let her go," Krueger said as the second phony cop, the one who had dropped his baton, recovered his courage and stood next to his friend. He looked like a man who had won a prize but was not sure how.

"Not a chance," the man replied. "Put down the gun. Now." The threat lingered in the air as the man pulled the baton, crushing Brandt's throat. Brandt's lips began to turn blue.

Krueger sized up his two opponents. Both smaller than he, but with the zeal of maniacs, they could easily overpower him.

But he did have Brandt. And her gaudy plastic trophies proved she was not as helpless as these two men believed.

Krueger nodded, a lightning-fast glance that gave Brandt a split-second's warning of what was to come. She saw it through tear-stained eyes and nodded in reply. Then Krueger raised his empty gun and threw it at the nearest man. It missed, barely striking his shoulder, but it provided Krueger the time he needed to reach down and grab the baton the phony cop had dropped earlier. So armed, the New York cop fell upon his foe, swinging the club, not caring where the blows landed, so long as they hurt.

Brandt's attacker took a defensive step back, and in so doing, lessened his grip. It was the one shot she needed. Simultaneously she stomped on his left shoe and drove her elbow savagely into his gut, enjoying the sucking sounds that came out of his mouth, knowing she'd left him winded. She spun and raked her nails across his face, drawing blood, and as he raised his hands defensively, she finally grabbed the sculpture and brought the rearing horse down upon his head. It left a red welt at the top of his skull, and he collapsed to the floor, conscious, but with no fight left in him.

Krueger, panting, dropped the blood-stained baton in disgust. His foe was bleeding from his nose, his lips were busted, and the remains of three teeth littered the floor.

"So how do you know self-defense?" Krueger asked, amazed at Brandt's swift and confident attack.

"I have a reputation with a few of the Neo-Nazi gangs," she said. Krueger noticed Brandt was still breathing calmly, suggesting she was fitter and tougher than most college faculty. "It pays to know how to take care of yourself, especially when amateurs like this are clogging up the gutters of Berlin."

Brandt shook her head dismissively, enraged that the men had violated her home and so casually assumed that she was easy prey. She had the look of someone who had often been underestimated in her life, and was left bitter as a consequence.

"Not quite," Krueger said, accurately assessing the situation. "They stripped and hung dead men from a tree, they found where you lived, and they either stole, or have friends who could provide, genuine police uniforms. Not bad for what appear to be addicts." Krueger totted up all these points like an accountant, and the grim balance suggested only one course of action. "We've got to leave," Krueger said, picking up his gun and wiping the blood from the baton. "More may be coming."

"But this is my home!" Brandt protested.

"And it will be again," Krueger said, "but right now, we have to get out of here."

Brandt stood with her hands on her hips in defiance. But suddenly her green eyes, which had narrowed to slits, opened wide. "I know where we can go," she said.

"It needs to be someplace secluded, someplace quiet," Krueger said. "I need to call Sam, and most likely Hawtrey too." Brandt was pacing around the apartment, tossing clothing and other items into a blue canvas bag. "What do you have in mind?" Krueger asked.

"Airport," Brandt replied.

"Did you just hear a damned word I said?" Krueger cried, but Brandt didn't reply. She pushed open her door, pushed past the worried neighbors with her nose in the air, and rushed to the lobby with Krueger, bewildered, following behind. "Trust me," she said, "this place is one of the most secure in the world."

Tessa Brandt gunned the car and sped out of her parking lot just as the sound of police sirens rose in the air. The real cops had arrived.

IT TOOK SIX LONG, drab hours to reach Frankfurt, but the journey had at least given Krueger time to rest. He slept well, and his dreams had been untroubled by the chaos of the last few days. He awoke to find a jagged grey skyline beneath a milky sunlight.

Not even Brandt's many conversations had woken him. She'd spent most of the trip on her cellphone speaking hurriedly in German, and though Krueger didn't know who she was talking to, the long wrenching laughs suggested it was a close friend or friends.

She's tough, Krueger thought. *A home assault would have broken most people's confidence and sapped their self-esteem. But this teacher? Yucking it up just hours later.*

"I should have used that time to make a few calls myself," Krueger confessed as he opened his eyes to find Brandt charging her cell phone. Outside, the sky was a vast grey smear.

The young German scholar smiled and flicked the turn signal; she was taking her green little Volvo off the Autobahn. "You needed to sleep," she said.

"Sam needs to know. So does Hawtrey . . . and Hassler."

"They'll all be told when we get you out of the country," Brandt said. "And there's too much heat on you in Berlin."

"On *us*," Krueger corrected her. Brandt grimaced, remembering the crazed savagery which had nearly ended her life. "So where are you taking me?" Krueger asked.

"Greystone Investment International," Brandt answered, before adding the words "private equity group" when she saw Krueger's vacant expression.

Krueger frowned as the Volvo drove over the Love Lock Bridge toward downtown. Vast skyscrapers, gleaming confections of steel and glass, rose up to meet them.

"You don't seem like a girl who parties with bankers," Krueger said.

"I'm not," Brandt replied, "but Barnaby Grimm isn't a banker."

Forty minutes later, Krueger and Brandt stood on a windswept helipad overlooking Frankfurt. Glum-eyed guards stood alert around them. Greystone, founded by Lord Anthony Leslie Grimm, had continental headquarters on the top floor of the Silberturm, a fantastical skyscraper that seemed to shine even in the dun afternoon light. Standing atop that tower, Krueger and Brandt could barely be heard over the din of the gusting wind.

But soon a sound louder still emerged: the throaty growl of a helicopter engine. Lights cut through the low-hanging cloud, and a sleek black chopper finally emerged, gracefully landing just a few dozen feet away from where Krueger stood.

The sole passenger gamboled out of the door before the rotor had come to a complete stop. His dark complexion and brown eyes contrasted with the light grey tweed suit he was wearing. His black hair was swept back, and a golden pocket watch twinkled from his vest.

"Tessa!" he cried in a deep baritone. "Welcome back!" Tessa smiled seductively and embraced him.

"Good to see you, Grimm," she said, before leading him to Krueger.

"Detective, this is Dr. Barnaby Grimm, formerly on the faculty at St. Andrews University. An expert on the antiquities and archeology of the Middle East, and a good friend."

"Please to meet you, pal," Krueger said, and was amazed to discover that Grimm greeted him without once staring at his chin. It was a welcome change from the minute winces and furtive stares he normally received.

"Pleased to make your acquaintance," Grimm said in an accent that suggested an expensive education. "May I press you to some afternoon tea?" Grimm asked, ushering Brandt and Krueger to the stairwell.

But Brandt grabbed his hand and came between him and the exit. "Actually, we are rather rushed, Barnaby. A swift departure would be most appreciated."

Grimm flashed a warm smile that lingered on his lips even as he returned to the helicopter. "As you wish," he said.

"Why are we hooking up with his guy?" Krueger asked Brandt as the rotor blades coughed back into life.

"Three reasons," Brandt answered, leading him to the open door of the helicopter. "First, he knows early Christian history like you Americans know baseball. He might shed some light on Krueger's quest for the Cross. Second, his dad is the third wealthiest man in Europe, which means he has ways to get us out of Germany without any entanglements with the police."

"And third?" Krueger asked.

"He's a lot of fun! We met back when we were both on faculty at the Smithsonian."

"Ah, so you met over organic hummus in some beige seminar room, right?" Krueger asked.

"Try bungee jumping in the Shenandoah Valley," Brandt spat as she slid into a soft, leather seat inside the chopper. Grimm was already opening a bottle of champagne as his helicopter left the pad, the pilot heading toward the sullen clouds above. He handed his guests each a glass, along with a set of headphones so they could continue their conversation above the din of the engine.

"So," the young professor said, "can I have some answers now, please? Seldom would I choose to interrupt a holiday in Ibiza, but your promise of adventure stirred my curiosity."

"Trust me, pal," Krueger said, "if it's adventure stories you like, you're gonna love this."

The cop sipped his champagne with incurious gusto. It seemed odd to quaff fine wine hours after a gruesome assault, but then, everything had seemed odd since the New York blast.

GRIMM'S CHOPPER LANDED on a bare airfield a few miles outside the city. Surrounded by wet fens and scrubland, it looked like a bleak and unfriendly land. But as the helicopter touched the greasy tarmac, Krueger caught site of a gleaming Lear jet idling on the runway. It was, he hoped, his ticket out of Germany.

"Fascinating," Grimm said, marveling at the papers Krueger had presented him with to support his ludicrous story. "Absolutely fascinating."

"So what do you think?" Brandt asked, but Grimm ignored her and kept repeating the word 'fascinating' as if it were a holy rite.

The three companions exited the chopper, and Krueger watched as the access door of the Lear swung open seductively. A flight attendant, with teeth like huge white gravestones, shimmied down the stairs and smiled.

"Are we ready to depart, Barnaby?" Brandt asked, but found her friend still lost in the papers. His mind, finely trained at Harrow, Cambridge, and Berkeley, was adept at tackling complex riddles, but his singular focus often left him forgetting other, more mundane, matters.

"Certainly," he said absently, as he came upon the blank sheet of paper, the one Trudy Krueger claimed was the last she ever received from her father. "And what is this?" Grimm asked.

Krueger explained the story, and as he did so Grimm shuffled toward the side of the runway, where a member of the ground crew was warming himself next to a fire roaring in an iron brazier.

"Fascinating," Grimm said, with a fey smile on his face. Brandt looked at Krueger to share her suspicion, and as she did so, the professor lowered the paper and placed it above the flames.

"Are you crazy?" Krueger yelled, charging forward and grabbing the paper as the flames began to lick it. Grimm did not resist and allowed the tall cop to take it from his hands.

"You nearly burned the damned thing!" Brandt said.

"Not quite," Grimm said, pointing to the document. Krueger looked down and saw, to his amazement, that the paper was no longer blank. It was covered in the writing of General Wolfgang Krueger.

- 9 -

MY DEAREST ELSA,

It is a ghastly thing to write this way, using my own water, but the Jews had great success evading the censors in the camps using this method, and evasion is now my utmost priority. I pray that you will discover the words I am writing.

I need to speak to you and Trudy plainly, so that you may know your husband, and so that you can see beyond the lies they shall tell about me. This is especially important as I have such little time left. My cancer has spread, my love, and I have just weeks left to live.

Darling, no one knows my heart as well as you, and you know that I joined Hitler and his band of criminals on the promise that they would help protect our Christian faith from the godless Communists. I wept bitter tears when I saw his troops smash their way through the museums and universities of Europe, but I was convinced it was for a holy cause, one that God himself had blessed. How else could one account for the string of victories Hitler won?

When I was ordered to Syria, I went with joy swelling in my breast, knowing that the Holy Spirit was leading me onward. I would, thanks to the al-Qalqashandi Fragment, find the True Cross, succeed where others had failed, and return the holiest of relics to our church. Held in common ownership by all God's children, the Cross would grant us all incredible power with which to make our fallen world a better one.

But God opened my eyes . . . before it was too late. Hitler's victories turned to bloody defeats, and Europe was soaked by the blood of innocents. Hitler's messages to me became more and more incoherent: one day I was to be promoted to the highest office, the next I was to return to Berlin to be hanged.

Finally, Himmler, Hitler's little rodent of an underling, dispatched an SS officer to oversee our work. God delivered him safely, of that I'm sure, for he soon revealed the truth that had been hidden from me.

This colonel confessed to me that Hitler did not want to save Christianity but to bury it. He and Himmler were building their black Camelot, a vile new religion with Nazi leaders as the new messiahs. Wewelsburg Castle would be both Rome and Jerusalem for this new black faith, where they planned to house the stolen relics of Christianity, draw from their power, and grind Christ's name into dust.

Hearing his words, my heart filled with dismay, as the truth, finally, was revealed to me: Hitler and his fanatics were spiritually dead. They sought the True Cross to obtain an everlasting life they did not deserve.

I felt utterly ashamed to have helped Hitler set this plan in motion. And so, knowing that Christ would accept no less from me, I sabotaged our search for the Cross. I pled ignorance and led my team in every direction apart from the one that led to the Cross.

Prayer sustained me in those dark times, my darling, prayer and the boundless love I feel for you.

As you know, the failure of the Syria dig ruined my reputation in Hitler's eyes and I was recalled to Berlin. No doubt I would have perished in one of the Fuhrer's exterminations, but the tide was turning in his war, and he had little time for a failed functionary like me. I was shuttled between various backwater posts, which was punishment enough as it kept me from you and Trudy. Even so, I succeeded in getting you both out of the country by the war's end before being apprehended by the Americans. I may have failed many times as a husband and father, but in this, at least, I was successful.

Alas, the Americans who captured me knew of my special service to Hitler, and they doubted my assurance that I did not know the location of the Cross. You know the rest of my sad tale.

But there is one thing you don't know. By the time I returned to Berlin in 1941, Hitler's Stormtroopers had raided my office, and it is likely they found information related to the Cross. A sharp mind, as sharp as mine, would easily be able to piece together what I left and learn the true location. If they do, then Hitler's black Camelot could rise from the ashes at Wewelsburg.

My love, it is for that reason that I contracted with a professor of science, a certain Dr. Gunther Volcker, who is working on the cutting edge of medicine. He tells me of a new procedure which can extend the lives of decrepit people, even the sick like me. I suspect that this man is a fraud, but I am desperate. I must not, I cannot allow Hitler's followers to abuse my work and seize the Cross.

For that reason, I shall be entrusting my body to Professor Volcker at the moment of my death. I have provided the guards here at Spandau with a large payment of cash, such that they will help facilitate the removal of my body to Volcker's laboratory. A pauper will be placed in the grave reserved for me in Berlin, to keep this conspiracy from becoming public.

My goal is simple: to remain here on this mortal Earth long after I have been called to Heaven. I cannot turn my back on an Earth I have put in such terrible danger. This is my penance.

I do this, my love, to atone for my many mistakes! I do not fear to meet my Maker; in point of fact, I long to kneel before Him and proclaim my love for He who died for us all. But I will deny myself the sweetness of His gaze. I cannot rest. I must keep watching!

When my watch is over, and if the Lord blesses us in eternity as He did in life, then we shall see one another again in a better place.

Until that time, my love,
Your Walter

Krueger, Brandt, and Grimm, the three chance companions, stood in the faltering light of dusk. Krueger looked punch-drunk, his mammoth jaw hanging slack, as if he'd been socked in the mouth by a prizefighter.

"How did you . . ." he asked in a small voice, as Barnaby Grimm removed a comb from him pocket and smoothed his immaculate black locks.

He looked nonchalantly at the cop. "Quite simple really," he said. "And I'm amazed that our good Dr. Brandt didn't test my theory beforehand."

"What theory?" she mumbled.

"Why, that Krueger was using the very first invisible ink known to mankind: human urine. Like I said, quite simple. You write the message you wish to keep hidden using a thin, wooden stick dipped in your own water. The urine then loses its color, but the acid scorches the paper and the text can be seen again if one warms the surface on which it's been written."

"Fascinating," Krueger said, oblivious to the fact that he'd appropriated Grimm's favorite word and was using it for himself.

"The technique was first used by spies for the Roman Empire, and it has lasted ever since. Inmates at the Ravensbruck concentration camp used the same method to get secret messages to their families outside."

"And General Krueger used it to," Brandt said.

"So it would seem," Grimm said, before leading his companions towards his Lear. "We should make haste," he said. "Having a mother from Ghana taught me a deep love of folklore and legends . . . but having a Calvinistic Scottish father taught me the importance of timekeeping too. We need to get you out of the country."

The expensive engine purred as the jet soared over the plains of Germany. Inside, Grimm was seated in a high-backed leather chair, a glass of something comforting next to him. Krueger, at Grimm's insistence, was laying on a sumptuous couch, buttery soft and piled high with cushions.

"You look drained, dear boy," Grimm said, as he put his hand on the cop's shoulder.

Grimm was right; Krueger's cheeks were the color of sodden ash. His lips kept trembling, as if he were talking furtively to himself. "Where're we going?" he asked absently.

"Wherever we wish," Grimm said, removing his tweed coat and donning a smoking jacket instead. It was disgustingly ostentatious, and Krueger would have taken a dislike to anyone else wearing it, but Grimm, for all his frippery, possessed a serious mind. "I can arrange transport to pretty much anyplace on Earth." Grimm removed a monographed cigarette holder from his pocket and began to smoke a fragrant tobacco.

"Why would you do this?" Krueger asked.

"The greatest curse of being rich is boredom," Grimm said unhesitatingly. "One can almost feel one's mind rotting amid the parties and vacations. It's why I went into antiquities. All the best adventures happened long ago, and I hoped to live vicariously through the heroes of yore. Alas, those dusty libraries are as dull to me as the lavish city cocktail bars. Adventure is still the one thing I struggle to buy."

They all fell into silence, leaving the stewardess to minister to their various needs. As Grimm began playing a delicate gavotte through the speakers, something which sounded like Bach, Krueger drank deeply from a mug of sweet-smelling tea and sighed as the sunset blazed gloriously through the window.

Krueger tried to forget the case, but couldn't. And sometime after seven, with the sky around him now a velvety blue, he found his muscles begin to loosen. He smiled reluctantly. It was in just this fashion, stretched out and comfortable as his mind raced along multiple pathways to the truth, that he had cracked many cases back in New York. It was not cutting-edge technology or deadly weapons that had helped Joe Krueger send dozens of verminous crooks to Riker's, but his beat-up couch and a frosty bottle of beer, with five auxiliaries waiting for him in the fridge.

"So how does this letter aid us?" Krueger asked, now eager for the mental marathon ahead. Barnaby began to look at him with a fey expression, as if doubting a strapping man with a bulldozer for a chin was capable of deep thought.

"Well," said Brandt eagerly, having waited impatiently for the opportunity to address the topic, "it tells us your grandfather is not the villain we supposed him to be. He got into bed with Volcker, I think, for honorable reasons."

"Perhaps," Krueger said, "but that doesn't help answer our two most pressing questions. Is my grandfather still alive, and if so, is he responsible for the terror attacks in America?"

"I'm afraid, dear boy," Grimm said, swirling his drink in his manicured hand, "that this text offers few clues to those twin mysteries."

"Then this has been a waste," Brandt said.

"Perhaps not," Krueger replied. "Dr. Grimm, can you tell us what the al-Qalqashandi Fragment is?" Grimm smiled broadly, luxuriating in the fact that he was now lost in a riddle his fortune could never have bought.

"Shihab al-Din abu 'l-Abbas Ahmad ben Ali ben Ahmad Abd Allah al-Qalqashandi was a medieval Egyptian mathematician and cryptologist. Amongst his many works was a partially completed biography of Saladin, the conqueror of the Crusader States, which we call the al-Qalqashandi Fragment. He died before he could complete the work."

"Why would General Krueger believe it to hold the key to finding the True Cross?" Brandt asked.

Grimm shook his head. "I don't know," he confessed. "The Fragment contains little new information of worth, save for the mistake he made about Saladin's children."

"What mistake?" Brandt asked.

"Almost every historical source records that Saladin sired seven sons, but al-Qalqashandi claimed that he fathered twelve. An obvious error."

Krueger leaned across the table and examined the paper. The words were lost again now that the paper had cooled. "So Brandt's right," he said. "This has been a waste."

Grimm, fluent in six languages, did not know what to say. "I'm afraid that is all I know of the Fragment," he mumbled finally. "If you wish to learn any more, I suggest an online search, or a trip to the Saladin Citadel of Cairo, which is where it is stored."

"Cairo," Brandt whispered, savoring the word on her tongue, trying to remember why that name had recently been mentioned.

"Cairo!" Krueger bellowed, leaping to his feet beside her. He turned his enormous face toward Dr. Grimm, and his eyes darkened.

Grimm watched in apprehensive fascination as Krueger emptied the pockets of his shearling and shuffled through the papers he had accumulated on his journey.

Krueger worked with a deft and expert touch. Fallujah had taught him that a lead in a case, even a small one, needed to be followed up promptly if it was to stay fresh. Years pounding the streets of New York had seared that lesson into his brain.

"Here!" he said triumphantly, bringing out a business card from Weber's wallet. It was for the Memphis Hotel in Cairo. On the other side, a hasty hand had written: *Room 41.*

Krueger allowed himself a smile. It was broad and lasted on his lips for many minutes. At last, he had his break in the case. Krueger knew it was likely a pyrrhic victory, but after days of delays, confusion, and retreats, it was nonetheless a welcome one.

"This means," Brandt said, "that the man ordered to kill you, and perhaps guard your grandfather's cryo-pod, was also in the city—"

"Where the key to finding the True Cross is hidden," Krueger said, finishing her sentence. "Hardly a coincidence."

"This merits an investigation, surely?" Grimm asked hopefully. "A detective of your caliber would not allow this opportunity to wither on the vine."

Krueger allowed himself another, smaller smile. "If you're willing, ready, and able, Dr. Grimm," he said, "I sure would appreciate a ride to Egypt."

Grimm leaned back and laughed. "It would be my pleasure, sir," he said, "though I haven't a clue what to wear. All my linen suits are back in the Balearic Islands."

"OKAY," O'BRIAN SAID, flinging the unwanted rind of a donut into the trash, "you can tell that hausfrau that there's no way Grandpa Krueger survived the cryogenic freezing."

Far above the Mediterranean Sea, shielding his eyes from the sparkle of the azure waves, Krueger was talking with his partner. Brandt was next to him, the repeated target of O'Brian's ribbing.

"You sure about this?" Krueger asked. "I mean, it's not like you're a Nobel Laureate or anything." Grimm had set Krueger up with video conferencing technology, meaning he could watch as O'Brian took his laptop in both his meaty palms and feigned dumping it in the trash.

"Unlike you, Joey, I know how to run an investigation. I hit up all my sources, called in a few favors too, which means this is coming not from me, but from the chief coroner, a professor of physics from NYU, and the chief science correspondent of the *Times*."

O'Brian was seated in the bullpen. It was just before seven in the morning, and the cops around him were too tired and too busy to notice that he was talking to their missing comrade. But O'Brian had nonetheless fitted his computer with a privacy screen and was talking in a barely audible hush. Slowly, he fanned out some recent print-outs over his desk.

"Let me count the ways that revival after cryogenic freezing is impossible. First, the obvious: your grandad died of terminal cancer. And last I checked, we still ain't found a cure for that, meaning even if we could wake him up, he'd still be meeting his maker pretty quick. Second: lack of suitable cryo-protectants at the time Krueger died. You remember them potholes on 51st, Joey?" O'Brian asked.

"Sure do," Krueger answered, remembering the damage they'd done to his Grabber.

"They sprung up right after last winter, right?" O'Brian continued.

"Water got into the chinks in the asphalt, froze, and caused those cracks to emerge. Well buddy, if he was frozen, the same thing would have happened to your grandfather's body. Ice molecules are bigger than water, which means when water freezes, it expands. All that water in your grandfather's body turned into ice when he went into his pod, meaning cells in his skin, his liver, kidneys, and brain all exploded. Heck, even bone cells are 31% water, meaning there's no way he could have walked, let alone lifted a 300lb bomb."

"I see. So what's a cryo-protectant?" Krueger asked.

"Something designed to stop what I just described," O'Brian said, "and the thing is, most of them are toxic to humans. So even if he used," O'Brian picked up a sheaf of papers and read from a text, "er, formamide, it might stop the formation of ice crystals, but it'd still kill him."

"What else?" Brandt asked, leaning toward the screen while tucking into a bagel.

"Next up: bacteria," O'Brian said, playing with his reading glasses. "It says here there are more bacteria cells in your body than human ones. Can you believe that shit?" O'Brian chuckled and shook his head. "Anyhow, let's say you revive a frozen guy . . . he's gonna be weak, right? Infirm? Just the kinda guy who'd die from the smallest bacterial infection, which is exactly what he'd get the moment all them bacterial cells defrost.

"And lastly, even if we found the cure for cancer, even if Krueger found a non-toxic cryo-protectant to make sure no ice formed in his body, even if he took the best antibacterial meds when he awoke, he'd still be brain dead."

Krueger shuddered at the use of the phrase. "And how do you know that?" he asked.

"The brain just isn't meant to be put on ice, Joe," O'Brian said, dropping the papers and looking back up at his friend through the screen. "It's called information-theoretic death; the moment when a person loses their memories, their emotions, and their hopes and fears. You scramble the brain, the way you would going through cryogenic freezing, you stop being who you were. That sounds like a pretty irreversible death to me."

O'Brian finished his report and drew up his papers, knocking his overflowing ashtray as he did so. The eunuchs at City Hall had banned smoking in all public buildings years ago, but he'd keep his dirty ashtray around as a form of silent protest.

"So you wanna explain why I'm telling you this over a screen and not in person?" O'Brian asked. "Last time we spoke you promised me you'd be touching down at LaGuardia."

"That's before we were nearly killed by a couple of home intruders," Brandt said, spraying crumbs over her cream dress.

"What?" O'Brian asked, listening intently as Krueger described his escape from Berlin.

"You're knee-deep in some kooky stuff," O'Brian said afterwards. "Better not tell me where you are headed. Don't want that kind of information flying through these screens."

"I'll call you when I land," Krueger said. "I may need some help learning more about those goons who were stripped and hung at the Volcker plant: Weber and Frick."

"You got it," O'Brian said, before quipping, "just think of me as your research assistant."

"How you holding up?" Krueger asked, drawing closer to the screen. He was freshly washed and showered and looked, for a fleeting moment, like the cop he was so proud to be.

"It's tough here," O'Brian confessed, and as his eyes turned to the floor, Krueger saw the weariness riven in his pallid face. His shoulders were slumped as if his head were too big for his body.

"Hang in there," Krueger said. "As soon as I've followed up this lead, I'll be home."

"Take care, buddy," O'Brian said, "and don't forget to check in with Hawtrey. I got a feeling she's one of life's good eggs. She might even be able to help you."

As O'Brian closed his laptop, he saw the round figure of his captain marching toward him. "Damn," O'Brian muttered under his breath. The captain was rarely at his desk before nine, but something had brought him to the office early. Something bad, judging by his complexion, for Hassler's skin was the color of beetroot. Watching him lumber forwards, the Irishman shook his head and pretended to tidy his desk.

"My office!" Hassler barked.

O'Brian usually ignored Hassler's wrath, responding, as the moment required, with either sarcasm, banter, or outright mockery. But the hardness in Hassler's flinty eyes suggested a simple "yes" would be best.

O'Brian followed Hassler into his office and found a pock-marked crone standing beside the captain's desk. Her face looked as if it had been carved out of dead wood.

"This is Maureen Gibbon, Internal Affairs," Hassler said, pouring himself into his chair.

Gibbon nodded. Her lips pursed as though she were sucking a bushel of lemons.

"So," Hassler said, before pausing to smile to himself. As the captain leaned forward, his great shoulders like heaving mountains of polyester, O'Brian thought he looked like a fat spider, marveling with hungry eyes at the fly it had trapped. "What's the latest on the Beaumont case?" Hassler said.

"Can we wait till after breakfast, cap?" O'Brian asked, playing for time. "I've been running on fumes for 36 hours now. Gimme an hour to digest something."

"You don't look like you'll starve anytime soon." Hassler snorted. "Now give me an update."

O'Brian sighed. "We're gonna speak to the complainant later today," he said, playing with his tie. He wanted to give the appearance of a man who didn't give a damn.

"Really?" Hassler asked. "Cause I spoke with Detective Saffineli last night, and he says he hasn't heard a word from you." Hassler grinned, satisfied that he'd caught his foe in a lie.

"Oh, come on, cap," O'Brian said, "you want me and Saffineli chasing a guy accused of smoking pot at the Juilliard School? This is shit best left to the uniforms, or better yet ignored completely."

Hassler had been smoldering with rage ever since Krueger had disappeared, and, suspecting that O'Brian knew more than he let on, had punished him with a series of dead-end assignments.

"So if you're not working the case I gave you, how have you been filling up your days?" Hassler asked.

"Well . . . it's been tough," O'Brian said, putting on such a virtuoso performance that he would have merited a scholarship to the Juilliard School himself. He looked pleadingly at his boss. "It feels like the world is screwed up, and its left me . . . bereft."

"I see," Hassler said, in mocking concern. "So is that why you're concerned so much about the afterlife? Because the search history on your work computer, which Gibbon here accessed on my order, shows you've been spending a lot of time reading about cryogenic freezing. You've also accessed many pages devoted to the True Cross. Are you getting religious in your old age, O'Brian?"

O'Brian remained silent. He'd faced a few scrapes in the past before and knew it was better to not waste words.

"Pricks like you think I'm not a good cop," Hassler said, jabbing his chubby digit on his desk. "You think I don't see those looks when my back's turned, hmmm? You and your pals in the bullpen laughing at my expense? Well guess what, buddy boy? I didn't get this gig because the chief liked my face. I got it through hard freakin' work."

Hassler repeated the last three words for emphasis, spittle flying from his lips.

"Hard. Freakin.' Work. And I can see you're in cahoots with Krueger. I can see it in that damned smirk. So how's about you hand over your cell phone so I can see who you've been calling?"

"How's about you let me call a lawyer?" O'Brian asked tartly in response.

"Trust me," Gibbon said in a voice so harsh it suggested she was not worthy of trust, "there's no need for lawyers. It will go better for you if you just answer whether you've been in contact with . . . someone."

O'Brian poked his finger in between his neck and his collar, a move he instantly regretted because he knew it made him look guilty. He was usually so nimble in his thoughts, even for a former boxer, but sat in Hassler's stifling office, he found himself caught between two options and could not decide between them. He could confess to his interaction with Krueger; after all, his partner had promised to call Hassler and explain. By refusing, he'd only be gaining a few hours before the captain rained down on him.

Yet O'Brian held his tongue. He suspected, vaguely, that Krueger was caught up in something of such enormity that Hassler would fail to understand. The less he knew, the better.

"I got nothing to say," O'Brian said, folding his arms to signal that the conversation was at an end. "All you got is proof I visited some odd websites, nothing more."

The office fell silent, as dust motes floated in the bars of buttery sunlight streaming from the windows. All O'Brian could hear was the strum of the clock, and the ringing in his ears.

Hassler turned to Gibbon, who shrugged with her thin, spindly arms. It seemed like a signal that she agreed with O'Brian.

"Get out," Hassler said, "and do your goddamned job."

O'Brian spun on his heals without a word. *Thank God I used my private cell*, he thought to himself, knowing that if he'd used his office line, they'd have proof of his complicity, and he'd now be headed to the cells.

Nevertheless, O'Brian knew that he was now being watched closely, and his ability to maneuver on Krueger's part was now greatly diminished. If he was going to assist his partner and get more information on those two dead Krauts, he'd need help himself.

THOSE RECENTLY ARRIVING at Cairo International Airport can expect the following: a long walk from their aircraft, beneath the blazing desert sun, to a stuffy terminal filled with sweaty, swarthy, indifferent guards, idly fingering machineguns. One moment they appear to be half-asleep, the next they are raving in such a high-pitched voice that those in earshot are convinced a terrorist attack is imminent. This is followed by a brief stop at passport control, too brief to be effective at screening all newcomers, and then the circus of retrieving one's luggage. Wearied by such a pantomime, tourists are then confronted by the cab drivers of the biggest city of the Middle East, who hustle for business like over-excited children at a lemonade stand, and drive like them too.

But Joe Krueger experienced something different. A sleek air-conditioned Mercedes was waiting on the runway when they landed, and it took him, Brandt, and Grimm to the terminal where their passports where checked over a cup of fragrant tea. Thereafter, they departed the airport in a Range Rover, driven by a suited behemoth in sunglasses. Fresh clothes were waiting for them in the trunk, and Krueger gratefully took a pair of linen pants and a navy shirt. They were both his size.

"How much does it cost to live like this?" Krueger asked.

"Surprisingly little," Grimm confessed, searching his phone for details of the Memphis Hotel. "People hear you have money, and they assume they will eventually be paid for their labors. But what they desire, really desire, is the proximity to the wealth they've been told I have. It's as if I'm from another world, and they want to be part of it, even fleetingly. I suppose I am, really. You know . . . I can't remember the last time I handled cash?"

"Well I hope you've got some on you now," Krueger said, "'cause this isn't a part of the world that always takes plastic."

"Relax," Brandt said. She was seated next to Grimm and put a reassuring hand on Krueger's knee in front. "Me and Barnaby have seen worse places than this."

"You sure?" Krueger asked, as the Range Rover suddenly pulled up next to a lopsided townhouse. The driver looked at his passengers in alarmed confusion, wondering if this hovel was indeed the place they intended to stay.

The car had stopped on a street that was soiled and choked with traffic, and the Memphis Hotel looked little better. Many buildings improve with age, taking on a quiet and determined dignity. The hotel, however, looked as though it was slouching, plodding bitterly through life, and waiting for its welcomed demolition.

"Are you sure . . ." the driver began, but Grimm consoled him, speaking beautiful Arabic.

Appeased, the driver escorted the three companions into the hallway, where the elderly proprietor, wizened and turbaned, greeted them with gusto. Seeing them so warmly welcomed, the burly driver left, assuring them all, but Brandt in particular, that he would be minding them during their stay.

"I think Berlin proves that we don't need him," Krueger said, suddenly desiring to remind the young scholar that he, too, was expert in using his fists. He lowered his chin as he spoke, as if such a small motion would hide its ugly size.

"Yes, yes!" trilled the old owner. "Beautiful room for you!"

"Beauty isn't what I desire, old boy," Grimm said. He was smiling broadly, but his eyes were fixed and determined. "It's Room 41 I want."

The old owner winced, and after a long list of compliments, he revealed that "room 41 is not available."

Grimm nodded and slammed a brick of notes onto the Formica desk. They were Egyptian pounds. "Is it available now?"

IT TOOK SAM O'BRIAN five long phone calls to discover the whereabouts of Colin Dubchek, before a put-out desk officer told him he was taking lunch in Central Park. The tall Irishman found him pecking at a peanut butter and jelly sandwich on a park bench, watching geriatrics play chess with maddening lethargy.

"Sup, kiddo," O'Brian said, affecting the younger man's accent.

Dubchek looked up to reveal he hadn't shaved since being banished from the FBI Field Office, and the resultant beard was coming in so patchy, he looked even more of an adolescent.

"Not much since Hawtrey threw me off the case," he said. "She doesn't trust me anymore."

O'Brian retrieved a gargantuan hot dog from the pocket of his sport coat and unwrapped the foil. "You got time on ya hands, I see?"

Dubchek nodded and threw the remains on his sandwich onto the ground. An assorted stew of birds landed and began pecking at the crumbs.

"Maybe you wanna job, then?" the cop asked, finishing his lunch in three bites and licking the mustard off his fingers. "I got two corpses—"

"Even the prehistoric tech at NYPD can identify a body," Dubchek answered petulantly.

O'Brian rolled his eyes and whistled. "Slow down, big hoss," he said. "I know who these guys are; I just need to know how they're connected. Nothing in their private lives suggests they would ever know one another. And yet they both tag-teamed and tried to kill my partner."

The word *kill* stirred Dubchek's interest. He was, despite his behavior in front of O'Brian, not a brat, but rather a good cop eager to prove it.

"I need the link that connects them" O'Brian said. "So can your fancy-pants machine up in the FBI building search the database for footage containing *both* these guys' faces?"

Dubchek smiled slyly. "Detective," he said, "I could find every girl you ever passed in the subway these last twenty years."

O'Brian smiled too, and soon, the pair of them were laughing like conspirators.

"Atta boy," the detective said. "Now I just need to get you back in your computer cave."

"You mean the offices of the FACE Unit?" Dubchek asked. "Good luck! Everyone knows I'm *persona non grata* there."

"Relax, kid," O'Brian said, "I've got a way to get you in."

- 10 -

TO HIS UTTER AMAZEMENT, Joe Krueger entered room 41 of the disgusting Memphis Hotel and found a little piece of paradise. Sure, the furniture was old and sparse, and he wouldn't have been surprised to discover a cockroach or two lingering in the wallpaper. But beyond the crooked bed, beyond the stained carpet and leaky faucet, beyond the open window, was the view that had captivated untold thousands.

Before him was the Nile, red in the afternoon sunlight, its shimmering beauty unspooling through the desert. Above was the sun, beaming in the cloudless cobalt sky. And there on the horizon, like spear points from the ancient past, were the pyramids of Giza.

"You want a glass of something?" Brandt asked as Krueger used his eyes to drink the beauty around him.

"I'm fine," he whispered, and meant it. Behind him, in the dusty, sand-strewn city, the Muslim call to prayer filled the sky. Krueger's heart ached as he heard it. It sounded like the kiss of heaven over the din of the city, a reminder, perhaps, that humankind was capable of something more, and something better, than the grubby wars that had scarred the Holy Land for centuries.

But Krueger's time to ruminate was ended by Grimm, who began circling the room clucking like a chicken. He would need time, he said, to arrange a private viewing of the fragment in the Citadel and was expecting to spend the rest of his evening attached to both his phone and his laptop speaking a variety of languages.

Brandt and Krueger therefore decided to leave and share a long, joyful dinner by a roadside café, where they listened to the din of a thriving city, and forgot the disasters that had brought them together in a foreign land.

It was past nine by the time they returned to the room, where they found Dr. Grimm playing with a collection of gadgets in the corner. His lips were pursed in annoyance while cobwebs of smoke creeped from his expensive cigarette.

"We are due at the Citadel tomorrow by mid-morning," he declared.

"So it was a productive day," Krueger said, opening the door to the balcony and admiring the desert scene bathed in a brilliant moonglow.

"Hardly," Grimm said. "I've brought an inspection camera, a thermal imaging camera, and a 3D stud finder, and they're all telling me the same thing: there isn't any secret passage, nook, or cranny, in this room. And there's no secret messages lurking behind the picture frames either; I've looked. Which leads me to conclude that the malodorous Memphis Hotel is not going to offer us any clues in our quest."

"Still, it was a good idea to visit," Krueger said, pointing to the inspirational view. So much blood had been spilt in these lands, and yet there was a beauty that endured here, a beauty that had drawn people in spite of the promise of revolutions and upheavals. The ancient desert and the glories it held had stolen the hearts of men from each faith and none.

Grimm joined Krueger on the balcony, and soon his eyes were shining with awe. "Yes," he said, "yes it was." He finished his cigarette, crushed the filter on the floor, then picked it up and placed it in his cigarette holder, where it joined several others.

"I'm sure you can leave that on the floor, pal," Krueger said. "Even a place like this has room service."

"Oh, of that I'm certain," Grimm replied absently, "but I always like to pick up after myself. We spoiled rich have a bad enough reputation as it is."

"Speaking of reputations," Krueger said, "it's about time I tried to salvage mine. How's about you enjoy another smoke on the balcony, Doctor? I've got to go inside and make a call."

Grimm nodded his acceptance, and Krueger entered the room. He asked Brandt for some privacy, and she joined her old friend out on the balcony, closing the door behind her.

It was past five in New York when Krueger made his call, the middle of rush hour, but he knew Lucille Hawtrey would still be at her desk. That's how it worked with professionals like her: they gave their all, every waking moment, till the bad guy was either in handcuffs or a body bag. Sure enough, when he reached the switchboard at the FBI Field Officer and asked to be put through to Jean Dupree, the sprightly assistant picked up on the first ring.

"I need to speak with Special Agent Lucille Hawtrey," Krueger said.

As a grand marshal in the savage combat that is fending off pesky callers, Jean was used to hanging up on people who had no business speaking with her boss. But the hardness of the voice, the swiftness and precision of the request, led her to ask, "And how do you know she is still in the office?"

"Because that's where I would be if I were in her shoes," Krueger replied. "Tell her this is Detective Joe Krueger. Trust me, she'll take my call." Jean forwarded the call, looking nervously at the door to Hawtrey's office. It had been closed since before lunch, and Jean hadn't seen her boss since then.

"Put it through," Hawtrey said with a ragged voice. She wore a crumpled black pant suit, and an untouched glass of Maker's Mark, generously poured, sat on a sheaf of papers next to her.

"Detective Krueger," Hawtrey said to the sound of deep breathing coming from her phone.

"I imagine you'd like to slap me right about now," Krueger said.

"I would if I weren't so busy," she replied curtly. "And I'm not sure much good can come from this conversation. It's too late for explanations. Your time would be better spent speaking to your lawyer about what you're prepared to accept as a plea when we haul you before a disciplinary court."

"I'm going to take my lumps," Krueger said defiantly. "And you'll soon see me in that courtroom. But first I want to explain what I've found. It may help with the case."

Hawtrey sighed. Before her were hundreds of data files, report sheets, and assorted miscellany that together formed a chorus line, mocking her for her failure to land the scum who'd bombed New York and Portland. But Krueger offered a brief respite from their taunting.

"Tell me everything," Hawtrey said.

Krueger did exactly as he was told.

"You are still in serious trouble," Hawtrey said, finally. Hastily drawn notes, taken with a blunt pencil, littered the table around her. What started as an occasional jot had turned into reams of scraggy paragraphs as Krueger's tale had turned more violent, and more confusing.

"That's what I figured. It'll probably mean the end of my career in Narcotics, perhaps even the force, but I need you to know I did it for the right reasons."

"Many of the greatest errors in history were made for the right reasons," Hawtrey said. "But if it's any consolation, I did some checking on your while you were gone. You've got a good record, Detective, lots to be proud of in that resume of yours. You may yet get through this."

"Thank you, Agent Hawtrey," Krueger said with newfound respect.

"Are you in need of assistance?" Hawtrey asked. She was still angry at what she perceived to be Krueger's dereliction of his post, but, like so many in the law enforcement community, she had an unbreakable desire to help the good guys when they were in distress.

"Perhaps," Krueger said. "The moment I've finished up in Cairo, I plan to head home, and you can put me in chains the moment I touch down. In the meantime, is there a way you could arrange for my grandfather's body to be exhumed? If we could check to see who is in that grave of his, it sure would go a long way to proving the truthfulness of his last letter."

"I'll get it done," Hawtrey said, making a note using her worn-down pencil. "Anything else?"

"I'd appreciate an update on the case," Krueger said.

"We've had over four-thousand tip-offs since we released that image of the suspect to the media. Each and every one of them was a bust. Even worse is the fact I've had the NGI database audited—twice—and it still confirms that the suspect seen in New York is most likely General Krueger."

"Urgh," Krueger said in response, as if he were severely nauseous.

"Our working theory is that the suspect used heavy make-up around his nose and ears, either with the intention of resembling General Krueger—or through sheer coincidence."

"That's awfully thin, ma'am," Krueger said.

"That's because it is," Hawtrey confessed. "But there's worse. A blog run by the Montana Freemen was posted late last night, claiming that the bomber was General Krueger. It mentions the possibility that he found the True Cross in Syria during World War II and was bestowed with eternal life."

"Who are the Montana Freemen?" Krueger asked.

"Neo-Nazi militia operating out of Butte," Hawtrey answered. "One of the smaller groups out West. Most of them are bitter, bored teenagers. Their Krueger post is a rant, but rants have a way of spreading online. I fear it's only a matter of days before a major media outlet, perhaps a supermarket tabloid, links the bombing to your grandfather. And when that happens, we better have some good answers, or we're going to be a laughing-stock. So whatever you are doing in Cairo, do it quickly."

"Understood," Krueger said. "Thank you."

"Don't thank me," Hawtrey said. "You're still going to be up on serious charges, and there's nothing I can do to stop that."

"I know," Krueger said, "but it's good to know I'm no longer thought of as a lunatic."

Hawtrey smiled and hung up the phone. She paused, surveyed all the material around her, which was gathering in volume each day like a spreading fungus. Finally, she set aside the ballistics, forensics, and intel reports that littered her desk, the data compiled using hard science and reason, and turned to her computer. Against her better judgement, she was soon researching the mythical powers of the True Cross.

IT WAS EARLY MORNING, and Krueger was awoken by a knock at the door. He rose quickly and found Grimm waiting patiently for him, decked out in a safari jacket and cravat.

"Breakfast?" Grimm asked, as he fixed the strap on his pith helmet.

Minutes later, over a handsome spread of dates, yoghurt, tea, and shashuka, Grimm turned to Brandt and Krueger, and handed them a single sheet of paper.

"What's this?" Krueger asked.

"The key information you need to know about the True Cross," Grimm asked. "If we are going to walk in your grandfather's footsteps, then we should at least acquaint ourselves with what he was searching for."

"I know, the Cross on which Jesus was crucified," Krueger said, and was surprised to find Grimm's eyes turn dark with annoyance.

"It is more than that," he said. "In the aftermath of the crucifixion, the cross became the central focus of the fastest growing religion in the world. And this new religion did not demand its followers bow to some remote, uncaring deity that they could barely comprehend. The cross was physical proof that this new God had walked amongst us and shared in our pains and fears. It was why, in the year 135, the Roman Emperor Hadrian tore down the cross and buried it in an old Jerusalem cistern. He wanted the physical proof of the existence of this new God destroyed. Later, he even built a temple over the site where Jesus died, the hill of Golgotha, in hopes of extinguishing the flame of this new faith."

"But he failed," Brandt said.

"Most certainly," Grimm answered. "For the Christians remembered Golgotha, and they remembered the Nazarene, the Prince of Peace, who died there. They also remembered where Hadrian had cast down the cross. And when the Dowager Empress Helena arrived in the Holy Land in 326, she rediscovered the it.

"She found three crosses there, for Jesus had been crucified alongside two thieves. To determine which of the crosses was the one True Cross, Helena ordered a gravely sick noblewoman to touch each of them. She regained her health the moment she touched the cross on which Jesus had died for our sins, thus proving to Helena and Christians throughout the ages that the True Cross had the power to grant unnaturally long life. And that power was bestowed upon Helena too, it would seem. She began her search for the cross at the age of 78, at a time when average life expectancy was in the forties, and after touching it, she went on to live another forty years in perfect health. There is simply no other record of any historical figure living to such an advanced age."

"But whatever its power, the True Cross was lost of the Battle of Hattin," Brandt said, finishing her breakfast and devoting herself to studying Grimm's handout. "Where Saladin destroyed the armies of Christian Crusaders in 1187 and seized the cross for himself. It has not been seen since."

"That's almost true," Grimm said, as if talking to a student he wished to see excel. "But don't forget Helena returned to Europe with a part of the titulus, and it remains at the Basilica di Santa Croce in Gerusalemme, Rome, the church which Helena founded before her death."

"The what?" Krueger asked.

"Forgive me! I am getting ahead of myself," Grimm said. "The True Cross consists of three elements: first the cross-beam, which Jesus was forced to carry to his execution after being convicted by

Pilot. Second, the vertical beam, which stood on the hill of Golgotha. And lastly, the titulus, the carved wood, which was hung above Jesus, mocking him as the King of the Jews. Helena kept a part of the titulus herself, and though the monks in the Basilica will not allow it to be subject to official dendrochronological analysis, the evidence strongly suggests that it is a genuine artifact."

Krueger snorted in disgust. "If you're so sure, how come those priests won't allow the experts to take a peek at it?"

Once again, Grimm turned his gaze on the officer. His lips, which so easily curled into a smile, curved downward into a grimace. "I would have thought that your unsavory experience in Berlin would have taught you than when mankind meddles with things he shouldn't, bad things follow."

Krueger, suitably chastised, kept his mouth shut. He turned to Brandt who winked, and the cop suddenly found his cheeks burning in shame.

"Of course, how the True Cross is related to the al-Qalqashandi Fragment I could not possibly guess," Grimm said. He wiped his mouth efficiently with a napkin and signaled for his turbaned butler to remove the remains of his breakfast. "But we shall endeavor to find out!" he said. "Come, our driver awaits."

Krueger found himself back in the Range Rover, with the sunglass-wearing wildebeest in the driver's seat once again. He navigated his way through noisy streets filled with cars whose dented fenders and loud horns suggested they were used to more than the occasional prang.

After a while, Krueger realized that the car was driving up a steep hill, and he looked out the window to find that the road was widening. High in the air were a pair of sleek, thin minarets, standing astride a wide dome.

"The Mosque of Mohammed Ali," Brandt said, reaching past Krueger and pointing with her finger.

She brushed the cop's cheek as she did so, and Krueger felt a frisson of excitement swell in his belly.

"It's the centerpiece of Saladin's Citadel. He ordered its construction in 1176 to protect the city from Crusader armies. It did its job. After the citadel was fortified Cairo was never again threatened by a Christian army."

The Range Rover eventually pulled up to a metal gate standing between two sandstone towers built into the citadel wall. Two guards wearing red berets emerged from their shaded office and looked at the car with a mixture of envy and anger before beckoning it forward. The gate creaked open on their order, revealing a vast genteel courtyard beyond, which looked oddly out of place amid the dust-strewn roads and menacing fortifications. The marble flagstones were polished, and around them were several parterres, bursting with desert flowers that glowed in their colorful bloom.

Krueger expected the car to turn toward the vast, golden mosque, seated ponderously in the center of the citadel. But instead the driver turned right, to a smaller, though no less ornate structure, with handsome porticoes and intricate carvings on the dark exterior wall.

"This is the Al-Gawhara Palace," Grimm said, "one of three museums in the citadel. And it contains the fragment, which will either make us famous or give us an embarrassing fable to tell each other in our old age. Either way let's go a take a peek."

Grimm led his companions onto the courtyard, ordering the driver to keep the car close. As he did so, Krueger saw a uniformed middle-aged man jog toward the car. He wore a crisp khaki uniform, and, though almost completely bald, had nonetheless applied cheap black dye to the little hair he had remaining.

"Greetings, greetings!" he said in heavily accented English. "I am Sharif, captain of the garrison. Welcome Professor Grimm. And you two? You must be his research associates?"

"Why yes they are!" Grimm said before either Krueger or Brandt could cut in. "We most deeply appreciate your hospitality and your willingness to let us see the al-Qalqashandi Fragment."

"Why yes! A supporter of the museum of such munificence deserves to see what his investment has purchased for posterity," said Sharif. "And it is so odd! I received a similar visit less than a month ago."

Krueger looked through his sunglasses at the captain and shared a nervous glance with Brandt.

"Who else has been here?" Krueger asked in too harsh a tone. He regretted it when he saw the momentary look of apprehension on Sharif's face.

"Oh, let's save that for lunch!" Sharif cried, recovering his smile.

THE EARLY MORNING clouds above threatened a storm, a tempest that the heat-ravaged city of New York desperately needed. But while the millions of people who called that city home toiled beneath the unrelenting sun, sweating as they waited for the deluge, one man was sweating in fear.

Shuffling nervously beneath the Doric columns of the New York Supreme Court, Glenn Chu stared with anxious eyes at the happy tourists walking the handsome sidewalks. None of them looked like the burly flame-haired cop who'd promised to meet him an hour ago.

"Mr. Glenn!" Sam O'Brian bellowed, not giving a damn that Chu had wanted to keep their rendezvous secret. He bounded across the street toward the marble steps of the Court, with some surly teenager in a ratty t-shirt following in his wake.

"This is not okay!" Chu whispered when Sam approached, tugging at the cop's deep red tie. "This is too big a risk!" Chu was perspiring so badly that his glasses, a pair of massive steel-rimmed aviators, had slipped to the end of his nose.

"Oh, and you don't think I was taking a risk helping you walk away from those charges?" O'Brian asked. "Heroin is a poison, pal, and to think you was peddling it through ya dry cleaning business!"

Chu swallowed hard. The teenager behind O'Brian looked as just as uncomfortable the forty-five-year-old Chinese.

"The Triads made me do it!" Chu pleaded.

"Sure, sure," O'Brian replied, "which is why I let you go free. But you remember I said someday I might need a favor? That's how this city works, see. Everyone helps each other out. And today . . . I need a little help."

Chu wiped his brow. The sun was fast disappearing behind a fat thunderhead, and if he didn't end this meeting soon, he was going to be late.

"This is my pal, Colin Dubchek," O'Brian said, "and he needs a ride."

Chu's lips curdled into a scowl. "You talk in riddles!" he cried, genuinely offended. "What you need? Tell me now!"

"Take it easy," O'Brian said, smiling earnestly. "Look, I know you are still working for that cleaning crew I fixed you up with after we shut down the dry-cleaning store. I know you're working the afternoon shift at the FBI Field Office. So if it isn't too much trouble, I'd like for you to sneak Colin here into the building."

"What?" Chu cried.

"I told you yesterday this was a waste of time!" Colin added. "This janitor hasn't got a chance of beating security."

Glenn Chu began to walk away, raving in his native tongue and waving his arms like a broken windmill in a hurricane. Chu had always possessed a strong sense of self-preservation, and it was stronger than his sense of self-respect.

"Calm down, Chu," O'Brian said, placing a fatherly yet firm hand on his shoulder. "Look," he said, staring at the smaller Chinese with earnest eyes. "You know I ain't like the others, right?"

"Sure," Chu said, and realized he meant it. O'Brian hadn't been amongst the sorry gang of uniformed cops who'd taken bribes when the Triads began squatting in his once-thriving store and used it to distribute their drugs. He hadn't been amongst those cops who'd laughed once they'd busted down his door and destroyed a business that had taken ten years of hard toil to build. No, O'Brian had been the one that made sure Chu's kids got Christmas presents that year, and that his wife was set up in a nice nail salon in Queens. Whatever else he was—joker, meathead, general asshole—Chu knew that Sam O'Brian was not a bad cop.

"I'm asking you to fudge the rules a little, I get it," O'Brian continued, before being interrupted by Dubchek.

"It's way more than that!" he cried, exasperated.

"But I'm doing it for a good reason," O'Brian continued, ignoring the younger man. "See, me and Dubchek here are working on a little side project, and with your help, we could nail the sucker who bombed New York."

"Really?" Chu asked. Thunder rattled across the skyline.

"Really," Dubchek said, sighing. "I know how it sounds, believe me I do, but it's true. We've got hold of something that the suits don't want to touch. It could be key to getting hold of the man who did this."

The rain began to fall, but O'Brian raised an umbrella and shielded Chu from the torrent.

"If I could . . . I would . . ." Chu pleaded. "But I don't know how."

O'Brian smiled and led Chu toward his car. "That's okay, Mr. Glenn," he said. "I sure do."

CAPTAIN SHARIF SERVED his guests with gusto. He offered the three companions lavash with cheese and olives, and did so as if they were long-lost friends. He finished this impromptu repast with a bushel of figs, of which he ate more than his fair share.

Indeed, Sharif's sunlit office suggested too much indulgence and not enough military discipline; it was stuffed with deep dumpy couches piled with soft cushions. An expensive sound system in the corner played Alan Jackson, which either meant the Egyptian captain was the world's most unlikely country music fan or that he'd picked a western artist at random in the hope of impressing his guests.

"It is an honor to have your support, Dr. Grimm," Sharif said as he poured out a fragrant tea.

"It's is only a meager contribution," Grimm said, waving away Sharif's ostentatious compliments.

The British expert had dropped a cool hundred grand into the museum's account before landing in Cairo—his way of guaranteeing an easy entry into the citadel.

"But I would, if you'd permit me, like to see what our investment is protecting," Grimm added. "After such a gastronomic indulgence, perhaps a walk to the exhibit halls?"

For man in middle age and the proud possessor of a gut, Sharif moved with incredible speed. "Certainly!" he cried in a placating tone. Krueger guessed that the captain had risen to such a key post in Cairo due to his willingness to move fast for those with money and guns, all while asking as few questions as possible.

Sharif opened the huge iron door of his office to reveal the courtyard. The smooth flagstones, laid centuries ago in perfect formation, were surrounded on three sides by tall walls. Opposite the office was the ornate, colonnaded Al-Gawhara Palace. Its spires were gilded and winked in their luxuriousness in the desert sun. The air coming down from the Muqattam Hills beyond smelled faintly of jasmine.

Not for the first time, Krueger was reminded of Iraq, and the scenes of beauty one could encounter with unexpected regularity amid the bloodshed and blasts. From the most spectacular mosque to the smallest engraving on a forgotten terraced house, the ancient world boasted aching beauty as precious as it was precarious.

"You mentioned that someone else had come to examine the al-Qalqashandi Fragment?" Brandt asked as they marched across courtyard toward the palace, pausing only once as Krueger returned to Sharif's office to fetch a bottle of water.

"Oh yes!" Sharif cried, beaming broadly. "A most welcome guest. Thomas Webber of Germany came here four weeks ago with the same request as yours. Quite a coincidence!"

"Thomas Webber the police officer?" Brandt asked, and Krueger shot her a look of annoyance. He knew that when a source was talking, you didn't dare do anything that shut them up.

"No," Sharif said. "Herr Webber is Vice President of Government Affairs at Pollux Solutions."

Krueger hastily turned and scribbled the name onto one of the papers in his pocket.

"Pollux is a large consultancy firm that's looking to establish itself in the Middle East," Sharif said, unhooking a large ring of keys from his Sam Browne belt. "Their extraordinary donation was their way of making themselves known here in Cairo, I suppose."

"Donation?" Grimm asked.

Sharif nodded but said nothing more. He was a gracious host, gracious enough to keep the secrets of those who bankrolled his museum.

Sharif and the companions reached the palace's colonnade, which was lined by flowers in large ceramic pots. Behind them were windows barred by thick iron rods. Turning right, Krueger saw a wide wooden door, the main entryway, which issued a ponderous creak as the Egyptian put his key into the lock and pushed it open.

"As per your request," Sharif said, straining under the weight of the timber, "we have closed the palace to visitors today. You can enjoy our exhibits without fear that the hoi polloi will interrupt your study."

Krueger led his friends into a vast, cool room with a long, lacquered floor and wood-paneled walls hung with portraits. It looked like the inside of a European palace. Straight ahead, past an arched doorway, was a library decorated in deep reds and greens. But Sharif took the party leftwards, past long tables covered with prized relics.

"The fragment is kept in this side room," Sharif said as he hustled them toward a little shaded alcove in the farthest corner. On one side of this small room was a bronze casting of the Eagle of Saladin, the heraldic symbol of the first Sultan of Egypt. On the other, locked in a glass case, was a large book, open to reveal a vast yellowing page decorated with a flowing Arabic script. The spine of the book was broken, and the page was sullied by a vast accumulation of ancient dust and debris. But the beauty of the text, carefully written and complimented by gilded images, was nonetheless impressive.

Krueger, whose relationship with God had been complicated by his witnessing of too many ungodly acts, felt something stir in his chest. He'd rarely glimpsed something so exquisitely precious, and it suggested a world beyond the one he knew—a world of angels, miracles, and God.

"The al-Qalqashandi Fragment," said Sharif proudly. "The first and only copy of this attempted biography of Saladin." The captain then pointed to another glass box hanging from the wall above. It contained a wax tablet. "Plus, the final notes taken by al-Qalqashandi before he died."

"Thank you," Grimm said gratefully. "We would like, if possible, to examine these documents outside of their protective casings."

Sharif nodded. "Please put on the gloves," he said, withdrawing three pairs of white mittens from his pocket. He then unlocked both the glass boxes and placed the wax tablet on a nearby table with reverential hands. "And don't move these documents into the sunlight, please. They must be kept shaded." Sharif shuffled out of the alcove, returned to the great room, and shut the blinds of the barred windows which faced onto the courtyard. Soft light from a sparkling rococo chandelier keep the place gently illuminated.

"We understand," Brandt said and smiled flirtatiously at the captain. He was so smitten, he did not realize she was hustling him out of the great room. Once he was back out in the courtyard, Brandt winked and closed the door behind her.

"What do you propose?" she asked.

"A patient reading of the text," Grimm replied. "This may take a while."

GLENN CHU DRAGGED his heavy janitorial cart across the greasy asphalt toward the loading bay of the FBI Field Office. This was where deliveries were made, mail was collected, and where the staff unworthy of the gleaming glass entrance at the front made their way into the building. It was five, and the black shadows were lengthening around the corners of the building.

"Evening, Chu," said a deep, rich voice hidden by the shade of the awning above.

"What?" Chu asked, spinning on his heels and looking in every direction with wide eyes.

"Easy, my man!" said the voice. A tall uniformed man emerged from the shadows, sporting large biceps and a badge that revealed he was guarding the building.

"Deroy!" Chu said, panting. "Good to see you! How is children? Good, good?"

"Sure," replied Deroy Clovis with a heavy hint of suspicion in his voice.

"You okay, Chu? You look a little peaky. The Mets giving you heartburn again?"

Chu burst into peals in fruity laughter. "So funny!" he said. "Yes, yes so funny!"

Deroy Clovis had known Glenn Chu for four years, ever since he'd come out of the navy and took a rent-a-cop job at the FBI Field Office. And he'd never know Chu to laugh as loudly or as long as he was right now.

"Okay," Deroy said, rolling his eyes and drawing out each syllable.

"No," Chu said, suddenly realizing his mistake. He caught site of the Beretta PX4 that sat menacingly in Deroy's holster, and the dull black metal reminded him how close he was to arrest and imprisonment. "It's . . . it's . . . home," Chu said, hoping it would be enough to mollify the security guard. Thankfully, it was.

"Oh, I get it, man," Deroy replied, patting the shorter man's rounded shoulder. "I got me two kids at home and one more on the way! The wife's giving me all sorts of crap!"

Chu nodded and shuffled forward toward the service elevator.

"Hang up, man!" Deroy cried. His brow was knotted in surprise and frustration. "Ain't you forgettin' somethin'?"

Chu's mouth hung open, revealing two rows of yellow teeth. He feared his bladder was about to release, until a loud voice, one that did not sound like his own, echoed through his mind: *The metal detector! The metal detector!*

"Oh," Chu said, smiling and waving his hand, trying to pass off his mistake as a minor lapse. "I *did* forget, Deroy! Don't ever get old like me. Those problems you have at home are a thousand times worse when you get old."

Chu yanked at his janitorial cart, yanked with all the strength he could muster. He could not, must not, allow anyone, even his buddy Deroy, to know how unusually heavy it was.

Pretending that the cart was as light as it typically was, Chu swung it underneath the imposing grey rectangle, staring at the red buttons that looked down from above like evil rats' eyes. He'd made this move a hundred times, and knew that the plastic wheels, the broom, the trash can, the mop, the dustpan, and the bottles of cleaning fluid would not cause the machine to sound its hideous beep.

But today was different, and if that kid Dubchek was wearing a belt, cufflinks, glasses, even so much as a collar stiffener, then the machine would pronounce judgement, like a mechanical God, and Chu's life would be destroyed.

With such a chill certainty rioting in his mind, Chu mouth grew dry.

"Carry on then, Chu," Deroy said.

"What?" Chu asked, blinking.

"Look, ya dummy!" the security guard replied. "The cart's through. You can go on up."

"Oh . . . of course!" Chu answered and left Deroy Clovis to wonder whether he too would become so absent-minded when he reached middle age.

The moment the elevator doors were closed, Chu felt the energy drain away from his legs, as if someone had slashed at them with a knife, and he fell onto his haunches. He only kept himself upright by holding onto the edge of the trash can.

"It's too hot in here man," Dubchek whispered. He was at the bottom of the can, a nasty pile of detritus camouflaging him from the video cameras that Chu knew were hanging everywhere in the building.

"The heat is on me!" Chu whispered.

But before he could protest further, the doors opened, and he was on the second floor: the first of five floors he was responsible for cleaning.

Silently, Chu took his cart into the nearest restroom, where cameras were banished, and the moment the door closed, Colin Dubchek emerged from the trash can wearing janitor's overalls and peeling a melon rind from his shoulder.

"I can't believe that worked!" he said.

Chu nodded but was too weak to speak. He turned the faucet and splashed cold water onto his red, sweaty face. "This too much for me," he whispered, wishing that he'd never met Sam O'Brian.

"Easy," Dubchek said to his new partner-in-crime as he pulled a baseball cap low over his head. "Remember, we're doing this for the best of reasons. And we are almost done. I just need thirty minutes with my old computers."

Chu and Dubchek left the restroom, looking like buddies working together. At Dubchek's insistence, they walked briskly and confidently to the room that contained the NGI database.

Confidence, Dubchek knew, was key to pulling off the whole caper. Once they reached the vast metal portal, Chu swiped his card on the nearby reader, and it opened with a hum. There was nobody inside, but a graveyard of takeaway food boxes on the work benches suggested somebody would be returning soon. Chu held the door and let Dubchek enter.

"Since the bombings there's been a lot of people here at night," Chu whispered. "I don't think you'll have your thirty minutes."

"I kinda figured that," Dubchek said, cracking his knuckles and removing the two pictures O'Brian had given him earlier in the day. "It just so happens I'm damn good at my job."

"Me too," Chu said. "I've got to finish my rounds on this corridor. When I'm finished, I come back and dump you outside."

"You got it, partner," Dubchek said, looking directly at Chu.

Together, they smiled. Somehow, they both knew they were working for the good guys. It helped them beat the panic swelling in their stomachs.

With Chu gone, Dubchek got to work. His hasty hands scanned the images, and minutes later, the computer responded with a prompt answer. The pictures O'Brian had given him were of Sergeant Thomas Webber and Herr Gunther Frick. Just like the cop had said.

Tapping feverishly at the black keyboard, Dubchek mounted a search of the database looking for images that contained both the dead German men.

The computer whirred in reply, processing the request Dubchek had given, filtering the terabytes of data it contained. Dubchek stared at the screen, willing it to hurry, listening for sounds outside, but only hearing his own ragged breath.

Dubchek heard a beep. The answer popped onto the surface of his screen.

Three images. Taken at two different occasions. Webber and Frick had long known each other.

Dubchek sighed in relief and hit the print button with a trembling finger. He grabbed the crisp sheets as they came shooting out of the printer.

Feeling the warmth of the pages, Dubchek smiled. He turned. And then he saw the person standing in the doorway with a gun pointing at his chest.

JOE KRUEGER YAWNED AUDIBLY. It was late afternoon, and he no longer cared if he disturbed Barnaby Grimm, who for four hours had been pouring over the al-Qalqashandi Fragment. The professor had found no secret code, no hidden message. He even tried heating the beaten leather on which it had been written, hoping that perhaps the 13th century author had used the same kind of invisible ink as General Krueger. It hadn't worked.

Krueger looked at Brandt and she rolled her green eyes.

"I am ready to pronounce the al-Qalqashandi Fragment a busted flush," Grimm announced grandly. "There is a solitary mention of the True Cross, where al-Qalqashandi writes that Saladin was victorious over the Crusading armies in July 1187 and seized it for himself. He took the cross back to Damascus and it was never seen again. But that is all the book says, and it's something we already knew."

"So what about this wax thing?" Krueger asked. With his gloved hands he picked up the tablet. It had wooden backing, chipped at the bottom, and was the size of single sheet of paper.

"Ah yes," Brandt said, "wax tablets were like notepaper in the medieval world. You used a metal stylus to write in the hard wax, and when you no longer needed the text you'd written, you'd heat the wax and scrape away the words leaving a smooth surface ready for the next time you needed it. There's nothing here that I can see," Grimm said, looking over the text carved into the ancient yellow wax. "Mostly idle ramblings. Poor al-Qalqashandi was dying when he attempted this biography, and I fear his mind was no longer as sharp as it had once been. Speaking of sharp," Grimm said, rubbing his finger over the broken wooden backing, "I fear I may have a splinter."

"Damn it," Krueger muttered, tracing his finger over the useless writing. He came to a line at the bottom of the page that did not look like the rest of the text. "What does this say?" he asked.

Grimm looked over his shoulder and raised an eyebrow. "Mmmm," he said, "that's very odd. Al-Qalqashandi wrote in Arabic throughout his career, but this line is in Greek. Ancient Greek to be exact."

"What does it say?"

"'Demaratus looks behind,'" Grimm said, "which could just as easily be a clue as it could be the ramblings of a senile man. I'm too tired to consider that problem now. Come, it'll be dusk soon, and I'm sure Sharif would like to see the back of us until tomorrow."

"Damaratus?" Brandt asked. "Is Dr. Barnaby Grimm forgetting his Greek history?"

Brandt clenched her jaw and took the tablet from Krueger's hands. Shaking her head at the two men in front of her, she squeezed her fingers between the tablet and its wooden backing, right where the crack in the wood appeared, and pried the two apart. The tablet fell away with ease, suggesting that someone else had done the same thing before. Brandt was left holding the wooden backing of the tablet and showed it to her companions with a triumphant smile on her face.

"Demaratus was the King of Sparta," Brandt said, before Grimm cut her off.

"Who, during the Persian Wars, smuggled a secret warning to the people of Greece that they were about to be invaded," he said.

Brandt, not to be denied her moment, pushed past Grimm and drew closer to Krueger. Her green eyes sparkled, and

Krueger found himself grinning like an addled teenager. "He did it," she said, "by writing a secret message on the wooden backing of a wax tablet."

SAM O'BRIAN WAS shouldered into the elevator by Munroe, the natty FBI agent who was still fixed up in a vest and tie. The other agent, a hulking blonde who looked like a linebacker, stood behind him with indifferent eyes. A Springfield custom pistol in the big guy's holster winked at O'Brian from beneath his suit jacket. It was proof he had nowhere to run.

Munroe and his lackey had picked O'Brian up at Anna's, a cozy Irish pub seldom frequented by the shrill tourists who clogged Manhattan with their neon fanny packs and selfie sticks. It was where he'd arranged to meet Colin Dubchek at seven. Instead, the two FBI pukes had sidled up to him in his booth, and moments later, they were riding in their Crown Victoria toward the FBI Field Office. They hadn't even bothered to tip O'Brian's waitress.

Standing silent in the elevator, O'Brian began to weigh his chances of avoiding jail time and realized they were pretty slim. There was no way he would let Dubchek and Chu take the fall for this; his imperishable honor demanded that he take the brunt of whatever the FBI was about to dole out.

The elevator doors opened, and O'Brian was hustled forward. Looking around, he saw smart corporate offices with nice wooden doors and comfy upholstered chairs. If he was being taken to an interview room, then it was going to be the nicest interview room he'd even seen. At the end of the corridor was a heavy mahogany entryway and closed blinds. Munroe knocked on the door and entered without waiting for an answer.

And then Sam O'Brian, against all his expectations, found himself in the plush offices of Special Agent Lucille Hawtrey. Colin Dubchek, his confederate and co-conspirator, was seated by the bookshelf, gripping a cup of coffee as if it were a life preserver. He didn't look up when Sam and the agents entered.

"I cannot believe," Hawtrey snapped, "that I am standing before an officer of thirty-three years' service, who has just attempted to illegally enter secure government property and steal confidential data."

Hawtrey rolled her eyes and signaled for Munroe and the troll that followed him to leave. The dun clouds outside were being slowly illuminated by a bright half-moon.

"With such recklessness, I'm amazed you've managed to catch a single crook in your life."

"It's that recklessness, ma'am, that's helped put some of the worst criminals in the city behind bars." O'Brian stood stiffly on his feet and clasped his hands behind his back. He knew he was going down for what he'd done, but there was no way he'd let anyone question his ability as a cop.

"That attitude is going to get you into deep, deep trouble," Hawtrey said, crossing her arms and turning away from O'Brian. She paused and let out a thin sigh that sounded very much like a hiss. "But not today."

O'Brian glanced at Dubchek, but the kid wouldn't lift his gaze from the coffee he was gripping. The poor guy must have taken a terrible fright when he'd been seized by Hawtrey's agents.

"As much as it turns my stomach to say this to a man who just tried to steal data from my headquarters, you and I are on the same side." Hawtrey shook her head, as if disagreeing with what was coming from her own mouth, and sat behind her vast desk. "I took a call from your partner, Joe Krueger last night. He told me everything."

"Then you know why I tried to get at your Next Generation Identification database?" O'Brian asked.

"Yes," Hawtrey replied tartly, "and if Krueger's damned Nazi general theory weren't the only game in town, I'd have you in a cell this second."

"Is he okay?" O'Brian asked, and his eagerness reminded Hawtrey, despite her fury, that these were decent officers she was working with—officers who wanted to stop the bomber as badly as she did.

"He's fine; just confused like the rest of us," Hawtrey answered. "I ordered General Krueger's body to be exhumed today, to try and disprove your partner's cockamamie theory."

The Special Agent sighed and poured two glasses of Maker's Mark. She didn't bother asking O'Brian if he liked bourbon before handing him a glass; he just looked like the kind of man who did.

"We are still waiting for DNA analysis, but a preliminary investigation of the remains shows that the man inside that coffin was approximately forty-years-old when he died. There're two gold fillings in his back lower molars, plus two bullet holes in his skull. General Krueger was 61 when he died, and according to his dental records, had fillings made only of porcelain. Oh, and when he died of throat cancer, there were no bullet holes in his head."

"So the body ain't Krueger?" O'Brian asked.

"It would certainly seem that way," Dubchek said, rising on uncertain legs. He took O'Brian's bourbon without asking and downed it. Hawtrey smiled in spite of herself and poured another two slugs of booze.

"So this guy was successfully frozen for all these years?" O'Brian asked.

"I don't know about that," Dubchek said, "but those two who tried to kill Joe Krueger were definitely Neo-Nazis." The kid pulled the print-outs from the pockets of his overalls and placed them on Hawtrey's desk. "This is what I broke in here for, ma'am," Dubchek said, shamefacedly. "I wanted to help Detective O'Brian answer the mystery of how Thomas Webber and Gunther Frick knew each other before they both tried to kill Detective Krueger. The answer is in these pictures."

O'Brian looked at the images, which had the grainy quality of a hidden camera.

"A rally of a Neo-Nazi group, held in Budapest in March this year," Dubchek said, pointing to the pictures. "These were taken by an undercover officer from Hungary.

"This group is mostly made up of young Eastern European males, keen on shouting in the streets and occasionally smashing a window shop, but little more. However, they have attracted adherents in all the major capitals of Europe, and there's been some increase in online chatter lately about procuring weapons, even fully automatic rifles. It looks like Webber and Frick were secret members of the group, perhaps even the leaders of the Berlin affiliate."

"Okay," said Hawtrey, thinking quickly. "That gives us something to work with. You're on the case now, O'Brian, and I want to see that you're as good a cop as I think you are. I'll speak with Hassler and have you formally seconded to our Field Office. Munroe has just set aside a desk for you. Go find it and get started straight away on finding out everything we can about these bastards."

"You got it!" O'Brian cried, elation stirring in his heart.

"And our other priority," Hawtrey continued, "is the Castor Group, the company which owns that disused factory where Krueger's body was allegedly stored. Dubchek, speak to our contacts at the Securities and Exchange Commission and see if we can't shed some light on who those creeps are."

Dubchek beamed and promised that he'd get onto the job. Together, he and O'Brian turned and left the office.

"And gentlemen," Hawtrey trilled, "one final thing. Don't tell anyone about this investigation. Anyone. If the press finds out, we will not only all be fired, but subject to the worst public ridicule imaginable."

HERE BE WRITTEN the tale of a boy who was given nothing, and given the world.

It was the 19th year in the reign of An-Nasir Salah ad-Din Yusuf ibn Ayyub, who the legends call Saladin, the man who had united the Muslim world in opposition to the Franks and the other heretical defilers of the Prophet, Peace be Upon Him. And though this kind and munificent Sultan, wise beyond his years, was still in the full flower of his manhood, he was struck with a fever which soon forced his humors out of balance.

Confined to a bed in his palace in Damascus, Saladin, following the teachings of our Prophet, Peace be Upon Him, dispensed with all his worldly wealth. Confirming his reputation as a man of unbounded kindness, Saladin rendered himself a pauper through his generous giving. By the time he was called to Paradise, he had just 1 piece of gold and 40 pieces of silver about his person.

The lands he had conquered were divided amongst his mighty sons: the eldest took Syria, while the next in line was granted Egypt. Aleppo, Palestine, and Yemen where likewise divided among the sons and kinfolk of the founder of the mighty Ayyubid dynasty.

But there was one amongst Saladin's loyal family who did not receive a gift of land from the mortally sick Sultan. The twelfth and youngest of Saladin's sons, whose name is lost to time, was not given so much as a scrap of desert. Born in 1178 by Saladin's dutiful wife, Ismat ad-Din Khatun, this boy was aged just nine when his father took to his death bed, and watched as his older, more ambitious brothers fought like jackals over the worldly wealth of this father.

The poor boy has been forgotten by our histories. His older brothers soon fell into quarrelling and warfare when their father ascended into Paradise. But the boy, without land and without arms, was ignored by our madrassas and men of learning, the ulama.

But Saladin was wiser than those who came after him and knew that this child was worthy of a special honor, one which was bestowed by God Himself.

In the hours before his death, Saladin was too sick to take food or medicine, save a little barley water. Left alone by his physicians, the conqueror of the Christian lands was visited by the Angel of

Revelation, the archangel Jibreel, who the Franks call Gabriel. Lo! Jibreel said unto Saladin: "do not be afeared. I have come with instructions of God, who wishes you to hide the remaining worldly goods of the Prophet Mohammad, Peace be Upon Him, and all the prophets that came before him.

"God granted you possession of these relics because He knew you would revere them and keep them from the covetous. But the ranks of the unclean are swelling, and they search for power they do not deserve. These relics can bestow might that no mortal can possess, and thus must be hidden forevermore. This is the last great task, asked of you by God. So hide the mantle and the beard of Mohammad, Peace be Upon Him, and hide also the Cross upon which Isa ibn Maryam, who the Franks call Jesus, was killed."

Thus Saladin summoned his youngest boy to his bed, and said unto him: "I have had a vision, and you shall not be accorded a piece of my empire, my son. Rather, I have for you a special task, ordained by God, and for his Glory." Saladin then ordered the boy to hide the relics of the Prophet, Peace be Upon Him, and also to return the Cross to the Horns, where the great warrior had first taken it from the Franks years before. Though Saladin thought the Cross was a gaudy relic worshipped by iconoclasts, he was sore afraid of Jibreel's wrath and ordered God's Will to be done.

Saladin's boy was a dutiful son and did as he was told. He buried that Cross in the mountain fastness, hidden from those who hungered for it.

Upon completing his holy task, the boy exiled himself to Karak, where he lived without heirs, for he did not wish his tale to be told. He ascended to Paradise soon after, to Firdaws, where he sat at the right hand of his father.

DR. BARNABY GRIMM drew a deep breath, as if he had just escaped from being trapped underwater for too long a time. He'd spent his evening translating medieval Arabic, and this last, and most important passage had left him bewildered. *I am*, he thought feebly, *on the cusp of an extraordinary discovery.* Grimm removed his cravat and wiped away the sweat sheathing his forehead.

"You've done it, Grimm," said Brandt, "you've written yourself into an adventure, one that will be remembered for as long as Christians walk the Earth." She gave him a sisterly kiss on his blushing cheek.

"We, together, may have done it," Grimm replied. He took several photographs of the secret message with his phone before returning both the texts to their glass boxes.

"So if this was all some vast conspiracy," Krueger said, "how come that mathematician who wrote the secret message knew all about it hundreds of years afterwards?"

"That question," Grimm said with a dreamlike quality in his voice, "and all others can wait until tomorrow. I need a long soak in a bathtub and a night's rest."

Grimm left the alcove and opened the blinds in the great room. A velvety mantle of blackness had fallen across the courtyard.

"Come," said Grimm, "let's go find our host and see about supper."

"Supper?" Krueger asked, jokingly. "It's approaching midnight, Grimm. You've been at this for quite a while, and I doubt we'll get so much as a dollop of hummus at this hour."

Grimm and Brandt walked the length of the room and headed toward the wooden entrance, walking past the chandelier and the portraits of Victorian emirs and khedives. But something, some shape lying in an unnatural angel, had caught Krueger's attention in the courtyard. He suddenly realized why Captain Sharif had not disturbed them during their long hours in the museum.

"Don't go out there," Krueger said sharply.

"Why?" Brandt asked, tugging on the brass door handle. But the door wouldn't budge. "Damnit," she said in her Germanic accent. "Sharif must have locked us in."

"I don't believe he did," Krueger said.

"Why?" Brandt asked. There was a hardness entering into Krueger's eyes, a hardness she had not seen since the attack in her apartment.

"Because Sharif's dead body is lying in the courtyard."

"What?" cried Grimm, stepping away from the door and approaching Krueger.

He looked through the barred window and saw the shape which had roused Krueger's apprehension. It was shrouded in shadow, but the moonlight, silver and bright, reflected off a pair of well-polished shoes and a sweaty bald head. Captain Sharif was lying flat on the deserted flagstones outside.

"This is some mistake," Grimm said. He snorted and flared his nostrils as he did so, giving the impression of a beast caught in a trap. Grimm rapped his knuckles on the windowpane. "Sharif?" he yelled, "come now man, open up! We need to be off at once!"

The rapping turned to a pounding, and soon Grimm was smacking the glass with both his trembling palms. Still, Sharif did not muster.

"What is happening?" Brandt cried, running toward Krueger. But before she could reach him, the lights went out, and her world turned into darkness.

- 1 2 -

IT TOOK A FEW SECONDS for Joe Krueger's eyes to adjust to the blackness, but those seconds drew out like a long and terrible epoch. With one unsure foot after another, he hustled his friends into the alcove, retreating from the windows and the sight of their dead host.

Thinking quickly, Krueger brought up his phone and used the sickly green light to illuminate his friends. Grimm was aquiver, his chest jerking with each ragged breath he took. Brandt was stood beside the wax tablet, her eyes closed and her hand stroking her chin. She looked like a professor pondering a tough question in class.

Krueger dialed O'Brian. No answer. He dialed again. But O'Brian was currently being hustled out of his bar by Munroe and unable to pick up.

Krueger tried Hawtrey too, but she was providing Colin Dubchek with a *gratis* lecture on the foolishness of sneaking into her fortress. She, too, failed to notice Krueger's call.

"Who else can we call?" Brandt asked, looking over Krueger's shoulder. The cop noticed that she'd cut her voice to a whisper, as if she shared his queasy feeling that they were no longer alone.

"Our driver!" Grimm cried and reached for his own phone. "He was once in Mubarak's army, you know! He'll damn-well save us." The light of Grimm's cell cast crooked shadows over his panicked face, and as he punched the numbers he looked to Krueger like a lunatic.

Grimm brought the phone to his ears, but with each ring his hopes faded, and his crazed smile melted away. Finally, Grimm threw the phone to floor, where it cracked apart loudly.

"Why does nobody pick up!" he cried in the tone a spoiled teenager.

"Shut it, Barnaby!" Brandt shouted, and her friend did exactly as he was told. There was something about a German giving orders that demanded an immediate and affirmative response. Suitably chastised, Grimm bent and collected the remains of his phone, ruing his stupidity.

"We need to know the layout of this place," Krueger said. "I don't know what happened to Sharif, but my guess is somebody does not want us knowing about that secret message."

"Could it be the same people from Berlin?" Brandt asked.

"I don't know," Krueger answered truthfully, "but if it is, we are in danger."

"Oh, God," Grimm whispered. He crouched low and wrapped his sweaty hands around his head.

"My phone has a flashlight," Brandt said. "Perhaps we need to find a way out of here."

Krueger nodded silently and stepped out into the great room. He played the light across the nearest wall and exhaled in relief when he saw no one approach. Next, he looked through the windows and found the courtyard still empty, apart from the corpse of Captain Sharif. The offices built into the citadel wall opposite, Krueger noticed, were as black as the palace, meaning the power was out, or had been cut, throughout the complex.

Shuffling forward, the sound of his footfalls masked by his sneakers, Krueger passed the long wooden tables and looked over the relics that were on display. Codices, monographs, and old coins and fragments of pottery were the dreams of an antiquarian, but for a man who fears he is being hunted, they offered nothing but mocking pity. Krueger chewed on his lip and picked up a shard of an ancient jug. There wasn't even an edge on it sharp enough to cut.

Past the tables was the entryway to the library on the left and the door leading to the colonnade on the right. Krueger pulled the handle, just as Brandt had done moments ago when the lights were shining and everyone was smiling, but the door was locked. And even a man as big as Joe Krueger would not be able to bust through those thick ancient timbers.

A sound came from the library.

Krueger's heart seized with fear, and he spun soundlessly on his feet. But he saw nothing but old bookshelves stuffed with ancient, useless texts.

Another sound, another creak, came from the room in front of him.

Krueger darted forward, a graceful move for someone so tall and brutish looking. He hunkered down next to the entryway, listening, hoping to hear anything beyond his own beating heart.

He did not have to wait long. A louder, longer creak came from the library, and its chilling immediacy prompted Krueger to action. He took the shard in his hand and threw it across the room. It struck the window opposite with a crack. Using the diversion, Krueger took a few precious seconds to peer into the room and play the flashlight across the walls.

His light illuminated the cavernous library and revealed a long wooden staircase in the left corner. A tall man, clad entirely in black, was descending those stairs, with the slow and sure approach of a professional. Carrying a C8 carbine in his gloved hands, Krueger thought he saw at least two other firearms holstered beneath his Kevlar vest. Even worse, the man was wearing night-vision goggles. Expensive ones, too, Krueger judged.

This was all Krueger could discover before the man swung his weapon toward the source of the light and opened fire. It was a series of short bursts, in between which the man continued to descend the stairs. As Krueger retreated back into the great room, the man gained the last step into the library.

Krueger saw that Brandt and Grimm had left the alcove and were fast approaching him. Brandt was carrying a large silver platter that occasionally flashed in the moonlight.

"It's all I could find," she whispered, offering it to Krueger as a weapon. "What's in there?"

"One man," Krueger replied. "Professional and well-armed." He took the platter, wondering how he could possibly use it to disarm the pro who was seconds away from finding them.

But Krueger's thoughts were interrupted by the sound a large clang, followed by an unmistakable hiss—one which Krueger had heard on too many battlefields to forget.

"Tear gas!" he said softly, trying not to shout. A large canister had struck the main doorway, and was now sitting, fat and wretched, on the opposite side of the room, vomiting its noxious contents into the air.

"I'm not supposed to die like this!" Grimm wailed, and Krueger could not help contrast the desperate, babbling weakling in front of him with the man who'd greeted him in Berlin days earlier. Back then Grimm has boasted coiffed hair, a refined tweed suit, a pocket watch, and expensive cigarettes in a monogrammed case.

An idea blossomed on Krueger's mind. It was shocking in its vividness and left Krueger feeling like a thirsty man after he'd taken the first gulp of water.

"Grimm, give me ya smokes!" he said suddenly. Krueger knew he had seconds to save himself and his friends.

The man in the library was probably standing patiently now, a smile lingering on his masked face. He'd likely heard what had happened in Berlin, understood the dangers that his targets posed, and was waiting for the gas to do its dastardly work. Once they were choking and prostrate on the floor, he'd enter and finish the job.

Krueger lunged at his confused friend, grabbed the cigarette case, and popped it open. Grimm's confusion grew even worse when

Krueger picked up two of the used filters and stuck them up his nose, one for each nostril He did the same to Brandt.

"Do not breathe through your mouth!" he ordered. Breath through your nose and let these babies keep that crap out of your lungs."

Grimm took the filters and did what he was told, ignoring the stink of stale smoke which assaulted his nose. He knew the alternative was far worse.

The gas grew into vast, billowing clouds. Before he was swallowed by this swelling yellowish mantle, Krueger retrieved the bottle of water from his pocket, the one he had taken from Sharif's table earlier in the afternoon. He poured the cold water over his eyes and did the same to Brandt and Grimm. It would not take away all the pain they were about the feel, wouldn't take away even a fraction of it, in fact, but it was better than nothing.

And then, the pall was over them.

It was like a thousand tiny pinpricks at first, jabbing remorselessly at Krueger's eyes. His mouth tingled, and as he brought his hand to his massive chin, Krueger noticed fat ropes of spit hanging from his lower lip.

But his lungs were not burning. His chest was not seizing up in pain. And he could still swing his silver platter with enough force to make that bastard in the library think twice about hunting him again.

Through the smoke, Krueger took Brandt and Grimm's hands and shooed them away, pointing further into the great room where the smoke had not yet spread. Suddenly alone in the agonizing mist, he squatted by the side of the library's entryway and waited for the man to arrive.

Through the swirling haze, past his tears and his raging pain, Krueger saw a black fleck that was the carbine's muzzle. The barrel came next, and when Krueger caught site of the fingers gripping the weapon, he lunged, launching himself using his mighty legs.

Krueger could not see his attacker's face. But the slow, unsteady way in which he fumbled his carbine proved that he was not expecting his quarry to still be standing. Too late, he raised his hands to fend off the assault, but Krueger brought the glistening rim of the platter down against the attacker's goggles. Soon they were loose, revealing wide brown orbs that were soon red and watering from the effects of the gas.

Desperate, the man raised his knee into Krueger's groin, and white, sickly pain crashed like waves over his stomach. The strength of his legs melted away, and Krueger fell forward, onto his enemy. Their arms tangled, their heads crashed, and soon both of them were falling onto the stone floor.

The man used his left hand to break his fall, leaving that side of his body momentarily exposed. And Krueger was the type of man who only ever needed a moment. Leaning onto his enemy, Krueger cast away his silver platter, punched hard into the man's kidneys, and finally gripped his man's face with both hands. Krueger ripped away his mask.

Too late, the man realized his error. Scrabbling violently on his back, the man tried to find the mask, the goggles, find anything that would stop the gas from filling his lungs and coating his skin.

Krueger could sense the man's rising desperation and methodically affixed both his meaty paws on his neck. He squeezed and realized, shamefully, that he was enjoying watching his enemy struggle. He could feel the man's pulse begin to quicken, his legs flying like two black eels caught on a fisherman's deck. The man's eyes shone with terror before filling with tears; the poor guy knew as he was perilously close to death.

Feebly, the man kicked again, his last and vain attempt to free himself. But this second kick, aimed squarely at Krueger's groin, was far weaker than the first, and the New York cop barely noticed it.

Krueger could not remember when Brandt and Grimm joined him, but after a time, he found his two friends at his side, pulling at his straining arms and trying to pry him away. He looked up expecting to see fear on Brandt's face, but instead, he found her wearing a hideous look of disgust. Krueger slowly realized that she was disgusted with *him*, and he sprang to his feet dismayed.

On the floor, a thin pleading wail escaped from the man's mouth, followed by gouts of thick, foamy saliva.

"Get the gun," Krueger whispered, weak and breathless.

Grimm thrust the weapon into his hands, and Krueger used it to fire on the lock of the exit door. By this time his vision was a blur of dark, shifting colors, but the bullets soon found their mark, and Brandt shouldered the door open.

The kiss of fresh air was divine, like the tender caress of an angel. The cool, jasmine-scented air soothed the exposed skin of Krueger and his friends and helped blow away the powdery compounds that were now stuck to their bodies with annoying tenacity.

Despite his many hurts, Grimm sprinted toward the body lying in the courtyard. He turned it over to see Sharif's dead gaze. The flesh of his neck was the color of the figs he had served so cheerfully hours before.

"Dead," Grimm mumbled through swollen and unsure lips. "Strangled."

"Use this water," Krueger coughed, handing his bottle to Grimm. He turned from the dead body and washed his face before passing the final dregs to Brandt.

"That . . . that was . . . this is . . ." Grimm said, before falling silent. He didn't have the words to finish his sentence.

"Crazy?" Brandt asked. She offered a weak smile, before looking back into the museum. The attacker had not emerged from the doorway. "Is he . . ." she asked.

"I don't care," Krueger said in a voice thick with slow-burning hatred.

Brandt's mouth hung open, despairing at the callousness of a man she was learning to admire. Krueger chewed his lip, before running back into the still smoking museum. He returned seconds later with his opponent hanging from his shoulder.

"Barely alive," he said with not a little remorse. Brandt hardly knew it in that moment, but beneath Krueger's barrel chest was a compassionate heart. He seldom sank into the degeneracy he'd glimpsed in desert terror cells and Harlem drug gangs.

"You figure this was a terror attack?" Brandt asked.

Krueger's answer was obscured by the rising sound of an unmistakable judder rending the air above. The companions each looked up into the moonlit sky.

Brandt pointed past the citadel wall high above. Circling in the vast blackness was a helicopter, with something long and metal pointing from its side.

Tessa Brandt did not have the expert vocabulary to describe it, but she sure knew a big, nasty gun when she saw one.

"GOT IT," HASSLER SAID slamming the receiver down with a pout.

Hawtrey had just broken the news that Sam O'Brian, the loutish thug one mistake away from early retirement, was being taken out of his department. Laughably, Hawtrey claimed that he was now taking part in the investigation of the New York bombing.

Just another one who thinks I'm a big dope, Hassler thought to himself. *The pair of them are probably laughing right now, congratulating themselves on having fooled me.* Hassler crossed his arms, trying to ignore the large belly which had ballooned since his last girlfriend had left back when Leno was hosting the Tonight Show. Feeling thoroughly sorry for himself, he scrambled out of his chair, looking for a moment like a turtle stuck on its back, and began pacing his office. He nibbled at a powered donut as he did so, halfheartedly promising himself that he'd cut out the junk food as soon as he'd figured out how to get his revenge on O'Brian and his missing partner Krueger.

Guys like them had always laughed behind his back. Like the kids back in Buffalo who'd chuckled at their short neighbor (they never called him a friend) when he'd said he wanted to be a cop, or the meatheads at the police academy who'd laughed when he'd collapsed into a ball of hair, sweat, and humiliation half-way through a post-Thanksgiving marathon. Laughing. Always laughing.

But Hassler had beaten them all. The commendations hung in his office proved it. So too did the pricey Ferragamo loafers he was wearing on his fat feet.

"I'll beat them too!" Hassler said to his bruised ego, his wormy lips creating a cloud of powdered sugar as he did so. He'd make an example out of Krueger and O'Brian. He'd show his team the price you paid for mocking and belittling Captain Cormac P. Hassler.

Chuckling, Hassler hoisted the last of the donut down his throat and closed the blinds to his office, denying the cretins in the bullpen any further opportunity to look at the captain they so obviously despised. *I always do my best work in secret,* Hassler thought. It was time for a little skullduggery.

TWO BRIGHT LED searchlights sliced through the night, and the helicopter drove down toward the courtyard.

"Get your asses running!" Krueger screamed to his friends.

"Run bloody where?" Grimm demanded. His pointed to the museum, bleached white by the chopper's lights. Smoke was still streaming in ratty plumes from the doorway.

"Captain's office!" Krueger said. He turned and saw the door, wondering if it was unlocked, and if he had the strength to bust it open if it wasn't. "Separate and run in zig-zags!" Krueger shouted as his friends darted toward the northernmost wall. His words were lost to the din above him.

Krueger took a hasty step forward, but then stopped, remembering the stricken man at his feet. Leaving a curse word hanging in the night air, Krueger stooped and picked up the armor-clad man who minutes before had been on the cusp of killing him.

Wrapping his long arm around the man's shoulders, Krueger barreled forward just as loud, short bursts of machine gun fire erupted from the chopper. As it echoed with chilling immediacy, Krueger charged forward in great alternating hops. Running leftward and then rightward, Krueger prayed his nimble-footed gait would reduce his chance of being hit.

His shoulder started to groan in protest at the great weight it was being forced to carry across the courtyard, but Krueger shut the pain out from his overladen mind. He could smell the sickly-sweet sweat on the wounded man as his eyes opened and closed with the dreamy regularity of someone dipping in and out of consciousness.

In front of him, Brandt reached the office door. With sweaty hands, she grabbed the handle and twisted it with a panicked jerking motion. But the door remained shut. Grimm was close behind her, and when he caught up, he flung himself onto the nearest office window, which unlike those of the museum were not barred.

The rotor blades above whirred as the pilot dragged his bird to the left, circling back toward the courtyard. Krueger's lungs felt red and angry.

He soon reached the locked door, and Krueger swiftly dropped the wounded man and shouldered it. The door didn't move in its frame, and the muscle in Krueger's arm blossomed into furious pain. Ignoring the damage he'd done to himself, Krueger turned and pulled the pistol from the wounded man's holster. A single shot reduced the lock to a shower of red sparks, and Krueger flung open the door. Brandt and Grimm charged inside, followed by Krueger, who dragged the wounded man inside by his belt.

Grimm raced across the room and grabbed the iron door, which opened onto the opposite side of the citadel wall. But it was locked, and far too thick for Krueger's gun to have an effect.

"Telephone!" Brandt cried, pointing to Sharif's desk. "Alert the garrison!" But when Grimm picked up the receiver, he was greeted by nothing except a dead line.

"Wires cut," he said, tearing open the draws of the desk. "We'll have the use the radio instead."

"Whatever you do, stay away from those windows!" Krueger ordered, dragging the wounded man closer to the far side of the office. He began lifting him onto one of Sharif's many couches, but as he did so, he felt something hot and wet pool in his hands. Dropping his load, Krueger saw the unmistakable sight of dark blood. A quick examination revealed that the attacker was dead, but it wasn't Krueger who had killed him: there were at least three bullets holes in his torn armor.

"These guys are desperate," Krueger muttered. Shaking his head in anger, he pawed the dead body, looking for a radio or cell phone. But there were none to be had.

Empty-handed, Krueger bounded toward Grimm, who was still ransacking the drawers in a futile search for a radio. Swatting away the doctor, Krueger lifted the desk and dragged it toward the wall farthest from the windows. He dropped it onto its side, shouting "we need a barricade," as he did so.

Panting, Krueger and his friends hunkered down behind the thick oak as the roar of the helicopter echoed in the sky above.

"Maybe Sharif has the radio clipped to his belt." Grimm wondered aloud.

"I'm not sure any of us should risk our life for a maybe," Krueger said. The windowpanes rattled ominously, as the courtyard outside flooded with the roving lights of the chopper. The pilot was likely positioning his bird to get a better shot at the offices.

"They are gonna be on top of us at any minute!" Brandt said. "There is no way out of this place!"

Krueger, clenching his jaw, was unwilling to voice his agreement with Brandt. He looked and saw the pistol still in his hands. It was a Glock, and on a bright, perfect day, Krueger could use it to shoot a big moving target like a helicopter with ease.

But it wasn't a perfect day. Krueger was trapped in a bloody hellscape in a foreign land, just the sort of place he had hoped to forget after his departure from the quagmire in Iraq.

"I'll go try to fetch the radio," Krueger said, looking at Sharif's dead body through the windows. "You teachers might be excellent in your fields, but I don't think you've got what it takes to escape these guys. They're kitted out in the pricey stuff which only mercs use."

Grimm nodded his acceptance, but Brandt blinked and recoiled as if she'd remembered something important. She began to mutter and plunged her hands into the pockets of her jacket. "Teachers," she kept saying over and over again.

Finally, Brandt found the object she was searching for and flashed a great joyful smile at Krueger, something which looked comically absurd amid such chaos.

"You sure we teachers aren't useful?" she asked, opening her hand.

Tessa Brandt was holding a laser pointer.

Krueger grinned, nodded his big chin, and beckoned Brandt to join him by the door. "These bastards are gonna swoop down into the courtyard any minute to give themselves a clear shot at the office," he said. "So when I get out, you point that thing straight at the cockpit. Don't worry about the guy operating the gun. If you do your job, then the pilot will be dragging that bird all across the sky to try and avoid your laser. They won't be able to get a good shot off."

Brandt was breathing heavily. She was still in pain from the tear gas, and sweat was streaking down her freckled face. But when Krueger asked if she was ready, her prompt and immediate reply was "yes." Brandt had been taught to fight bullies ever since she sat at her grandfather's knee, and that imperishable commitment was burning brightly in her eyes as Krueger opened the door.

The whoosh of the rotor blades filled Krueger's ears, and he stepped forward gingerly with his pistol raised. With Brandt waiting expectantly by the door, he shuffled forward, emerging into the light and away from the citadel wall. The wind whipped in the courtyard as he did so, and moments later, the fat black belly of the chopper descended. The masked gunman was clutching his weapon, but he did not expect to see Joe Krueger less than forty feet away with his own weapon raised. Krueger opened fire just as Brandt flashed her laser pointer toward the cockpit.

Almost immediately, the chopper started to sway, and the gunner was flung from his perch. He was forced to grab the interior bulkhead to stop from falling onto the flagstones below.

Krueger took the opportunity to reload and spewed another half-dozen bullets at the helicopter. It rose higher into the air, as if meaning to retreat, but the gunner suddenly returned to his weapon and sent a burst of furious fire out onto the courtyard.

Krueger darted rightward, running away from the death-dealing gun in nimble, lifesaving leaps.

"Keep your nerve!" Krueger shouted back to Brandt, who was flashing the scorching red light from the office doorway. It had its effect, and the bird swayed again, a tremor which sent the machinegun fire uselessly into the ground. The flagstones cracked and jostled, but Krueger remained safe.

Her confidence began to swell, and Brandt took a step forward toward the menacing helicopter. She was joined by Krueger alongside her, who, realizing he had just a couple of shots remaining, raised his Glock and fired, aiming for the gunman's chest. But the chopper barreled forward as he did so, much more violently than before, as the pilot tried vainly to keep Brandt's hateful laser from burning his eyes anymore. As the bird pitched forward, looking like it was caught on the crest of a sudden wave, Krueger's bullet struck the masked man in his face. He fell back into the belly of the chopper, the suddenness of his collapse proving that his wound was fatal.

But Krueger didn't have time for elation. Without pausing, he raised his pistol and aimed at the cockpit, but before he could fire, the pilot wrenched his chopper backwards, and the long black tail boom struck the flagstones. The result was as instantaneous as it was terrifying. The rotor tore into the ground, dissolving into flecks of deadly shrapnel as the blades churned uselessly. The fuselage erupted into a sheet of flame, which hungrily devoured the bird and sent sizzling sparks into the air.

As the inferno swelled, Krueger sprung backward, dragging Brandt back toward the office and the meager protection its walls offered. He felt white-hot debris fly past him with deadly velocity, but reached the office door without injury. Breathless, Krueger turned to see the cockpit erupt into a spew of flame as the windows blew outwards. The door trembled as the chopper's fuel was eaten up by the blaze. Soon, nothing remained of the black menace except the clattering debris skating across the courtyard.

"I didn't get the radio," Krueger said dryly.

"I don't think we need it anymore" spoke an awestruck Grimm, who looked at Krueger as if he were one of the Grecian heroes he was so fond of studying. "That blast will bring the whole bloody Egyptian army down on top of us."

IT WASN'T QUITE THE WHOLE army. But to Brandt it sure felt like it. Two regiments of the President's personal bodyguard soon arrived at the Citadel as the smoldering ruin of the courtyard was buzzed by F-16s. Swarms of paramilitary police ran through the offices of the late Captain Sharif, as if they thought the mere act of looking busy would assuage the panic of a city that was soon flooded with violent rumor. Handling their guns nervously, they discovered Grimm's driver dead in the parking lot, alongside the bodies of Sharif's garrison of seven soldiers.

Krueger was bundled into an armored Land Rover with enough force to suggest that the authorities did not believe his story about being a humble associate of Dr. Grimm. His two friends were placed in different vehicles, and together, they formed a formidable motorcade, which raced toward an unknown destination on the outskirts of Cairo. It was approaching midnight, but the attack on the Citadel meant that neither Krueger, nor anybody in the panicked Egyptian government, would be sleeping that night.

Eventually, the clatter of metal gates signaled to Krueger that they had reached their destination. Sure enough, the truck pulled up amid the serried ranks of green canvas tents, and a mustachioed officer dragged him into the desert air with the business end of a revolver digging into his ribs. Muttering curses in a low Arabic growl, the officer led Krueger to an ugly one-story barracks.

Inside was nothing but greenish strip lighting, which carved dark lines on Krueger's face. His friends looked equally haggard as the surly officer escorted the three companions to what he mockingly described as a lounge. But Krueger knew a holding cell when he saw one. The room was spartanly furnished with a single splintery table and too few chairs. The solitary sad and greasy window, set high above, was barred by rusty iron.

"Wait," the officer thundered as he shut and locked the door, as if the three friends had any other choice.

In the silence that followed, Krueger silently pointed to the farthest corner from the door. As they huddled, Krueger brought his hand to his mouth.

"They're scared," he whispered. "They wouldn't have made this rookie mistaken if they weren't. You don't put suspects in the same cell before interrogation. It gives them a chance to get their stories straight."

"I'm not sure that our story needs much straightening," Grimm replied. "We don't have anything to hide from the authorities."

"We told a few lies to reach a precious artifact and then tore it apart without asking," Brandt said. "In this febrile atmosphere, that might be enough to keep us behind bars for a while."

"I think you are right, Tessa," Krueger replied. "I know this part of the world. It's unstable, and when attacks like this happen, governments tend to react rather badly."

As if to confirm Krueger's claim, the door suddenly and violently swung open. An officer strode into the room, colder and more refined than the first, flanked by thuggish brutes on either side of his epauletted shoulders.

"Good evening," he said in a cut-glass English accent, with just the right amount of condescension to suggest there was nothing good about it.

"Officer," Grimm said in his smoothest and most ingratiating voice, "if I may—"

"No, you may not!" roared the officer, cutting him off. "How did you bring down the chopper? Tell me!"

"We just barely escaped with our lives," Brandt protested, "and many others were not so lucky. If I were you, I'd be trying to identify those attackers and figuring out if more attacks are planned."

The officer snorted and pointed to the door languidly. His thugs closed it. "Do not tell me how to do my job," he said. "One of the great treasures of my country has just been attacked, and if you want me to believe that you had no part in that disgrace, you had better start providing answers."

Tired of the pantomime, Krueger lunged at the officer, throwing Brandt's laser pointer into his unsuspecting hands. "That's how we saved ourselves!" he cried. The officer took a defensive step back, terrified as raw rage spread across the freakishly large face of his prisoner. "It's a laser pointer!" the face yelled.

"How?" asked the officer, weakly. He was growing unsure of himself in the face of Krueger conviction.

"That is a 5-milliwatt laser, bud," Krueger said. "It may not sound like much, but it can cause permanent retinal burns at fifty feet. And trust me, we were a Hell of a lot closer to the chopper than that."

"I see," said the officer, chewing his lip thoughtfully.

Suddenly, the door swung open, and the man who had originally hustled Krueger and his friends into the room reappeared. But the snarl of his face had been replaced by a simpering dread. He galloped toward his superior and whispered into his ear. Krueger saw drops of sweat drip from his hairy ears as he did so.

The officer finished his report and fled the cell without waiting to be dismissed. He left behind the senior man, who was fast losing his refined appearance. The color drained from his cheeks as he caught a bad case of the fidgets. He couldn't decide where to put his hands; one moment they were resting on the table; the next they were massaging his temples.

"You!" he said finally, pointing to Grimm. "Come here!" The officer was trying to recapture his authority, but when he took Grimm's arm, he did so with a respectful and soft touch. He led him toward the door as if he were the maître d' at a Chelsea eatery. The officer paused only once, to place the laser point on the table with an undue reverence.

Grimm, the officer, and the two thugs left, but they did not lock the door, leaving behind a bewildered Brandt and Krueger.

"Take a seat," Krueger said, exhaling. "Looking at that guy's face, I think we've caught a break."

Krueger sat on the floor marveling as what a strange thing authority could be. It was invisible, and yet everyone knew when you had it . . . and when you didn't.

Thirty minutes later, Dr. Grimm returned. One of the thugs followed behind him, carrying three large coffees. Brandt leapt forward and took one, sipping even though the drink was still scalding hot. "Just what the doctor ordered," she said.

"Yes," replied Grimm, "literally."

The thug left silently and closed the door.

"So what kind of trouble we in?" Krueger asked as the closed.

"Very little," he said with an insufferable smugness. "My father personally manages the Egyptian President's investment portfolio over at Greystone, and some enterprising fellow must have made the connection between him and me. One quick phone call secured our release. I expect we'll be out of this rat hole momentarily."

And so it proved. Just as dawn was breaking beautifully over the tawny dunes, a man entered the cell with breakfast. He then took their formal statements with little fuss, using an old Dictaphone to record their nightmare in the Citadel.

The return to Cairo was an altogether more pleasant affair. The President had dispatched his personal Rolls Royce to drive the trio back to their hotel, where they found an armed guard and their belongings fastidiously packed. Three hours later, Grimm's jet was back in the air with three tired, grateful passengers safely inside. Below was the golden vastness of the desert and beyond, the silent, sparkling majesty of the Mediterranean.

"It's a good job you were with us," Krueger said to Grimm as they sat together. "I don't know how we would have gotten out of that fix if it weren't for you."

"Yes, you do," Grimm shot back, staring into his empty hands. "You'd have found some way to escape, just like you did in the Citadel. All I could do was wail and make a fool of myself. It wasn't me that got us out of the clink. It was my father's money."

Krueger placed a comforting arm around Grimm's shoulder. "Your first time in a fight like that is always your worst. Trust me; I know."

Krueger was not lying. Ten weeks in boot camp and two months in Army Ranger School hadn't been worth a pail of goat's spit the moment Krueger stepped onto the sun-scorched streets of Fallujah. The sound of your drill instructor is terrifying, but not so terrifying as the sound of an IED blowing up your best friend. And when that happens, everything that instructor told you just drains away, replaced by red panic seizing control of every synapse in your brain.

Grimm coughed, embarrassed. "Well, I'd like for us to resume our search for the Cross," he said, "which would mean landing in Jerusalem. But I think we ought to confer with your allies in America first, don't you think?"

Krueger nodded. "Why Jerusalem?" he asked.

"Because," Brandt said, returned from the bathroom wearing a clean linen blouse and a refreshing smile, "the Fragment claims Saladin's son returned the Cross to the Horns."

"The Horns?" Krueger asked.

"The Horns of Hattin," she answered. "The twin peaks of a dead volcano which overlook the Hattin plain. It was there that Saladin vanquished the Crusaders and took the True Cross. And where, if al-Qalqashandi is correct, it was buried."

"It's in Israel," Grimm added.

Krueger thought hard, wondering what next step to take. Making a mental survey of his predicament, he realized the danger of continuing the pursuit. There was obviously some high intelligence directing the conspiracy, throwing its agents against Krueger and his friends without remorse.

"I need to speak to Hawtrey," Krueger said, realizing that his brow was dripping with cold sweat.

THIS WAS FAR EASIER said than done, for at exactly the same moment Krueger boarded his jet in Cairo, Lucille Hawtrey was getting onboard a private plane heading to Washington. It was too damned early to be up, but she was, according to the White House Press Secretary, due to give a presentation to the President regarding the progress of the investigation. In truth, she was due to receive one almighty tirade from a Commander-in-Chief who was getting very bad press. The failure to name a single suspect, let alone make an arrest, was driving his poll numbers downward faster than any sex scandal.

But she was not going alone. Sam O'Brian and Colin Dubchek followed her onto the plane, functioning on little more than energy drinks and adrenalin. Hawtrey told them it was because they were key to the investigation, which was only half true. The real reason Hawtrey brought them along was because they both knew she had started to dabble in Krueger's Nazi conspiracy, and as such could easily destroy her career. Hawtrey needed them to do their job, but she also needed to watch them.

But despite Hawtrey's unwelcome trip at an ungodly hour, the indefatigable Ms. Dupree succeeded in connecting her group to Krueger and Brandt, and they were soon eyeballing one another through a video conferencing screen. It was the first time each person who'd helped investigate the mystery were all together.

"I thought you were returning to New York?" she asked waspishly as dawn broke slowly over the Eastern seaboard. It appeared even the sun was slow to move in the humidity.

"Something happened," Krueger said.

"What something?"

Hawtrey's plane had landed in the sweaty capital of the nation by the time Krueger had finished his incredible tale. A car was idling on the asphalt outside, waiting to take the senior agent to her jeremiad. But Hawtrey didn't flinch. She was processing the tale, cataloging and filing the relevant facts with the same tenacity that had won her a scholarship to UVA in the first year that storied college started accepting female students.

"I am grateful that you survived the attack and escaped Cairo," she said. "But I am nonetheless wondering how your alleged discovery aides us in our search for the bomber?" Hawtrey's eyebrow rose like spider's leg.

O'Brian, incredulous, threw his hands up in the air, while Dubchek coughed nervously.

"Ma'am," Brandt said finally in a timid voice. "Whether we believe that General Krueger is responsible for the bombings or not, it is clear that a group of people is determined to halt our investigation into the whereabouts of his body."

"I agree," Hawtrey said, "but that is not an answer to my question. The world's press, not to mention our angry President, are starting to suspect we are fools. We've had three weeks to find the terrorist, and all we have to show for our efforts is a handful of clues to an ancient mystery. So why should we be investigating this True Cross nonsense at all?"

The pilot cut the engine on Hawtrey's jet, and the conference table was plunged into a deep and unwelcome silence.

"Because it's the only lead we've got in this damned case," Krueger spat finally, and nobody argued with him. "All of us here," Krueger continued, "have no choice but to accept the fact that my grandfather, somehow, is bound up with these attacks. Maybe he was successfully revived from the cryogenic freezing. Maybe he was resurrected through the power of the True Cross. Or maybe this is all one big lie and he spent the last half-decade in South America with Elvis Pressley faking the moon landings. We don't know. And until we know where he is, I've got a bad feeling that America won't be safe."

"He's right," came a firm, mahogany voice from beyond the screen. Dr. Grimm emerged and sat next to his friends, wearing a velvet robe and monogrammed slippers.

"Jesus," O'Brian said, "are you guys heading to the Playboy Mansion?"

"Let's stay on topic, please," Hawtrey said, who nonetheless made a mental note to include this ridiculous tidbit in that evening's Maker's Mark-infused debrief to Mr. Hawtrey.

"The point," Grimm continued, "is that while we cannot yet draw a clear line between the bombings and the disappearance of General Krueger, the overwhelming evidence is that they are linked." Despite the hard edge of confidence in Grimm's voice, his face was drawn and pale, and he moved slowly, as if his robe were made of glass.

Hawtrey sighed. "Show him the tape," she said to Colin Dubchek, who ferreted away at his laptop in response to the order.

"We are sending you some footage to view," Hawtrey said, "taken in Atlanta last night."

Krueger's cell phone vibrated, the signal he'd received an email. It contained a link to video footage shot outside a tall gated building.

A figure darted suddenly across the screen; his silver head bowed, his gloved hands holding an enormous black haversack. *Grandfather*, Krueger thought with sickening certainty.

The video was shot with a cell phone, and whoever had recorded it followed General Krueger as he was pursued down a street past the building. A crowd had formed behind him, and they were yelling curses in English and Yiddish.

"This is General Krueger," Brandt said, watching the video with a mixture of fear and curiosity churning the pretty features of her face. The man ran onwards, his movement lithe and graceful even under stress. To Brandt, this proved that it was the refined Prussian general who was being pursued.

"We don't know that," Hawtrey replied icily. "All Atlanta PD are able to tell using CCTV footage and witness statements is that the man in that video attempted to break into the synagogue on Peach Tree Street yesterday afternoon. A group of worshippers chased him out of the building."

"Caught him before he could plant his bomb," Dubchek said to himself.

The video was still playing as he spoke, and the crowd, fearful and angry, finally caught up to the bowed figure. Suddenly, an ogre bounded into view, roaring obscenities. His bare arms were enormous and sunburnt; his biceps were the size of roast chickens.

"Who the heck is that? King Kong?" Krueger asked.

"Professional weightlifter," O'Brian answered. "Served in the Israeli army. Over seven feet tall. Weighs 450 pounds."

"You don't say," Brandt said, as she watched the brute jab his hulking hand into Krueger's chest, but the General just looked bored by the attack. Krueger's look of boredom seemed to enrage the weightlifter. Finally, he grabbed Krueger's arm, the one carrying the haversack, and that's when it happened.

General Krueger, dead for half a century, took hold of the man's neck with his free hand. Krueger's fingers appeared to gain little purchase on the corded muscle of the strongman, but he nonetheless started to choke. The crowd, which had gathered around the spectacle, erupted in shrieks of fear. The witness shooting the footage on his cell phone yelped in surprise and dismay.

As if dispensing with a ball of cotton candy, General Krueger tossed the weightlifter to the ground just as a burgundy Honda came screaming around the corner. The car pulled up, its tires smoking, and Krueger entered the rear passenger seat with the huge haversack resting on his knees. The weightlifter was left heaving on the asphalt, red, trembling, and wide-eyed. The video cut out shortly thereafter, as the crowd's chorus of frightful cries rose to a shuddering crescendo.

"Impossible," Grimm said.

"I've been hearing that word a lot lately," Krueger said, and Hawtrey nodded her agreement.

"A foiled attack?" Brandt asked. She settled in her seat and covered her head with her hands, as if she were wearied, perhaps even diminished, by what she had just witnessed.

"Yes," O'Brian said to her through the screen. "It looks like the bomber was caught before he could strike, which is good news. But the bad news is this recording shows he has greater strength than anyone I've ever met, and I've been boxing in the toughest gyms in Brooklyn since before I left high school."

"Why are you showing me this?" Krueger asked. It seemed every day he was confronting proof of the enormous power of his enemies.

"To prove to you that this bomber is a mean SOB, Joey," O'Brian answered. "We need to light a fire under your butt. Whatever you need to do in the Middle East, do it quickly. This ain't a field trip."

Brandt slammed her hands on the desk with a sharp judder. "Damn you!" she screamed. "We know that! I almost died trying to get to the bottom of this!"

"Okay relax!" Hawtrey bellowed as she rose to her feet. "I'm already late to meet the President." Hawtrey scowled and signaled for the plane door to be opened onto the splendid summer sun outside. "Krueger, I am indulging you once more. Don't make me regret it. Get to Hattin. See what you can find there and report back. I'm sending Munroe to Atlanta to see what he can discover about the abortive attack at the synagogue, if indeed that is what it was. O'Brian and Dubchek will continue searching for more information about the Castor Group, the business which owns that hideous lab in Berlin."

Dubchek whined like a chastised teenager. "But ma'am," he said, "there's nothing more we can do. Our liaison with the Securities and Exchange Commission got us nothing but a big fat goose egg. The Castor Group is a shell. Registered in Belize. The company address is a PO Box in some ratty barrio."

"Well, here's another one for you to search, Colin," Krueger said, withdrawing a crumpled card for his crumpled shirt pocket. "Webber allegedly got into the Citadel claiming to be a manager of an international consultancy. It's called Pollux Solutions. You might have more luck finding out about those guys."

Dubchek carefully wrote down the name, checking that he had spelled it correctly.

"Pollux and Castor," Grimm muttered, "how very curious." Krueger noticed that his friend's hands were beginning to tremble. He was, Krueger realized, struggling to gain mastery over his rising fear.

"What you say?" O'Brian asked through the screen.

"Pollux and Castor were ancient twins," Grimm said.

"Excuse me?" Hawtrey asked. The last of her patience was spent.

"Castor and Pollux were the mythical twins from ancient Rome," Grimm said. "So it's odd that we should be discussing both those storied names. Of course, today most people know them from their supermarket horoscopes."

"How so?" O'Brian muttered.

"Because," Grimm continued, "the images of Castor and Pollux represent one of the astrological signs." Grimm coughed and realized with embarrassment that he was wasting his friends' time. "They represent Gemini," he said, expecting to finish his point, and was amazed when Sam O'Brian, an obvious hardboiled philistine, erupted with a hundred angry questions.

CURT DENNILSON, THE 55-YEAR-OLD founder of Gemini, sauntered into his office, where, for the last decade, he had calmly straddled one of the biggest companies on the face of the Earth.

North of Oakland in California, Gemini was headquartered on a far-reaching promontory of rock, facing the Golden Gate Bridge. The campus, built by Dennilson after he'd made so much money he no longer had to worry about overruns and budgets, was a sleek silver skyscraper. A gorgeous behemoth of steel and glass, which glowed pink during the beautiful fall sunsets, the building was a giant semi-circle. From above, it looked like a fingernail pairing or a half-moon, and within its walls was more computer power than most nation states.

From his spacious, spartan office, Dennilson saw the wide azure San Francisco Bay. On clear days, he could glimpse Silicon Valley beyond. He liked that his business was far from the heart of the Valley and was instead perched like an outsider looking in. It reminded him of where he'd come from.

Not that Curt Dennilson liked to recall his past. He talked about it often, especially to starry-eyed journalists who would go on to write hagiographic accounts of the tech titan. But he spoke without remembering, reciting passages as if they were from another person's life. He'd tried hard to forget the hunger, the humiliation, and above all, the piteous glances.

Following his family's disgrace and retreat from England in the austere 50s, Dennilson's harried mother had finally settled with relatives in California. And there, forgetting that she could no longer afford the life of relaxed leisure to which she had become accustomed, she became what Dennilson detested most of all: a mooch.

This mooch gave birth to her son after a dalliance with an aimless beatnik, whose far-left ideology appealed to a woman who detested being asked to pay for anything. The hippie soon departed, and the son he sired was dragged around the West Coast by a surly mother, who bitterly refused to accept that it was her own mistakes that had led her to such misfortune.

Passed from one exhausted relative to another, Dennilson's mother died drunk and penniless, and at her dismal funeral, her young son never forgot the well-camouflaged look of relief in the eyes of those who claimed to be mourning her. And as tears sprung from his young eyes, he told himself, he *swore* to himself, that he would never become the parasite that his grasping mother had turned into.

Two subsequent years of frustration as an art student at a cheap community college proved fruitless, and the succession of catering jobs that followed only served to improve Dennilson's bank balance but not his self-esteem. But a job lifeguarding at Fort Funston in the early nineties proved much more promising, as it gave him a chance to meet the Prince of Pennsylvania, Bill Frost, who bonded with Dennilson over their mutual love of surfing.

A scion of a famous East Coast banking family, Frost had come to California to bring some button-down sensibilities to the freewheeling computer industry. He soon invited Dennilson to join him in his first venture: bringing banking online. His young friend came with few academic credentials, but was armed with a white-hot desire to succeed—one which the languid Ivy Leaguers did not. This desire drove him to work nights, weekends, and holidays, and he was soon as good an expert on computing as the grads Frost had been liberally hiring.

Of course, it was that same white-hot desire that Frost admired which led Dennilson to lead a buyout of the company and force his former mentor back to Pittsburgh. But, as he looked upon the gallery of photographs of himself shaking the hands of Presidents, religious leaders, and Oscar-winning actors, Dennilson knew it had all been worth it.

With a half-smile, Dennilson flipped a small switch tucked into the corner of one of the picture frames. Slowly, the wall whirred and spun, revealing a secret panel behind the beaming pictures.

Behind them, hidden away from prying eyes, was *The Storm on the Sea of Galilee* by Rembrandt van Rijn. Framed with ornate gilded wood, it was the Dutch master's only seascape, depicting Jesus, serene and ageless, calming the waves of a churning Sea of Galilee. It was also, Dennilson knew with devilish delight, the most expensive stolen artwork in the world.

He'd picked it up from the thieves who'd lifted it from a Boston Museum back when he first started to make good money. They were ignorant of its worth, and Dennilson paid just a fraction of what it would have cost on the open market. He'd dabbled in the black market ever since, and in his San Francisco home, which reporters breathlessly reported as looking 'humble' and 'down-to-earth," was stolen artwork, secretly stored, worth over half a billion dollars.

Once, when he was a wide-eyed student of limited means, he might have been disgusted with himself for having squirreled away precious works like a miser, but he was world-weary now, and he knew that the stale-breathed oafs trudging through museums with their screaming brats could not appreciate works like his stolen Rembrandt.

There was a knock at the door, and Dennilson returned the wall to its original appearance. Sinking into his chair, he watched as Preston Gates emerged, looking like a paler, shorter, and fatter version of his boss. Thunder was growling on his brow.

"We have a problem," Gates said, wiping his sweaty upper lip. It was late, and only a few key lieutenants were still in the building.

"I really hope not," Dennilson replied. He'd just finished his afternoon run and was eager for a few moments in the shower before confronting any of the miscellaneous problems, which gathered on a CEO's desk like scum in a drain pipe. "What is it?"

Gates slammed a pile of photographs on Dennilson's glass desk. They showed the smoldering husk of a helicopter. "Someone is poking around our Middle East operations," Gates said.

Dennilson threw up his hands. "The same people in Berlin?" he queried.

Gates nodded with both his prodigious chins.

"I thought we put John Decker onto this?" Dennilson asked, tossing the photographs back to Gates. They proved that he was close to being exposed, and he was eager not to look at them.

"We did," Gates answered. "Major Decker took two of his best into Cairo. They were killed in this attack three hours ago."

Dennilson sucked in his breath. "Jesus," he said. Even seated in his office, surrounded by the gimcracks that proved his wealth and power, he could feel those damned investigators drawing closer to his work.

And secrecy was key for what he had in mind.

"Our guys couldn't stop some New York cop and the Ivory Tower dame he picked up in Berlin? What the Hell are we paying them for?"

"This isn't just a cop, Curt," Gated replied, pulling a folder from beneath his flabby, sweaty arm. He opened it to show the records he had discovered. "Joseph Krueger did two tours in Iraq and three in Afghanistan, and he walked away with a lot of medals and a lot of practice fighting. He's not some meter maid."

Dennilson chewed his lip and grabbed the file from Gates. His shower would have to wait. "So what's he found out?" he asked glumly.

"He knows about the Volcker-Blum factory. And given that Decker failed to stop him, we must assume he knows what's contained in the Fragment."

"Well, if that's true, then he'll be going to Hattin next," Dennilson said looking up. A dark smile bloomed on his face, twisting his handsome features. "And that's where we will stop him."

"Curt," Gates said bitterly, "we sent three top-dollar mercenaries to kill him, not to mention our friends in Germany, and none of them gave this Krueger so much as a paper cut."

Dennilson sighed and reached for the phone. "Relax," he said. "We are going to try something a little different."

"THIS IS RISKY," Hawtrey said to Sam O'Brian, who had the look of a dog eager for permission to go chase a ball. He'd been waiting for two hours for Hawtrey to get out of her early morning meeting so she could green light his plan, and they were now all racing back to the airport.

"It sure is," O'Brian agreed, "but I'm not going in with a gun drawn. Just lemme go speak with Dennilson. Maybe look around his fortress out in California. Call ahead for me. Tell him we're about ready to release the artifacts we recovered from the blast site in New York. It's the perfect cover."

"I'm sorry," Hawtrey said, "but I need more than the word 'Gemini' to pull the trigger on this one. It could just be one heck of a coincidence."

"Or maybe not," Dubchek said, swinging his laptop around to show a web page to his boss. "While you were being yelled at by the President, I was doing some digging into Mr. Dennilson's private life."

"Oh Jesus," Hawtrey said, as the pressure on her temples blossomed into a headache. "I wish you hadn't told me that. Do you know how many guys his money has put into Congress? And how many are now on the Homeland Security Committee?"

"Don't worry, ma'am," Dubchek replied. "I didn't leave any fingerprints, but it did take a few hours trawling the dark web to find it." The wiry young men pointed to a scanned image of an old document.

"So what is it, professor?" O'Brian queried.

"Something that someone doesn't want found," Dubchek answered. "It's a docket from US Immigration officials working at Ellis Island, proving Dennilson's mother landed there in 1951, aged 23. She's listed as Mrs. Clara Dennilson. But, in fact, she was Lady Dennilson, sister of Lord Haw-Haw!"

O'Brian knitted his brow and sighed. "This isn't some costume drama on PBS, kid." He snorted. "Just tell us what it all means."

Dubchek rolled his eyes and resumed his report. "Lord Haw-Haw's real name was William Joyce. He was a British fascist who fled to Germany in 1939 and began broadcasting Nazi propaganda to Britain, after which the Brits gave him the nickname Haw-Haw. He was broadcasting right up till the day the British seized Hamburg in 1945. It was there they found and executed him for treason. His family was disgraced, of course, including his sister, who was rather fond of Hitler herself. She divorced her husband over it and came to America to try and escape the scandal."

"You see!" O'Brian said to Hawtrey suddenly, jabbing Dubchek's screen with his chubby finger while he bounced in his seat like an excited toddler. "You said yourself that the evidence points to these attacks being motivated by Jew hatred. Well here's the second bit of proof linking Dennilson: he's the nephew of Hitler's favorite limey fascist."

Hawtrey pursed her lips. "Dennilson *was* awfully keen to get back the art he had lost in the New York blast," she said slowly, as if arguing with herself. "If he was led to believe that we were ready to return the remains of his acquisitions, I'm sure he would welcome you with open arms."

"And while Detective O'Brian is touring the Gemini campus, I can follow up on Pollux Solutions," Dubchek said. "If there is a link between them, Castor, and Dennilson, then I'll do my best to find it."

Hawtrey's car crossed the Potomac River, its water still and dark. Two police Crown Victorias raced past in the opposite direction, speeding toward the city with their sirens screaming.

Perhaps they were heading to a robbery or an assault, one of the thousands of low-level crimes that beset the great cities of the greatest nation on Earth. But the sound of those wailing sirens chilled Hawtrey's blood regardless. She was, like everyone else, being eaten up by the fear that more attacks were coming.

"Okay let's do this," Hawtrey said with finality in her voice. "But on two conditions. First, neither of you speak a word of this. If people discover we are seriously looking at a link between the bombings and the True Cross, we'll be laughed at. But if it's discovered we're nosing around Dennilson, then his lawyers will be on us like leeches—and so will the members of Congress he bankrolled. Heck, the governor of California was the Best Man at his wedding."

"You got it, ma'am," Dubchek said. "What's the second condition?"

"That you go with O'Brian to Gemini," Hawtrey answered. "You'll have to do your investigating of Pollux while you are on the road, Dubchek, so you'd better be handy with that laptop of yours. It's not ideal, I know, but I don't want O'Brian going in there by himself."

"I didn't know you cared," O'Brian said as Reagan National Airport came into view outside.

"I don't," Hawtrey answered. "But I need someone to keep an eye on you. One mistake, and Dubchek will tell me. And if he doesn't, he'll be out without a pension, just like you. The two of you will be in a line to collect food stamps before Christmas."

O'Brian leaned back, waiting for the punchline, waiting for Hawtrey's face to break into a smile. But it didn't. She was serious.

"You got it," O'Brian said, suddenly realizing his mouth had gone dry.

THOUSANDS OF MILES away, Joe Krueger was watching with fascination as Barnaby Grimm's plane descended toward the Israeli capital. Below was the glimmering sprawl of Tel Aviv, where modern towers loomed over narrow, ancient streets in sweaty, immediate proximity. Beyond was the white surf of the Mediterranean, crashing onto beaches so old they had been fought over by men using bows and horses and then tanks and guns.

Grimm was seated next to him, busy chewing his lip. The academic kept bringing his hand to his face defensively, while his eyeballs swiveled, unable to focus on anything.

Post-traumatic stress, Krueger thought bitterly. It was a curt and malignant phrase, the phrase uttered to too many heroes returning from too many battlefields. There was, Krueger knew, more horror in the world than a mortal mind could accept, and in homes great and small (mostly small) across America, men bigger and badder than Grimm were still haunted by the grotesqueries they had seen. It was little wonder that the dashing professor was so troubled.

"Rest easy," Krueger whispered, placing a hand over Grimm's.

But Grimm instantly recoiled. He spluttered and closed his eyes. "This is a bad idea," he declared.

"You know," Krueger said, "there's no shame in admitting your fear."

"I am not afraid!" Grimm cried, before realizing the absurdity of his claim. "Well," he said, "I am not afraid anymore."

Grimm's raised voice drew the attention of Tessa Brandt, who was sitting at the front of the aircraft. She approached her two friends and sat next to them.

"This is a waste of time," Grimm said, looking at Brandt and asking, silently, for her support. "The Fragment is quite obviously a fake."

"How do you know?" Brandt asked.

"Muslims do not believe in the Resurrection!" Grimm shrieked. "In the age of Saladin, they mocked Christians for believing Christ was crucified. After they seized the True Cross, they mocked it as a fake relic of heretics. Why would a devout Muslim like Saladin go to such lengths hiding it?"

"Because," Brandt said patiently, "he was visited by an angel. And as a devout Muslim, he would have wished to do the bidding of Jibreel. After all, it was Jibreel who came to Mohammed with the revelation, which would ultimately become the start of the Quran."

"There is no other source to corroborate what we just read," Grimm said stiffly, changing the subject.

"Which would explain why the Cross has not yet been found," Brandt answered. She was speaking like a teacher and reached out to take Grimm's hand. But he jerked back.

"There are just too many questions. Too much uncertainty!" Grimm said. He was staring at his shoes and refused to meet the gaze of his companions as he grew angrier. "It's most likely an utter fantasy!"

"People tend not to kill for the sake of a fantasy."

"Oh no!" Grimm said. "Tell that to the men killed in Iraq and Israel and a hundred other dumps just because they worshiped a different deity!"

Brandt pounced, enraged and bewildered by her friend's behavior, and slammed Grimm against the bulkhead. "Do not blaspheme in a land like this!" she said, discovering her own voice was rising.

The stewardess approached, ready to tell her guests to affix their seatbelts, but seeing the argument before her, she retreated to the galley.

"Take it easy," Krueger said, placing his muscular hand on Brandt's shoulder.

"I am getting out of this nightmare!" Grimm declared, rising and heading toward his private office at the back of the fuselage. "Tessa, you and the ugly freak can go get yourself killed, but not me!"

Grimm locked himself away, leaving his insult to hang in the air.

Freak.

Krueger fell into his seat and silently buckled his belt.

Freak.

So there it was. Grimm hadn't, couldn't see past Krueger's physical deformity. He was, and would forever be, a *Freak*.

"He . . . he's just . . ." Brandt said, taking a seat next to the cop and trying to apologize for her friend's crude remark.

"Don't," Krueger said.

So Brandt didn't.

They landed in silence, and when the door opened and glorious sunshine flooded in, Brandt began wordlessly departing. Krueger, wounded, followed her with his head bowed, as if he was trying to hide from the world the disfigurement that would mark him as different forevermore.

"Joseph," Grimm said in the thin voice from inside the office. "Would you come see me? Please?"

Krueger sighed. He knew what the world expected of guys like him. Big guys, with dirt under their fingernails and a six pack of domestic beer in the fridge, were expected to laugh at insults and bullying. But that was easier to do when your chin wasn't the size of Rhode Island.

"Please?" Grimm asked again.

Krueger gritted his teeth and opened the door.

Inside, Grimm stood next to a wash basin with his head bowed. He gripped the porcelain tightly. "I am so sorry," he said.

"I get it," Krueger replied, not bothering to look at the man before him. "You were angry." Krueger's voice was flat and hard.

"That was unspeakably cruel of me," Grimm said, "and someone in my position should know better."

"I get it," Krueger repeated.

"Yes, and I get it too. That's what makes my remark so much more wretched."

Krueger didn't understand what Grimm was saying and was still trying to decipher it as the academic turned to face him.

But the man he saw was different. Upon Grimm's smooth forehead was a wide white oval, and more white spots, like giant tears, cascading down his left cheek. His left hand was almost entirely white also, save for a few, final vestiges of blackness at the fingertips.

"Vitiligo," Grimm said, answering the question posed by Krueger's shocked expression. "The slow destruction of my skin pigment. Incurable, I'm afraid, and the doctors tell me that it'll get progressively worse."

"I'm sorry," Krueger said, genuinely.

"It's quite alright," Grimm said. "I can camouflage these ugly things with makeup, at least until the disease is more advanced. Which is more than I can say for you. That's why my remark was so despicable." Grimm approached and offered Krueger his hand. "I said it because I was scared, just like you knew I was. Unlike you, I've never faced a gun before. And unlike you, I've never had to walk the streets without my deformity covered. I tried it once as a teenager, when my skin first started turning white. It was . . . not a good experience."

"People can be cruel," Krueger concurred.

"And leave you with a rather, shall we say *brittle*, self-esteem," Grimm said. He pursed his lips and looked shamefacedly at the floor. "You are a fine man, Detective Krueger," he said, "and as long as you have need of a foolish peacock like me, I will be by your side."

"It's your fortune and brilliance that have gotten us this far, Dr. Grimm," Krueger answered. "I doubt I'll get this job done without you hanging around."

The two men embraced, and the resentments and stresses fell away in those tender moments, like leaves falling from a rotting tree.

Waiting on the asphalt of Ben Gurion Airport, Brandt looked disbelievingly as Krueger and Grimm descended with their arms around each other. Grimm was looking his usual glamorous self, having applied the makeup that hid his affliction from the world. Krueger, whose massive chin would never be hidden, nonetheless gilded it with a wide and generous smile.

"I won't ask what happened back there," Brandt said with a half-smile.

"Oh, please don't," Grimm replied. "There's no time to dwell on those ugly moments. Come, we have a cross to find! And hopefully find some time for afternoon tea, as well."

Two hours later, Krueger found himself in a different world. Perhaps it was his weariness, which had settled over his mind like shroud, but he felt as though he had stepped back into an earlier age, far from the glitzy capital with its cars, computers, and unwelcome haste. Krueger and his companions were now in a lush, fertile land filled with names freighted with history. Nazareth. Galilee. Haifa. And, of course, Hattin.

"Nearly there!" Brandt shouted, as the open-top Range Rover took her and her companions north toward Lake Tiberias. But Krueger, seated behind the closemouthed driver, didn't hear her. The wind screamed in his ears, and around him, he saw an achingly beautiful vista. He wore the smile of a traveler who'd finally arrived at his destination and found it exceeded his expectations.

"We got here far more quickly than I expected," Grimm said in despairing tones. He sat in the rear next to Krueger and was wiping the back of his neck with his silk cravat while sucking his teeth.

"Trouble?" Krueger asked. Grimm raised an eyebrow.

"What happened in Cairo last night counts as trouble, dear boy; this is a mere trifle in comparison. Nevertheless, it has me concerned."

"What does?" Krueger asked. The road began to climb steeply, and on the bright blue horizon, the detective caught site of two grey hills, stiff and proud, with a large cleft in between.

"I just remembered something: our utter ignorance," Grimm said languidly. "All we know is that Saladin's son returned the Cross to 'the Horns,' which we are assuming refers to the Horns of Hattin." Grimm raised his hand and pointed toward the horizon.

"And?" Krueger asked.

"And it's a big place," Grimm answered. "I don't know how to begin the search, or where to look. And I'd prefer going into this dig with a little more information."

"It's not much, but perhaps a little history could help," Brandt said, turning to face her friends.

The wind whipped strands of hair over her fair freckled face, and they looked like threads of gold in the sunlight. Krueger couldn't help smiling at the sight.

"According to legend," she said, "the True Cross was seized by troops serving under Taqi-ad-Din, Saladin's nephew. Saladin gave him command of the right flank of his army, which occupied the lands around the village of Nimrin during the battle of Hattin. Maybe that was where Saladin's son buried the cross?"

"Well it's not much," Grimm replied, "but better than nothing. We'll begin our search there the moment we are headquartered. I've rented a large farmhouse in the Lower Galilee. It should suffice as our base of operations."

"What about security?" muttered Krueger darkly. Beneath his sunglasses, his eyes grew cold, remembering the horror of the night before.

"A team of five men is waiting for us, led by a former CIA operative who joined my father's company back when he was selling penny stocks and living in a bedsit in Walthamstow. He can be trusted, and so can his men. They know what we are up to here."

"They know about the Cross?" Krueger bellowed.

Grimm waved his hand. "Please! I may not be Secret Service material, but I know how to keep a secret. All they know is I'm on one of my usual jaunts and Papa wants to keep a close eye on me."

Brandt allowed herself a little giggle. "Doesn't your dad get mad at you wasting his cash like this?" she asked.

Grimm leaned back and laughed. It was a giddy, weightless sound, and the nicest thing Krueger had heard since before he arrived in Berlin. He found himself chuckling right along, but didn't know why.

"Oh my dear, Lord Grimm positively loves what I'm doing! Do you know how many of his friends have kids that are addicted to drugs and sports cars and yachts and other utterly boring possessions? Back at the club in London, all they talk about is the price of vulgar rehab facilities on the West Coast of America and how they can arrange for their feckless offspring to become gainfully employed. By comparison to them, I'm a complete darling. Papa likes nothing more than to hear about my adventures."

Grimm trailed off, as the last word, the word which had driven him on trips around the world, left his lips. He knew now that adventure was not a sterile romp bought by tourists in the certainty that their safety was guaranteed. It was often something worse, something black and bloody. His smile shriveled away, leaving behind a wan, wearied face.

"The farmhouse is five miles away," he said bluntly, and said nothing more.

The Range Rover turned off from the main road and sneaked up a winding, crumbly path shielded by large palm trees. Dust hung in the air like a miasma, and Krueger covered his mouth with his keffiyeh. The path climbed higher and eventually levelled out to reveal a wide terrace next to a red keep. The thatched roof was golden beneath the glowing sunlight, and idle chickens clucked around the kitchen door. Three men, each wearing sunglasses and blank expressions, stood expectantly amid a large pile of crates.

"This is where we'll be staying," Grimm said, bounding out of the Range Rover and heading toward the group of men. "I had a devil of a time finding a rental and getting the equipment shipped here in time, but I think I about just pulled it off!"

"What equipment?" Krueger asked, to which Grimm winked impishly.

"You'll see!" he cried.

Krueger leaned back into his seat and sighed. The view from the terrace beyond was exquisite, a chorus of verdant colors, all soaked in the rays of a warm sunset. Green tilled fields lay beneath tufty golden hills and the sky was dotted by small fluffy clouds of brilliant white.

"Not too bad," Brandt said to Krueger. "As long as it's safe."

"I'll be here for you," Krueger said but cringed and turned away the moment the words left his lips. He hated how they sounded once they'd been spoken; they suggested the feelings firing in his heart, the feelings he wanted to remain hidden. Brandt, after all, could see his face, could see his gruesomeness. Only his ex-wife had ever claimed to be able to see beyond that ugliness, and now she was living with a handsome square-jawed gym rat in a Manhattan high-rise.

Brandt seemed to sense Krueger's unease and placed a comforting hand on his knee and squeezed. It was a tender moment, all too small and brief an act after so much chaos. But it cheered Krueger's heart.

"Come on," she said smiling. Together, they approached Grimm as he started to issue orders like a scout master at a jamboree.

"Nope, I don't think we'll need that metal detector. But the sifting boxes will certainly be useful. Get them unpacked tonight. And that ground-penetrating radar is crucial, absolutely crucial. I want each of the handheld floor scanners operational and the cart-mounted system ready by daybreak."

The men, who had the bearing of world-weary mercenaries, looked uninterestedly at the younger wiry man. His enthusiasm was clearly not infectious. Nonetheless, they figured it was an easy paycheck from an easy client, so they got to work unloading the crates.

"Where's Clipper?" Grimm asked as the men began their chores. He took a slug of water from his flask and offered it around the group.

"Opposite side of the property," one of the men replied, "scoping out the area."

As if summoned, the man called Clipper came running into view from the side of the farmhouse. He was dressed all in black, with a revolver tucked into a holster on his waist and another around his ankle. He had a flat gut, thinning red hair, and a navy tattoo on his exposed forearm.

"Splendid to see you, old boy!" Grimm said. "We've got a devil of a task on our hands. We've got some pricey equipment to help us find the thing, but even so, it's going to be tough work."

"Maybe not," Clipper said, thrusting his binoculars into Grimm's hands. "I think someone else beat us to it." Krueger and Brandt approached, nodded to Clipper, and watched as Grimm used the binoculars to stare in the direction to which his security chief pointed.

"Bugger me," Grimm said, handing the binoculars to Krueger. "We might have just caught a break."

Krueger used the high-power lenses to look at what had caused the two men such surprise. He did not struggle to find it. Two miles away was a stretch of land surrounded on all sides by razor wire. Desert tents were inside, their canvas doors flapping lazily in the soft afternoon breeze. And at the entrance to this compound, erected high above the fence, was a sign with four chilling words:

Pollux Solutions Welcomes You.

IT WAS LATE, AND THE CICADAS were in symphony outside. Krueger sat in the kitchen of the farmhouse, nursing a mug of coffee. Grimm's mercs eyeballed him nervously; they'd been told they were providing security on an archeological dig site. But the presence of the burly New York cop suggested something more to the gig—something menacing.

"The place looks deserted," Brandt said. She stood by the window next to Clipper and Grimm looking at the Pollux compound in the valley below. The sickly strip lighting above made her look more even tired than she was, as if it were drawing the nutrients from her freckled skin.

"Or maybe it's just meant to look deserted," Krueger said. The man next to him, a twenty-something blonde buzz-cut in khaki, took a seat next to him and nodded.

"Boss," Clipper said to Grimm, "if we are going to help you, then we need more than just the story you fed us while we were en route."

"Sure do," spoke the buzz-cut.

"It was all true; I assure you," Grimm said, pouring himself a coffee from the pot on the stove. "We are here to retrieve a precious artifact. Or, at least, discover what became of it. Those fellows down in the valley appear to have already gotten their mitts on it."

"Just like we feared," Brandt added.

"Those Pollux boys don't play nice," Krueger said evenly. "We locked horns with some bad guys in Berlin and Cairo, and we've got reason to believe they were mixed up with that company. They came with some high-priced toys too. Choppers. Explosives. They've got deep pockets and plenty of experience."

"Care to elaborate?" Clipper asked. Krueger looked into the dark brown eyes of the former CIA officer. There was experience in those eyes, Krueger could see, experience doing cold, nasty things in the dark corners of the world.

Joe Krueger was sitting with a fellow warrior.

"I can't tell you the purpose of our mission," Krueger said, "but if you've got the stomach for it, I can tell you the problems we faced before we got here."

Clipper stared at Krueger silently and clasped his hands on top of the table. *Sure,* Krueger thought. *This guy has the stomach for these sorts of tales.*

TO AVOID DETECTION, O'Brian and Dubchek took a commercial flight to San Francisco. Seated amongst the summer vacationers and harried businessmen, the two lawmen tried to snatch as many hours of sleep as possible. The last 48 hours had been a blur of daring deeds, confessions, and discoveries—both welcome and unwelcome. Even for O'Brian, the rough-hewn New Yorker, it had been a wearying slog.

Having taken off at ten, they arrived on the West Coast a little after lunchtime. Rubbing sleep from his eyes, O'Brian flicked on his cell and found a text message from Hawtrey:

I spoke with Dennilson. Explained that the artifacts from the blast are ready to be released into his custody, provided he gives you proof that they belong to him. That's your reason for being there. Dennilson is expecting you. Use the time wisely. Report back when you are finished.

O'Brian shoved an elbow into Dubchek's ribs and he awoke with a shudder. "Rise and shine," O'Brian said.

Dubchek looked worse than when they took off. His young face was now creased and wan, and his lips were tightly pursed. His short black hair was a scraggy mess, and his eyes had the deadened gaze of a sedated patient. Robotically, Dubchek reached for this laptop, a Dell C640 with a tough black outer case. Massaging the bridge of his nose, he switched it on and began beavering away at the keyboard, which rattled like lose teeth.

"You're quite the raconteur, aren't you, pal?" O'Brian asked.

Dubchek did not bother to look up. "Talking is your strength, pops," he replied. "This is mine. If there's a link between Castor, Pollux, and Gemini, then I'm the one who's going to find it."

O'Brian volunteered to drive the rental, an Impala with the sickly-sweet smell of cheap air freshener, to the Gemini campus. They pulled up before the main entrance of the giant crescent moon at 2pm, its glass exterior ablaze in the halcyon light.

"Nice bit of real estate," O'Brian said, shrugging his shoulders as he killed the engine.

The Pacific breeze kissed their faces as the two exited the car, and O'Brian chuckled as he saw a curvy blonde bounce out of the doorway and head toward them with a grin plastered across her heavily painted face.

"It's a diversionary tactic," Dubchek said, eyeballing the woman. "Dennilson's sending us the eye candy so we relax, let our guard down, you know?"

"Kid," O'Brian said, resting his thick forearm on the roof of the car, "I've got three ex-wives who'll tell you I know more about women than any man has a right to. I can handle myself around a beaut like her."

"Hiiii," trilled the woman in a light, cheery California accent. She wore a pale-yellow suit and azure earrings to complement her eyes. "I'm Ashley Parr, assistant to Curt. And he's so excited to meet you!"

Of course, Dennilson was nothing of the sort. He stood far

above, looking down on the tiny silver speck parked in front of his domain. His fists were clenched.

"Don't destroy this," he whispered, his voice as quiet as the hiss of a snake. "It's too important."

Preston Gates emerged, his sneakers squeaking on the immaculate floor. "Our newfound friend has just arrived," he said.

"I know," Dennilson spat, pointing out of the window.

"No," Gates responded, "the *other* friend. The one you summoned from New York."

"Perfect timing," Dennilson replied, a small, nasty smile creeping upon his lips.

"I don't get it," Gates said. "Why do we need *him*? We've got a small army on our payroll; all ex-military, ex-Secret Service. They'll gladly kill O'Brian and Dubchek for us. Why do we need that prick you brought over on your private plane?"

"Maybe I don't want them dead," Dennilson said.

Gates' face drew pale. "But," he stammered, "In Israel . . . we have . . ."

"Relax," Dennilson snapped, angered by the stammering. "We need options to end this. Violence is one. Our new guest offers us a second."

"Which is?" Gates asked, grumpily.

"Public exposure and ridicule," Dennilson said, his tanned face deformed by his scowl. "Besides, I like . . . collecting people," the magnate continued, savoring the words. "He'll be good to have in my pocket."

DENNILSON REDISCOVERED his smile by the time he arrived in the atrium of his campus. And his eyes were no longer shining with rage; they possessed instead the good humor that had made him the toast of many a celebrity-infested party. He shook O'Brian's hand fulsomely, looking once again like the simple surfer who'd made good.

"Good to see you again, Detective O'Brian," he said in such a voice that the cop almost believed him. "And Agent Dubchek, welcome to Gemini. It's great to see you both, especially since it means our art, or what remains of it, can be brought back to San Francisco, correct?"

"That's about right," O'Brian said. "All's I need is to see proof that what we saved from the blast is yours."

"No problem. No problem at all," Dennilson said, leading the two lawmen through the entrance to his campus. Young, earnest techies, wearing shorts and trainers were walking around with eyes that sparkled with the same shimmer as the glass overhead. Only the security guards, wearing ear pieces, blazers, and, O'Brian assumed, firearms, gave a hint of the power within the building.

"You seem confident you can get me proof these artifacts are yours," O'Brian said, as Dennilson and Parr turned left, away from the t-shirt clad kids, and toward a cavernous elevator. "I mean, it's not like you picked these things up from Gimbels and got a nice receipt for 'em."

The elevator had polished brass railings and a blaring TV screen on the roof, advertising the sundry products and services Dennilson offered to the world's billions. *You can't escape Dennilson's tech even when you're catching the elevator*, O'Brian thought.

"Oh, that's just a trifle," Dennilson said, his smile concrete and immovable.

"Some of the items are still pending analysis by our lab boys back in New York," O'Brian continued, "and if, at any point, we have reason to believe they serve as evidence in our ongoing investigation into the bombing, they are subject to immediate recall."

Dennilson remained silent and nodded. "Acquisitions," he finally said, and before O'Brian could determine who the magnate was addressing, he felt the elevator slowly descend.

Voice activated elevator, O'Brian thought. *Very nice.* But he didn't speak. For some reason, he didn't want to give Dennilson the pleasure of hearing a compliment. So they all sank lower in silence.

Eventually, the elevator came to a stop and opened to reveal a small low-ceilinged entrance room, dimly lit by a handful of lamps. A vast metal door was closed fast opposite.

"Not many people think of this as my most important work," Dennilson said, "but I do. It's here I preserve humankind's best achievements and protect them from those barbarians who would see them destroyed." The group entered the darkened foyer, and the elevator door closed.

"So what you got down here?" O'Brian asked, "Dracula's coffin?" Dubchek rolled his eyes. Parr remained expressionless.

"Oh, far more than I could inventory for you," Dennilson said. "But feel free to take your time perusing our collections."

"You know, I might just do that," O'Brian said with a chill hint of menace in his voice. "But first, the receipts, if you please."

Before Dennilson could act on the request, the elevator doors opened once again, and Preston Gates emerged. At last, O'Brian caught a hint of some emotion in Dennilson's face; as he saw his underling approach, concern mingled with anger shone in his eyes.

"Curt," Gates said, wearing a wolfish smile that revolted Dubchek. "It's time."

Dennilson's anger was swept away by confusion. Clearly, O'Brian saw that the entrance of this flabby sidekick was not part of the show he'd choreographed.

"Of course," Dennilson said, masking his puzzlement like a man who was well-trained in fooling an audience. "Gentlemen, it appears the pressures of running a business have returned once more. I must bid you adieu." Dennilson said no more and re-entered the elevator, thunder roiling on his brow. Gates stood next to him, and as the doors closed, O'Brian caught site of his disgusting grin once more.

"I'm so sorry!" Parr said in her voice like sunshine. "But I can certainly help. If you come with me, I'll show you the End Use Certificates. Everything is in order."

Parr placed her hand on a blinking screen next to the door, and moments later, the air filled with the humming of gears. Slowly, the shining metal door opened, revealing a black portal. Overhead strip lights coughed into life, and the shadows were cast to the corners of a vast, echoing storage hall.

Motes of dust hung in the air as the group stepped forward, Parr's designer heels clipping on the poured concrete floor. Dubchek was struck by the smell as he entered the cavernous, shadowy hall; it was not the offensive odor of rot or decay, but rather, the musty smell of age.

It was the smell of history.

"Curt Dennilson has sponsored over three dozen archeological digs across the world," Parr said, in a breezy, well-practiced voice. She'd clearly given this speech many times before.

Parr led the two companions past long lines of shelves, piled with wooden crates and objects shrouded in thick sheets of canvas. Far above, in the recessed corners of the hall, O'Brian saw several red shining lights, alien like the eyes of a spider, and he knew that many cameras were watching him. Parr's smile could not eclipse the fact that he and Dubchek were unwelcome strangers.

Parr was continuing her monologue without pause. "He has invested in work currently ongoing in such places as Turkey, Iraq, and Southern Italy," she said, pointing to the brass signs studded at various intervals on the storage shelves. They proclaimed ancient names as if they were captured prisoners. Pompeii. Anatolia. Hillah.

To his side, Dubchek was slouching along. He was wise enough to know that staring at his phone or laptop on a tour like this would be considered rude, but he still couldn't quite bring himself to pretend he was interested in the artifacts around him. But then suddenly, something caught his attention on the shelves. He said nothing, and Parr didn't notice. She was too busy with her recitation.

"Now, to the side here we have all the documentation you gents will need," Parr said, concluding her facile remarks.

Lining the wall of the hall were banks of shiny, white oblong boxes. Parr ran her finger along the edge of the one of the boxes, and a beam of blue light followed in its wake. The box opened to reveal card folders expertly stored.

"End Use Certificates, Customs Declarations, and affidavits signed by some of the world's leading authorities on ancient art, all confirming the provenance of everything you see here."

"And where are the documents pertaining to the New York exhibit?" O'Brian asked.

"Here," replied Parr, lifting a thick folder and handing it to the cop with a smirk. "Everything is above board."

"It sure is!" Dubchek cried in a loud and unexpected voice that startled O'Brian. He turned and saw the young man had a big smile on his face, as if he'd suddenly caught a nasty case of charisma. "Now is there a room where we might look over these forms?" he asked brightly. "Just a formality, you know."

"Oh, there is a small table in the vestibule we just left. You can work from there if you like?"

"Sure," purred Dubchek. "We have a long inventory here, so it might take a while."

Parr silently led them back to the small entryway next to the elevator, making sure to seal the mammoth door behind her, which guarded Dennilson's horded treasures. But to O'Brian's consternation, she didn't leave the duo alone to work. Instead, she sat on a high-backed chair in the opposite corner, retrieved her phone, and began scrolling through whatever pages that assistants to potential criminals read.

The presence of the sunny Californian was silent testimony to the threat O'Brian and Dubchek faced.

Wordlessly, the duo fanned out the assorted papers on the table. O'Brian didn't have a clue what he was looking at. Half of it was written in foreign languages, and even the English was indecipherable.

Don't worry.

Dubchek wrote the two words on a piece of paper and passed them to O'Brian with a wink. The cop read them expressionlessly.

O'Brian wrote back. *You find anything?*

Sure, replied Dubchek. *According to those brass signs, they've taken a big delivery of items from Hattin.* Dubchek added, *That's where Krueger is headed.*

O'Brian could feel a tingling inside his head. Somehow, whether by accident or by design, they were drawing closer to the conspiracy. Nonetheless, he mastered his burgeoning excitement and passed his colleague a skeptical note.

Coincidence, it read. *CD already told us he was busy in plenty of old foreign joints.*

"Oh, buddy," Dubchek said loudly, making sure Parr's ears picked up his words, "did I tell you I just collected my new car? She is cherry. Here, take a peek." Dubchek brought out his phone, and confusion washed over O'Brian's rugged face. The young techie brought up a photograph, but it wasn't of a car; it was of the interior of Dennilson's fortress. Dubchek had taken a secret snap of the thing that had caught his attention, and looking at it, O'Brian could see why.

The photo showed big crates sat above the brass sign which read *Hattin.* And on the side of each of them were two words: *Pollux Solutions.*

THEY WERE BACK AT their hotel, pacing Dubchek's room, too excited to eat the gargantuan plate of wings the New York cop had impetuously ordered. After keeping their pantomime going for two hours, O'Brian pronounced himself satisfied with the End Use Certificates Parr had presented and hustled himself and Dubchek out of the billionaire's lair.

"So we've got a link between Gemini and Pollux Solutions," O'Brian said. "And evidence that these Pollux guys have been nosing around Hattin."

"I think I have something else too," Dubchek said. "It's on the website."

"You told me the website was junk," O'Brian said, pouring himself a coffee. It was cold, and night was fast descending, but he knew it was going to be a long night.

"It is," Dubchek said, "just like the Castor site. Full of meaningless words that even a Princeton MBA couldn't understand." Dubchek helped himself to the coffee. "But they are both registered to the same person, Clive Dromney, out in Belize."

"Who the Hell is that?" O'Brian asked.

"I don't know," Dubchek said. "But he is also the owner, according to Belize government directories, of the barrio where Castor has its PO Box."

"This is great stuff, pal!" O'Brian said, savoring the spectacle of the net drawing ever closer.

For the first time since the bomb shattered the peace of New York, O'Brian finally felt as if they were on the front foot, panicking their enemies instead of reacting to their every move.

"So we've now got links to all three of these businesses. Not a bad bit of detective work." O'Brian allowed himself a chuckle. "We need to tell Hawtrey," he declared, "and see if we can raise Krueger back in Israel."

"My phone is charging," Dubchek said.

"Mine's hooked up in my room," O'Brian replied. "Lemme go fetch it." He turned, opened the door, and found the yawning black maw of a pistol pointing at his heart.

"At last," said a dark, familiar voice.

LUCILLE HAWTREY WAS picking over her untouched dinner when the call came. She hadn't heard from either Krueger or O'Brian, and even the indefatigable Colin Dubchek's phone was dead.

Jean Dupree put it through. "Director Cullingworth is on the line," she said.

Hawtrey sighed; she was too busy to listen to that nasal Massachusetts whine anymore. The owlish, bespeckled head of the FBI had sat so close to her during the morning meeting with the President she'd been able to smell the tang of his deodorant.

"Put him through," she replied, closing her eyes as she did so. She had less than a second to gather her thoughts before hearing the hesitant voice on the end of the line.

"Lucille," FBI Director Alan Cullingworth said. "Thank you for taking the call." His whine was as bad as ever.

"Alan," Hawtrey replied.

"So I just finished talking to Mark Griffiths," Cullingworth said, referring to the President's angry, preternaturally young Chief of Staff. "He has a message for you."

"The guy has my number," Hawtrey replied icily.

"Yes, yes," Cullingworth replied.

There was a pause, and Hawtrey imagined her boss fiddling with his metal aviators, something he did when he was nervous, which was often. Fifteen years using computer algorithms to successfully bust white-collar criminals had brought Alan Cullingworth to the apex of the FBI, but he'd never once busted the grubby, violent terrorists who Hawtrey dealt with every day. Away from his spreadsheets and databases, Cullingworth had the bearing of an anxious, over-wrought accountant.

"Of course," Cullingworth said finally, "but he thinks this would sound better coming from a friend."

"And when can I expect to hear from this friend?" Hawtrey asked.

Cullingworth replied with false, hasty laughter. "We are all so grateful for what you've done," Cullingworth said. "Really, we are."

Cullingworth continued speaking, but Hawtrey didn't hear him. Her heart began to pound so hard it felt like it was trying to escape her chest.

It's like a bereavement, Hawtrey thought, as she looked down and noticed with surprise that her spare hand was trembling. *My career is being killed. All that's left is the mourning.*

Hawtrey grabbed the desk with her trembling hand, embarrassed to have shown such weakness, if only to herself. "Are you canning me, Alan?" she asked, cutting into his long eulogy.

"Nope . . . oh heavens no!" Cullingworth replied. "But we would like you to consider . . . leaving the case with your head held high. The President wants you to know there are many lucrative jobs in the private sector waiting for you if you choose to leave the right way . . . well remunerated, big benefits package, plenty of vacation. I imagine you need a rest having worked like a fiend these last few weeks!" Cullingworth's quip fell faster than a plane without wings.

"If the President wants me gone," Hawtrey spat, "he's going to have to grow some cojones and fire me."

Back in Washington, Cullingworth heard these words and cringed. Ensconced in his sumptuous, air-conditioned office, he broke into a sweat. Even from so far away, Hawtrey's fury was terrifying to hear. "He can't fire a . . . a . . ." Cullingworth spluttered.

"A woman?" Hawtrey yelled, before realizing she'd happened upon the right answer.

The President had already caught the dickens in the press for stuffing his Administration with male chums. If he were seen to bring down one of the few leading female law-enforcement officers in the country, it'd play havoc with his already shaky polling among women.

"So the President doesn't have confidence in me," Hawtrey said, drawing out each word with increasing anger, "but won't get rid of an agent he thinks is hampering an active investigation because it won't play well?"

Cullingworth, wishing more than ever to return to the comfort of his spreadsheets, remained silent. "The politics," was all he managed to mumble.

"Forget it," Hawtrey said, leaning forward over her desk. "And forget your goddamn politics too. I'm not leaving until either you or the President dismiss me."

"Now Lucille," Cullingworth said. He lowered his voice and spoke in greasy, ingratiating tones—the same tones he'd used during his Senate confirmation hearing. "Our President did not go from first-term Governor of little old Delaware to most powerful man in the world without knowing a few tricks. If he wants someone gone, he knows how to get them gone."

Cullingworth, tired of playing with his aviators, began smoothing his slicked brown hair.

"Which is why the White House leaked your resignation letter to a friendly reporter twenty minutes ago. The networks will be running with the story during this evening's broadcasts."

Hawtrey suddenly felt breathless, as if she were suffering a massive, unexpected heart attack. The strength she'd possessed before taking this hateful call seemed to be melting away.

"If you deny the report," Cullingworth said, warming to his role as Administration stooge, "it'll make you look like a confused fool, too proud to know when to quit, which is sure going to have an impact on your future employment prospects. And if you fight us, then we'll be ready. All it takes is a few well-chosen phrases in the right publications, phrases like 'unbalanced' and 'unhinged' to put an end to your reputation."

"Smears?" Hawtrey screamed. "Is this it, Alan? You're going to smear one of your deputies in the gutter press?"

"You've lost the President's trust," Cullingworth said, eager to end the call now that he'd shared the ugly truth. "And he has a right to surround himself with people he thinks can get the job done. You don't fit that description, Lucille. So, it's time to move on. Now, if you want to play nice, then say so, and the President will make sure to open the right doors for you now that you're leaving the Bureau."

"Alan," Hawtrey replied, "ask any of the crooks I've busted, and they'll tell you I never play nice. And someday real soon, the bastards who tore up the Meyer Center will know it as well!"

Hawtrey closed her eyes and imagined her timorous boss

cowering in his leather chair. She opened them in time to see two agents, Cullingworth's minions, enter her office without pausing to knock.

"Anything else?" Cullingworth asked as his troops drew forward toward Hawtrey's desk.

"Yes," she said bitterly. 'When your pal Griffiths was in Congress, what part of California did he represent?"

"San Francisco," Cullingworth answered, wondering if his agent had suddenly lost her mind.

MIDNIGHT HAD LONG passed, and Lower Galilee was still and dark. The farmers were all asleep, waiting for the dawn when their toil would begin anew. Even the tall grasses seemed to lay still. Above, the moonless night was black and glowering.

For Joe Krueger, it seemed as if he had returned to the war without end. Iraq. Afghanistan. Desert voids in which high-minded policies were ground low into the dust. He stood surrounded by armed men, clad in armor, night-vision goggles covering their eyes. He held a Tavor with sweaty hands, remembering the last time he patrolled the Middle East with a rifle, and how he had desperately wanted to be rid of such a thankless, ceaseless task.

But now he wasn't protecting his fellow Rangers and veil-hidden women from mindless fanatics. He was now protecting his friends, Grimm, and Brandt, and doing his damnedest to protect his homeland too. Together, they were going to search the Pollux compound.

Clipper had led them to the floor of the valley, descending from the terrace in single file. The old pro had been told about the violence in Berlin and Cairo, and finally understood why Grimm had ordered him to Israel.

"Well," Krueger had said, after finishing his tale in the farmhouse's kitchen, "I sure as Hell am not waiting for those sons of bitches to get the jump on us. I propose we go take a look at what they are doing out there."

"Okay," Clipper had replied, "but if we go in, we go in my way." There was something fierce and determined in Krueger's features, something which the old CIA man respected.

Hours later, Clipper was leading his posse toward the encircled Pollux compound. With a stiff hand signal, he dispatched two men to explore the main entrance, which was locked tight and protected by a traffic barrier.

The two men fleetly sped toward the entrance and were soon lost to the grey-green blackness of Krueger's night vision.

"We'll try the back entrance," Clipper said in a hard whisper.

"I don't think there is one," Grimm said, and in the pause that followed, Krueger sensed that Clipper was smiling beneath his keffiyeh.

"We are going to make one," he said. "Wait here till you're called for." Without pausing for a reply, Clipper led another of his mercs toward the northwest corner of the compound, leaving the buzz-cut, Levi, as the unhappy chaperone of the civilians.

The anxious quartet stood amid the whispering grasses of the pensive valley, with nothing but the shadows for company.

Words, hasty and fierce, came spewing out of Levi's earpiece.

"We have an entrance. Let's move," he said.

Sauntering like a jaguar close to his quarry, the eager merc led Krueger and his friends to the farthest corner, where they found a massive opening cut into the fencing. Clipper stood at the breach holding a metal detector, moving its search coil in long, sweeping curves close to the earth. His deputy was examining the entry he had made with his cable cutters, looking for the ominous glint of a trip wire.

"Okay, listen up," Clipper said. "We need to scour every damn inch of this place. So you stay behind me and Macintosh at all times. You don't touch anything . . . you don't step anywhere without my permission. Clear?"

To the three who'd had first-hand experience of the skullduggery surrounding the True Cross, no warning was needed. Like timid sheep, Grimm and Brandt followed in Clipper's wake, even going so far as to tread in the footsteps he left behind in the dirt.

Pollux had built a half-acre compound in the valley, fixed up with sumptuous living quarters inside sturdy tents, and archeological equipment of such cost and splendor that even Grimm was envious. Through the flapping doorway of one particularly large tent, Krueger glimpsed microscopes, rotary lasers, and a theodolite standing proud on its expensive tripod like a creature from an H.G. Wells novel.

Inch by agonizing inch, Clipper led his team forward. The entire compound remained bathed in darkness, leaving Krueger and the others dependent on the greasy green light of their goggles to guide them forward.

Krueger's vision was suddenly eclipsed by a piercing white blaze which exploded across his ken. Snatching the goggles and pulling them down, he saw the beams of two flashlights being played around the front of the compound.

"We're in boss," came a disembodied voice. "No guards. No security safeguards. Place is deserted."

"We'll see," Clipper said, pulling down his own goggles. "Take it slow up there, Wren. Looks like these boys had plenty of cash. I can't believe they'd leave all this stuff unprotected."

"Look at this!" Brandt said, pointing toward the center of the compound. Clipper brought his light to shine on where Brandt was pointing, revealing a gaping maw in the earth, surrounded by guide ropes. A backhoe was idling beside it, alongside a small platoon of picks which Pollux's minions must have used to make the hole.

Grimm and Krueger stared silently at the pit, the brown earth piled like funeral pyres along the edge. Even the mercs, who knew little about the reasons behind their infiltration of the compound, knew better than to ruin the moment with idle chatter. Something vast and cold inside told them that this was sacred ground. Their tongues lay still.

Brandt discovered that she was breathless. With a trembling arm, she pointed Clipper toward the pit, and holding the metal detector, he gingerly stepped closer. Krueger and Grimm gathered closely behind him, so close in fact that that could hear the former CIA man whispering a little prayer.

The metal detector remained silent. The night breeze fell away. And then, finally, Brandt, Grimm, and Krueger stood at the edge of what looked like a vast menacing grave.

It was empty.

But they knew—they *all* knew what had been inside that hole, lost for centuries to the adherents of the faith. Without a shred of proof, without using any of the pricey and somehow anachronistic technology standing idle in the tents, Krueger knew that this was the place where Saladin's nameless son had returned the True Cross. An odd sensation ran through his torso, as if his body was undulating in chill waters. Krueger swallowed hard and wondered if the breath of God was gusting through his soul. That moment, Krueger knew, stood in the darkness with the bombs and bullets of the recent past forming a tapestry of horror in his thoughts, was the closest he had ever come to the Divine.

"They have it," Brandt said finally, shattering Krueger's reverie.

"Yes," said Grimm, "and I fear they've had it quite a while. These piles of dirt are dry. So too is the earth in that pit. Freshly dug turf would be moist to the touch. My estimate is that this excavation took place at least a month ago."

"Right before the first bomb went off," Brandt added, though Krueger has already performed the macabre math in his head.

"It would be nice to know that for certain," Krueger said.

"Indeed," Grimm said, turning toward Clipper. "My friend, we need as much information about this place as we can find. When did they get here? When was that hole made, and what was inside it? Perhaps your men could be useful in searching this place?"

With Clipper's numerous and varied warnings thundering in their ears, his four deputies were ordered to find anything that might explain what had been in the pit, and where it had been taken. Computers, paper records, and discarded phones were hungrily searched for, so great was the need to know what had transpired in the enemy camp.

Levi found his heart pumping lustily as he began the search. Leaving Clipper to watch over the three wackos, he retreated to the deserted northeast corner. He played the beam of his flashlight across the ground, and saw tracks emerging from the farthest tent, made by what he guessed were several pairs of big, booted feet.

"Hi there," he purred playfully, not bothering to ignore his excitement. He removed his glove and touched the tracks.

They were moist. They were recent.

Levi barreled forward into the tent, heedless of the danger. He'd been yearning for just this sort of action ever since the army had honorably discharged him.

A large wooden bureau stood close to the entrance. A few papers flapped forlornly on the ground beneath it. *At last!* Levi thought. *No more babysitting rich folks. Back to proper soldiering!* Without thinking, he yanked open the topmost drawer, triggering the bomb which had been left there. The young Tennessean was vaporized before he realized his mistake.

The roar of the bomb swept through the valley like a hurricane. Macintosh, Clipper's able assistant, was flung into the fencing as the orange flames, thick and ferocious, grew among the tents. He landed on the floor in a heap and did not move.

Brandt screamed. So did Grimm. But Krueger didn't hear them. The air was filled with the din of fire and ruin: the wind gusting, the debris falling, the fire chuckling in delight as it fed on Pollux's inventory.

The fire touched Macintosh's leg, and finding that he did not resist, it promptly consumed him.

And that's when Krueger realized how foolish his thoughts of God had been.

He was nowhere near Heaven.

He was in Hell.

- 16 -

CURT DENNILSON WAS STRIKING back against his enemies, but on the morning after Sam O'Brian had paid him a visit, the morning after Lucille Hawtrey had been canned, one foe remained to be defeated.

In the sweaty suburbs of Atlanta, Agent Munroe was admiring the neat, well-tended gardens surrounding the Temple Beth-El. Since he'd arrived in Atlanta yesterday, he'd spent his time investigating the aborted attack, and his only reward had been the sheen of sweat that was now covering his back. Nonetheless, his necktie and vest remained steadfastly in place.

He'd been checking into his hotel room the night before when the news of Lucille Hawtrey's dismissal began reverberating around the echo chambers of cable news. Sleep suddenly became an impossibility, replaced by a series of gossipy phone calls with colleagues in New York and Washington. With no boss left to report to, Monroe spent the night listless and confused. The case was far more frustrating than anything he had encountered at Quantico, and this unwelcome sojourn to the sweaty South had only made the situation worse.

The young FBI agent had been partnered with Officer Butterman of the APD for his tour of the synagogue, who, despite his calorific name, was a slender, wiry man. Butterman had extended Munroe every courtesy as he wasted his hours in Atlanta and was rounding out his fine service by offering a long list of eateries where Munroe could take his lunch.

"Now, Mick's next to the Olympic Park has the best friend chicken in the city," Butterman intoned, despite being so thin Munroe doubted he'd ever sampled a friend morsel in his life. "But the next best place is—"

Munroe never had chance to learn what the next best place was. A hulking Escalade came screaming around the corner from the intersection, its engine filling the air with thunderous rage. Munroe took a defensive step back. Something about the swiftness of the turn suggested this was not a drunk driver . . . that, in fact, the driver had a deadly sober reason for driving so recklessly.

The Escalade sped further down the quaint Southern street, its hood a vast mirroring black. The engine grew louder, roaring like the king of the savannah, pronouncing judgement on a lame beast. Munroe raised his gun, and Officer Butterman did likewise. Too late they opened fire, spewing bullets into the massive windscreen as the car mounted the curb and barreled toward them. But the driver, hidden from view by the tinted glass, would not be denied his prize. As the air filled with the sounds of swift carnage, Munroe and Butterman turned and ran, hoping to reach the safety of the synagogue walls. But the car slammed into the FBI agent, clipped his right leg, and sent his hapless body flying into the gorgeous blue sky. He fell to the ground, his body making a wet cracking sound as it did so.

That sound—that ghastly horrific sound of something precious breaking beyond all hope of repair stayed with Butterman for the rest of this life. He remembered it, years later, when his pension was safely tucked into his bank account and his grandkids were scrabbling at his scrawny ankles. The grisly wetness of the sound of Munroe's body falling imbedded itself in Butterman's mind like an evil tic.

The Escalade halted, then reversed and rode over the stricken body without hesitation or regret. It was back on the road and speeding away from the attack in seconds, leaving Butterman alone and scared, his throat cleaving. He grabbed his radio and reported Agent Munroe's murder with trembling hands.

PRESTON GATES ENTERED Dennilson's office wearing a small, nasty smile. The television screens breathlessly reported the departure of Special Agent Lucille Hawtrey from the investigation of the Meyer Center bombing. Curt stood, hands planted on his slender hips, watching the drama unspool. The Golden Gate Bridge stood firm in the morning sun, impassive and imperious.

"It's done," Gates said.

"I know," Dennilson replied, pointing to the blaring screen. The anchors were wide-eyed. The chyrons beneath them were flashing.

"All of it," Gates said, taking a step forward and standing between Dennilson and the television. "New York, Atlanta, and Israel," he said, his nose wrinkling as if he'd just sniffed rancid milk. "Our problems have been disappeared. Just like O'Brian." Gates stood waiting for a word of thanks for his boss. But the word never came.

"See to it that there are no more delays," Dennilson said with a newfound malice. He grabbed his underling, cringing at the crusty, unclean feel of his t-shirt, and pushed him out of the way.

Gates sloughed away angrily, leaving behind a man deformed by his greed. In that moment of Dennilson's black triumph, the façade of the idle surfer was gone.

THE BLAZE SPREAD triumphantly, its hungry flames wrapping themselves in the tents and equipment. Raising his hands, vainly trying to ward off the heat, Krueger stumbled forwards and grabbed Brandt roughly by the arm.

"This way!" he said, pointing to the front exit, where two of the mercs had already evacuated.

"No!" Brandt replied, falling to her knees. The fire was close now, so close that the heat was searing Krueger's nose. Worse, it was throwing up smoke in great, dense billowing clouds, which spread over the compound like fat sentries ready to choke the invaders. "It isn't fair. It isn't fair!"

Brandt repeated these words as she pulled herself free of Krueger's grasp and slid to the ground in despair. Wailing, she clutched the grass near the open hole and looked inside once more, as if expecting the cross to appear.

"It's not fair," she said once more, but this time in a thin, defeated voice.

Through the haze, Krueger could see the anguish in his friend's eyes. It was not just the fire that was causing her to weep; it was the injustice of seeing such a special site raped by a murderous and uncaring enemy.

"Listen, Tessa," he said over the roar of destruction, "nothing will be gained by losing you to the blast!"

Krueger saw Clipper limp past him, his left arm smoldering and bloody. He was dragging Grimm toward the exit, whose mouth was hanging agape. The professor's cotton jacket was a charred ruin.

Krueger got down on his haunches and ran his meaty hand through Brandt's blonde hair. "Let's go," he said softly. "Let's go make this right."

Brandt didn't have the strength to lift herself from the ground, but she did allow Krueger to pull her up to her feet and lead her to the exit, where they joined the other survivors.

By the time they got there, the compound was lost to the thick, choking smoke. Tall orange flames licked the night sky.

"Macintosh didn't make it?" one of the mercs asked and was answered by Clipper's cold stare. "I'm afraid not, Wren," he replied.

"Oh Christ!" Wren said. "Oh Jesus! What the Hell are we into here?"

"Back to the farmhouse!" Clipper ordered. "And let's be quick about it!"

Despite the burn to his left arm, the old CIA hand led the team back in good order. When they arrived, he ordered everyone to take a seat in the kitchen. Krueger helped Clipper remove his shirt and began tending the burns, which ran in smoky red tendrils from his hand to his neck.

"So what the Hell were we doing down there?" Wren cried in a rage that Krueger could understand. He and his team had arrived in the expectation of an easy job and big paycheck. Now Levi and Macintosh were dead, and Clipper was badly burned up.

"You'll get an explanation!" Clipper said, wincing as Krueger began bandaging the wounds. "But not now! When we are all safe. We've got to leave."

"And just leave our boys back in the valley!" Wren said. "Is that what you'd do if I was dead? Just leave me?"

"Yes," Clipper said without remorse or pause.

Wren, deflated, sank in his seat. Grimm, who'd never had to confront death before but was fast becoming a close acquaintance, stepped forward.

"Their families will be well taken care of—" he began, but Wren cut him off in a rage.

"Screw you, prick! Macintosh has a baby daughter at home! You think she'll give a shit about your millions when she finds daddy ain't coming home?"

Grimm, chastised, retreated to the back of the room.

"They knew the risks," Clipper said, the last of his bandages in place. "And they wouldn't want us to risk our lives to collect their physical remains. They are in a better place. For us, however, the dangers are manifold. Not only do we remain a target for the people whose camp we just infiltrated, but the Israeli police are now going to be very interested in our presence. Unless we move quickly, I foresee us spending quite a while in a prison cell far from home."

"I have a plane in Tel Aviv," Grimm said hopefully.

"I know you do," Clipper said, "because that's where we are heading. People, you have five minutes to gather your things. In six minutes, I will be out of the front door, and I won't be coming back."

Clipper insisted on driving, despite his wounds. He raced down the steep defile toward the road leading to the capital. On the left, piercing the darkness, the fat orange blaze devoured the compound and whatever secrets had once been hidden there.

"So is there room on the plane for all of us?" Wren asked Grimm from the back seat.

"It doesn't matter," Clipper said, cutting off the professor before he could answer. "We're flying commercial."

"What?" Wren exclaimed.

"I've got to be honest; I'd rest easier with you alongside us. Could use you," Krueger said. He was seated upfront and nodded darkly toward Clipper as he spoke.

He saw two fire trucks pass, their sirens destroying the serenity of the night sky, barreling toward the fire.

"Sitting back on that Lear jet with a martini sounds pretty sweet," Clipper said, "but splitting up is the best thing to do right now. It'll help to confuse whoever planted that bomb, and it'll also make it easier for us to hide once we reach the airport. Professors Grimm and Brandt leaving the country with a friend is one thing; leaving with a squad of surly mercenaries is quite another."

"So what the Hell are we gonna do boss?" Wren asked. "Wait around at Ben Gurion till the cops feel our collars?"

"Not a chance," Clipper said. "Your employer Dr. Grimm here is going to get on his phone right now and buy us tickets for the first plane out of the country. First-class all the way. Right, boss?"

Grimm nodded. His mouth was dry. Fumbling, he reached for his phone and got to work.

"You know how tough security is at Ben Gurion is, right?" Brandt asked. "They'll know you've been handling weapons the moment they swab you."

"Oh, doctor," Clipper answered. "I know Israel and the rest of the Middle East better than any Imam or Rabbi. Somehow, they always have need for guys like me around here. Don't worry, we have fresh clothes in the back, clean passports, and a bolt hole in the capital where we can get clean before heading to the airport."

Silence fell over the companions as they raced toward Tel Aviv. The sky was beginning to lighten; a sliver of pink, like a comforting sheet, glowed on the horizon.

Without speaking, Krueger reached for his phone and dialed Hawtrey. He got no answer. He didn't get an answer when he tried again fifteen minutes later, or an hour after that when dawn broke gaily over the ancient land.

Krueger didn't know it, but while he'd been escaping from the bomb blast, Hawtrey had been sparing verbally with Cullingworth before being eighty-sixed from her job. Krueger was trying to call her on a phone that had been confiscated. With no words from the FBI Special Agent, or from Sam O'Brian out in San Francisco, Krueger's mood grew darker.

Clipper's Tel-Aviv "bolt hole" turned out to be a cute one-story home. Krueger sighed when he glimpsed the swimming pool, its waters shimmering in the morning light. But with enemies surrounding him, and a bomb site behind him, which the Israeli government would soon connect to him and his friends, he knew his dip would have to wait. Within ten minutes of arriving, Clipper, Wren, and the other merc emerged from the front door of the house looking clean, well-dressed, and bearing passports that proved they were part of a congregation of Ohio Presbyterians. Clipper slid into the driver's seat and drove his companions the short distance to the parking lot beneath Ben Gurion airport.

"You are heading to Newark via Gdansk," Grimm said, forwarding the tickets he'd bought to Clipper's phone. "Take off is in two hours." The professor extended his hand to Wren, which the merc examined with fey curiosity before shaking it firmly.

"I'm sorry it ended this way," Krueger said to Clipper, taking his good hand and shaking it. "But I promise you that mission wasn't in vain. One day . . . you and me . . . we'll share a drink, and I'll tell you about what we are doing. Those men you lost fought a fight worth having."

Clipper smiled wearily—a smile of an old, clever man, and he scratched at his stubble. "You know something, Krueger?" he said. "I believe you. There's something about you. Perhaps it's your earnestness. Don't worry about my boys. I'll get them home. And I trust Grimm to take plenty good care of Levi's ma and Mackintosh's family."

"Oh, he will," Krueger said in agreement. "I'll make sure of that."

Clipper embraced Krueger, sealing a swift friendship borne of shared sacrifice. "I'll see your sorry ass soon, big man." With his promise hanging in the air, Clipper led Wren and his other merc into one of the crowds of tourists heading toward the airport. They were soon lost amid the beiges and the khakis, looking like a trio of innocents heading home.

It was soon after that that Krueger discovered Hawtrey's fate. He couldn't ignore it; the news was blaring from every screen in the airport. He grew desperate and felt a film of sweat spread over his forehead.

Easy, Krueger thought to himself. The soldiers in the terminal were trained to spot people who looked sweaty, shifty, and agitated. Feeling lousy was one thing, but looking so lousy you get hauled before Israeli soldiers would be something several orders of magnitude worse.

"What are we going to do?" Brandt asked.

"Say nothing till we are onboard Grimm's jet," Krueger whispered.

It was midday by the time Grimm, Brandt, and Krueger boarded their plane. Grimm, needing to file a flight plan, claimed that Cannes was his destination. Truthfully, he didn't know where he was going.

Nor did Krueger. Hawtrey was not returning his calls. Even worse, neither was O'Brian.

"What time is it in San Francisco?" Brandt asked.

"It's 2am," Krueger replied. "But that doesn't matter. When I call, Sam picks up. Period."

"Not today," Brandt replied. She looked at her friend, saw the concern he wore on his brow, which he tried manfully to hide. He knew Brandt and Grimm were depending on him. "So . . . so where are we going?" Brandt asked.

The questions stoked a fierce and terrible rage in Krueger. He desperately wanted to pound his fist into the leather seat and scream *I don't know!* But to do so would be to admit failure—to admit that he had led these civilians into a conspiracy he could not escape or expose.

Luckily, Krueger's phone trilled, the signal that he had received a message. He read the following:

Staying at the Excelsior Hotel in San Francisco. Caught a break in the case. Very big. What did you find in Israel? Can you meet us here?

The message was from Sam O'Brian.

Krueger cried out in delight. The man, above all others, he knew he could depend on was still in the game.

"How long will it take us to get to San Fran?" he queried as the plane levelled out in the sky.

"A little over fifteen hours," Grimm guessed, "plus an hour or more for refueling in Europe. We might need to take on an extra pilot, too."

"Good. O'Brian's found something at Gemini headquarters. Wants us to head there now."

"Then let's do it," Grimm said. In just a few days, he had undergone an extraordinary change. No longer was he a languid member of the idle rich. He had an edge to him now, flinty, dark, and, considering the threats they all faced, entirely welcome.

Krueger grabbed his phone and dialed O'Brian but got no answer. He left a message promising that they were headed toward San Francisco. Doing rough math in his head, Krueger estimated when they'd touch down the following day.

"About 6pm your time, buddy." Krueger spoke into the phone. "I'll keep trying you. When you get this message, call me back. I'm guessing you've heard about, Hawtrey, right?"

Krueger began charging his phone and leaned his seat back, desperate for a moment's repose. He may have failed to find anything in Israel, but Sam's message suggested he found something.

Good Old Sam.

"GODDAMMIT, HE'S calling me!" Preston Gates said, looking at Sam O'Brian's phone in his hand. "I knew this was a foolish idea!"

Preston Gates, trapped in the bowels of the Gemini headquarters, was overtired and overworked. His complexion, pale despite his years living under the California sunshine, was even worse than before. His pallor was that of a corpse.

The room was small, windowless, and unventilated. It was not part of the guided tours, which Ashely Parr gave with her well-practiced charm. No, none of Dennilson's coquettes ever came this far down into the subbasement. For only a select handful of the magnate's closest associates ever went into the shadows beneath the glimmering rows of computer banks and open-plan offices, which so mesmerized the world's media. And those few were selected based on their willingness to do dark deeds for their boss.

This was where Dennilson brought disloyal staffers for what he euphemistically called a *frank exchange of views*. This was where men suspected of industrial espionage were interrogated. This was where Dennilson shook the grubby hands of tyrants, crooks, and gang masters, anyone who could help him acquire art or larger profits for his business.

Getting Sam O'Brian and Colin Dubchek into this dismal hole had been a struggle. Dennilson had to resort to using a few of the burly men he kept on retainer for precisely that sort of ugly affair. But now that they were locked to their metal chairs, restrained with plastic binders, there were never going to escape.

"What's the matter? You don't have the balls to take a phone call?" O'Brian asked, and his captor stared at the cell phone, unsure how to proceed.

Gates, full of an impotent rage he could not express, slammed his fist into the cinder block wall. He whimpered when he felt the flood of hot pain surge through his hand, which made O'Brian chuckle. It sure felt good to laugh. It reminded him of better times.

Heavy keys jiggled on their chain outside, and soon the door that barred O'Brian's escape opened. The portal was filled with the huge menacing figure who had seized O'Brian and Dubchek back the hotel.

"You've screwed me!" Gates said petulantly. "Krueger's going to suspect a trick."

"Relax," replied Captain Mac Hassler. "This whole thing will soon be at an end."

COLIN DUBCHEK COULD NO LONGER feel his butt. The steel chair that the grim-faced thugs had chained him to was a cheap contraption, something you'd see in an underfunded public school, and not designed for comfort.

He wriggled silently, trying to get the blood flowing once more in his backside, watching in dismay as Hassler waddled into the room.

Armed with a computer, a connection to the internet, and his ironclad commitment to the Constitution, Dubchek was a fine FBI operative. He'd joined the Bureau fresh out of Vassar College with a fixed and immoveable idea of what bad guys looked like, and how the technology of the 21st century could defeat them. But as he sat in Dennilson's cell, watching as tech titans and cops exposed themselves as corrupt, self-serving crooks, he realized how wrong he'd been.

You didn't need a spreadsheet to find monsters; you just needed to look hard enough at the guy sitting next to you.

"Hey!" Gates said, pointing at the New York cop. "I'm talking to you! This crappy plan of yours is going to backfire."

"Relax, snowflake," Hassler said. He took one of the spare metal seats and slurped at the coffee inside the Styrofoam cup he was carrying. "Just string Krueger along with those text messages. He'll bite."

"But what happens if he keeps calling and I don't pick up? He'll get suspicious."

Hassler grimaced. The coffee was cold and tasted like burnt wood. "Listen, I'm making the best of a bad situation, alright? You failed to apprehend those clowns in Israel, so I'm coming up with a Plan B on the fly." Hassler thrust his lower lip forward in a pout. He really was good at feeling sorry for himself.

"And what you gonna do when Krueger arrives?" O'Brian asked.

Dennilson's punks had beat him pretty badly when they and Hassler seized him, and his nose was caked in dried blood. And O'Brian suspected that he'd be receiving a few more love taps before dawn. But would he be facing anything worse? Hassler was corrupt, that much was obvious. But was he willing to murder, too?

"Shut your pie hole," Hassler said. Dubchek looked up expectantly, eager for an answer to O'Brian's question. He'd taken a few hits too. "You're gonna be exposed; that's what gonna happen," Hassler said finally.

He realized that describing O'Brian's fate might cause the tall Irishman more distress, and the thought pleased him.

"Yep," Hassler said, "once Krueger is in town, we'll apprehend him and bring him back here. It'll be a nice little reunion for you. Then Mr. Dennilson's associates will help show you the depth of his disappointment." Hassler chuckled mirthlessly. "After that, I'll take you back to New York and expose you. Yes, the media is gonna love it. While your brother officers were working round-the-clock, risking their lives to bring the terrorist to justice, you were wasting police time sniffing around a cockamamie conspiracy theory. You'll be out of the force by Labor Day. And Dubchek will be gone, too. You'll be the butt of the jokes on late night TV. And with no pension, you'll be dirt poor, too."

Gates listened to Hassler's monologue with growing anger. As the portly cop finished issuing his threats, the young crony bounded over and jabbed a finger in his chest. "Who the Hell do you think you are, prick? You got here a few hours ago and already you're issuing orders! Screw you."

"Get lost," Hassler said, waving away Gates' eruption. "I'm working for Dennilson, not his gofer. Me and him have got a deal. I expose the multiple felonies these crazies have committed in pursuit of their conspiracy theory, and that ends a nasty problem for him. In exchange, I get handed a nice chunk of Gemini stock. You don't figure in those plans, so get outta my face."

"They should be killed!" Gates announced with the haughty air of a blue-blooded magistrate. "They *will* be killed."

Dubchek felt his stomach grew cold, as if it had suddenly been filled with ice. But Hassler simply laughed, a loud, cutting bray that echoed sharply from the cinder blocks.

"Kill them?" Hassler cried. "You're as crazy as they are! I don't know who you think I am, but I'm not going to start killing cops just to please your pudgy, pimply ass. They get beaten, and then they get fired. Nothing more."

O'Brian, who'd been listening raptly to his two captors argue, tilted his head like a confused dog. *So, Hassler draws a line at killing*, he thought. *Guess he doesn't know everything Dennilson has been up to.* O'Brian shuffled excitedly in his seat. If he could prove to Hassler that his newfound sponsors were in fact terrorist killers, he might convince the captain to help him escape. It was a long shot, but until Krueger arrived, it was all he had left to take.

"So, captain," Hassler said, "I never figured you'd be so squeamish about murder. After all, your new bosom-buddy Dennilson has put more people into their graves than Jeffrey Dahmer."

"What the Hell did you say?" Hassler asked, draining his cup of its vile contents. He was jet-lagged and underfed, and had little stomach for any of O'Brian's needling.

"Sure," O'Brian continued. "He tried to have your officer killed while he was investigating in Berlin. He tried again in Cairo using a team of mercenaries. And if you'd dig the wax out of your ears, you might hear the proof that Dennilson is the man who organized the bombings. Yup, your boy sure is a ruthless SOB. I'd watch my back if I were you. He might try to weasel out of that sweet deal you negotiated for yourself."

"Shut up!" Gates cried, striking O'Brian with the back of his hand. But it didn't hurt. Gates was a weakling, with dainty hands attached to stubby, flabby arms. O'Brian laughed.

"What the heck is he jabbering about?" Hassler asked, rising to his feet.

"Nothing," Gates said, lying unconvincingly.

"It's just like Dennilson said when he called you. These jerk-offs are wasting time, wasting money, and even worse, committing dozens of crimes here and abroad. They're embarrassing you and the nation. And for what? Some shitty story about the True Cross! We called you in because we didn't want them to shame the country anymore, especially if the world's media discover they are harassing such a renowned figure as Curt Dennilson. Curt and I thought you had the balls to help bring this pantomime to an end. We were right about you, weren't we?"

Hassler paused, chewing his lip as an uneasy silence fell over the room. O'Brian stared at him with a raised eyebrow, while Gates' mouth curdled into a rancid smile.

Finally, Hassler returned the smile, though his eyes were still laden with apprehension. Silently, he turned and left the cell, more certain than ever that he didn't like Gates, and hating the thought of being in cahoots with him. Faster and faster, he sped down the corridor, eager to leave the building, eager to forget the terrible question that was now thundering in his mind. *Am I just a stooge?*

UNABLE TO TALK, the text read.

"Dammit," Krueger whispered to himself. It was late afternoon, and the plane was idling on a runway in Frankfurt, having just been refueled.

"You okay?" Brandt asked, her eyes creased with worry. She'd travelled so far, so fast that Brandt was now far beyond typical jetlag. She felt as though she was wrapped in a black smog, peeking out from beneath the billowing darkness at a world she barely understood.

"It's strange," Krueger said as he showed Brandt the text. "O'Brian has many weaknesses, but an inability to talk has never been one of them."

"How many times have you tried calling?"

"More than a dozen. It goes straight through to voicemail each time. I've gotten a few texts in respond, urging me to hurry to Frisco." Krueger's speech degenerated into a series of low grumbles as he settled into his seat. He tugged at his seat belt and closed his hands, hoping for a moment's repose.

Something didn't sit right.

JOE KRUEGER ARRIVED in San Francisco at 7 in the evening. Without weapons, without the patronage of Lucille Hawtrey, without any clue as to what O'Brian had discovered, he exited the plane.

Standing in silence, Krueger and Brandt waited beneath a summer rain shower as Grimm obtained a rental car. He pulled up in a black SUV and opened the doors wordlessly. As Krueger was about to step in, Brandt pulled at his arm.

"Whatever happens," she said, "you're a great man. You did your very best."

Krueger was too tired, too numb to respond, but nodded to show his deep appreciation. Despite O'Brian's triumphant messages, Krueger didn't feel as if he were close to ending an investigation in glory; he felt as if he were taking the perilous steps his enemies had planned for him to take.

The Excelsior Hotel was a redbrick townhome lit up like a Christmas Tree in the middle of Mission Bay. Krueger could picture the inside: creaking wooden staircases, narrow corridors, rooms cramped with too much chintzy furniture. It would not be easy to escape from.

Great to know you are here, partner! Come up to room 7 ASAP. O'Brian had sent this last text message ten minutes ago. Krueger had followed it up with a call, which had not been answered.

"Tell your partner you won't enter the building until you've spoken to him," Grimm urged, seeing the confusion on Krueger's face.

"No," Krueger said. "There's a chance that he's telling me the truth—that for the last day he's been surveilling people, or apprehending people, or spying on people, or doing something which meant he couldn't talk."

"He couldn't take just a minute to return one of your calls?" Brandt asked doubtfully.

"Well I'm going up there," Krueger said. "I know it's probably a mistake. But I'm tired, Tessa. I'm tired of fumbling around the edges of a conspiracy like a blind man. I want answers. Even if it means putting myself in danger."

"Well, you won't be going alone," Brandt said.

"I know," Krueger replied. "Grimm is coming with me. But *you* are staying in the car."

"What?" Grimm and Brandt both cried together.

"That's right," Krueger said. "If Dennilson is the man behind it, then he's going to think twice about killing a fellow playboy. It'll be easy to cover up the death of a police officer, but the death of a European princeling would be a tough thing to make disappear, even for a billionaire."

"And why am I being forced to stay here?" Brandt demanded.

"Because I need eyes on the front of the hotel," Krueger said, his voice hoarse. "You see anyone suspicious going in or out, you call me. And if you don't hear from us once we are inside, fly back to New York and confess everything to my boss, Mac Hassler, over at NYPD."

THE HALF-EMPTY bottle of Pepto-Bismol felt fat and useless in

Hassler's pocket. He'd spent the last hour drinking it in the hope of soothing his sour stomach, but it hadn't worked. Ever since his confrontation with Preston Gates that morning, he'd been sick with worry.

Hassler stood waiting in the Excelsior, where he'd captured Sam O'Brian and Colin Dubchek on behalf of his new, wealthy benefactor. Now he'd been sent to repeat the trick and bring Krueger, and whoever else was following him, back to Dennilson's campus. Hassler was eager to finish the job and see the whole sorry gang exposed and disgraced. But still, his stomach protested in angry vehemence. He couldn't help worrying that he'd picked the wrong side in a battle he did not comprehend.

"You okay?" spat the hulking thug standing next to him. Hassler pursed his lips and nodded.

When he'd captured O'Brian, Dennilson had given him command of a security team who had the look and bearing of seasoned pros. But for the Krueger job, Gates had left him with a half-dozen raggedy hillbillies, sporting long beards, bandanas, and death metal t-shirts. One lanky man clung to the corner of the room like a perennial vine and fidgeted with his gun using trembling hands. If there were any bloodshed, or worse, any death, then the public outrage Hassler was hoping would pour over Krueger's head would undoubtedly hit him too.

His stomach growled again.

THERE WAS NO ONE at reception. The hotel bar was closed. His several loud calls for help went unanswered.

"Dammit," Krueger said, standing in the hallway of the hotel. Grimm was next to him holding a tire iron, which he'd taken from the rental. "This isn't a good sign," Krueger whispered, feeling stupid for stating the obvious.

Shaking his head, his silently unlatched the glass case behind the reception desk, which held a heavy fire axe. Looking more like a condemned man headed to his execution than a cop on his way to breaking a case, Krueger led Grimm up the stairs to the guest rooms. His head was bowed low. Though he gripped his newfound weapon tightly, he knew it wouldn't shield him from the gunfire he expected.

"Room Seven," Grimm whispered, as he gained the last step leading to the first floor of the hotel. The lamps on the greasy walls were grimy and dim. Someone was playing a Giants game loudly in their room. Scanning the scene, Krueger caught site of the door with a brass number seven nailed into its timbers. With a steady hand, he pointed and led Grimm onwards.

The corridor filled with a leaden silence as the duo drew closer. Krueger knew he still had a chance to escape, to flee what he suspected would be an ambush. But it was too late now. He'd fought hard against this conspiracy. Now his hunger for answers was too great to ignore. Joe Krueger knocked the door.

Behind him, the door to room number six flew open. Like demons summoned from Hell, a half-dozen black-clad brutes barged through the portal, waving guns and knives with callous disregard for the danger they posed. Each eager to claim the prize, they grunted and brayed, pawing Krueger's body like meat.

With a well-timed swing, Krueger guessed he could have taken out three, perhaps four, of his attackers. But his muscles were wearied from travel, and his mind had been dulled from too much toil. He surrendered to his captors and allowed his hands to be bound by a plastic cord. Uncaring hands grabbed Krueger's wallet and phone, which soon disappeared amid the chaos.

"Unhand me," Grimm said, shouting in a very British accent as he was deprived of his tire iron. He hoped the sound would alert the other guests in the hotel.

"Shut ya yap," one of the men said, slamming Grimm's head into the wall.

"Take it easy!" demanded Mac Hassler, as he slowly came into view. He suddenly felt very embarrassed to be seen in league with such men.

"Captain!" Krueger yelled angrily.

Hassler looked at the floor in response and began a speech he'd been practicing since he'd boarded Dennilson's jet for San Francisco.

"You thought you were smarter than me, didn't you Krueger? Ignoring orders, running around in Europe and the Middle East? And for what? To create havoc and show us all such disrespect! Well, it's over. We are taking you back to New York where you'll answer for what you've done."

Hassler spoke in a dull, quiet voice. No longer convinced of the righteousness of his cause, his mettle began to buckle.

"You are making a terrible mistake!" Krueger said. "Jesus, Mac, what have you done with O'Brian and Dubchek?"

Hassler turned away, not wanting to meet Krueger's ferocious gaze. "You'll see them real soon," he muttered. "They are in the subbasement of the Gemini campus."

"So, you're taking us there?" Krueger asked.

"Sure," Hassler said, rubbing his temple. "Mr. Dennilson would like a few choice words with you before your trip back to New York. I can't promise it'll be pleasant, but it's what you deserve." Hassler signaled to the closest of the guards. "Let's get them out of here."

"He's the one, Mac!" Krueger bellowed. "Dennilson blew up the Meyer Center!" Hassler, his porcine nose in the air, descended the staircase. Krueger tried again. "The world is gonna know you aided a terrorist!" he said.

Hassler snorted and dismissed the threat with a shake of his head. "Because you're going to tell them, is that right?" he asked. "Krueger, who do you think is gonna believe you? A freak whose dereliction of duty dismayed his brother officers? Who selfishly chose to chase ghosts around Europe while his nation was at war?" Hassler laughed and could see the rage in Krueger's eyes melting into a rending sorrow. The captain turned his back and continued descending the stairs.

"Help!" Grimm cried but was slammed in the ribs for his trouble.

"Save ya voice, sweetheart," one of the thugs said. "This joint is empty. We paid the owners to take the night off, and the guests were all rebooked in other joints. So no one is coming to your rescue."

"Who are these guys?" Krueger demanded as he was dragged down the stairs in Hassler's wake.

"Dennilson's security," Hassler said, buttoning his sport coat.

"Bullshit," Krueger spat. "Billionaires don't pay amateurs to handle their security. For Christ's sake, look at these people, Mac! They look like the meth dealers me and you were busting in upstate New York. Hell, this guy's got a Totenkopf tattoo on his freaking hand."

Hassler's eyes scanned the man closest to Krueger, the one with his hands around Krueger's left arm. Sure enough, skull and crossbones glowered from his fist. Hassler thought it was a gang symbol; he was too stupid to know it was the mark of Nazis.

Using the fire escape in the back, Hassler led his team to an idling black Escalade waiting beside the hotel. Krueger and Grimm were shoved into the middle row of seats and swiftly flanked on either side by burly guards. Despite the Escalade's size, they sat so close that Krueger could smell their rank breath, which reminded him of toilets in a concert hall. Hassler, the ringmaster of this stinking troupe, climbed in next to the driver, while the remaining men were told to remain and clean up the crime scene.

"Headquarters," Hassler said to the driver, flatly.

In silence, the car turned onto the road. With a brief glance, Krueger saw that the rental car was still parked across the street from the hotel, but it was empty. Had Tessa Brandt been captured too? Or had she followed Krueger's orders to flee if something went wrong?

Please God, he thought, *please let her be okay.*

The Escalade sped north toward the Golden Gate Bridge, passing the undulating hills of the city.

It was long past nine, and the traffic was thinning out. Hassler's driver made good time as they passed through the city.

"We'll be fine, old sport," Grimm whispered, patting Krueger's knee with a firm and steady hand. If the doctor was scared, his face did not show it.

But as the Escalade crossed a wide intersection, Krueger caught site of a gleaming SUV bounding forward from the side street on the right. It was the rental. He turned in time to see Tessa Brandt at the wheel, her jaw thrust forward, her blonde hair tied back. She wore an expression of such fury that even Krueger, who was fast falling in love with her, was, for a brief moment, both transfixed and terrified.

Brandt slammed the car into the side of the Escalade with such force that its rear wheels jumped into the air. The doors caved inward with a grinding crash, as the windows shattered and showered the occupants inside with milky shards. Metal squealed. Inside, Krueger was jolted sharply to the left, and he slammed his head into Grimm's shoulder, leaving behind a bloody smear.

"What the Hell!" someone yelled as the Escalade began to settle, rocking on its springs, before a momentary stunned silence filled the air.

It was soon replaced by a violent screaming. "Oh, God, help me!" the man seated next to Krueger began wailing. His right knee had been badly mangled by the crash. Bones jutted out from his black jeans at unnatural angles.

A cacophony of car horns filled the night sky. Vaguely, Krueger heard the pitter-patter of unsure footfalls and suspected that people were running toward the site of the crash.

Krueger ignored the wounded man next to him, trying to think quickly how to turn this unexpected crash to his advantage. Around him, the men were grunting and whimpering, making the noises that scared bullies make when their plans go awry. Only Hassler maintained his composure and exited the car with his gun drawn.

With his hands tied behind his back, it was impossible for Krueger to escape. Trapped, he witnessed Hassler circle the Escalade, taking a moment to peer into Brandt's car and see if anyone was inside.

It was empty, and Hassler sent a litany of curses flying into the air.

With his attention focused on his corrupt captain, Krueger failed to notice Tessa Brandt pull open the left-side passenger door. Armed with a baseball bat, she pulled the shocked guard next to Grimm from his seat and flung him to the asphalt. A swift strike to his shoulders reduced him to a simpering pile. Grimm saw the sudden opening and barreled out of the car, with Krueger fast behind him. The driver was too stunned to offer pursuit.

Brandt used her pocket knife to slice open the plastic cords that bound Krueger and Grimm's hands. Then, with her bat raised high, Brandt led them back toward the rental car, where Mac Hassler waited with his gun raised. The arc light above lit up the miserable architecture of his face.

"Hold it right there!" he yelled into the night sky, as raindrops began to fall.

"You can't stop us," Krueger said, inching toward the car.

"You think I'm too scared to shoot you?" Hassler asked. He chuckled, as if trying to mask his rising dread.

Krueger shook his head and took another step forward. Thunder chuckled in the sky. "No," Krueger answered. He put a hand on the busted hood. "I think you're too good to shoot us. You may be a lousy cop, but you sure aren't a murderer."

Krueger opened the side door and let Brandt and Grimm into the car, leaving Hassler standing in the rain with his mouth agape. Krueger was right; the old captain had the heart of a fool, but not that of a senseless killer. Thus, he did not stop their escape.

In spite of the collision, Krueger found that the rental was still drivable. And as he pulled away he left Hassler all alone, feeling the rainwater sodden his jacket, hearing the wail of the police sirens pierce the air, sensing the confused glares of passersby.

"What are you doin'?" bellowed the driver of Hassler's Escalade, who'd finally rediscovered his composure. He watched in dismay as Krueger drove the rental toward the Golden Gate Bridge.

Summoning the last vestiges of his courage, Mac Hassler returned to the car and found that the engine was still running despite the crash. Relieved, he ordered his driver to follow. Hassler didn't know what his next step would be, but he hoped that it would, at last, be a good one.

WITH HEADLIGHTS SLICING the blackness like a blade, Krueger's car approached the outer fences of the Gemini campus. Krueger gripped the wheel with a rage kindling in his heart. His weariness still hung over him, wrapping him in an unwelcome blanket, but he was beyond feelings of fatigue and of pain. He wanted answers now. His mind would not let him rest until the conspiracy has been laid bare.

And Sam O'Brian had to be rescued.

"You wanna tell me what happened back there?" Krueger asked Brandt. "This car was empty when we passed the hotel with Hassler. I was worried about you."

Brandt smiled and kissed the wound on Krueger's forehead. "I did alright by myself, don't you think?" she asked playfully. "Soon after you headed into the hotel, I saw that Escalade turn into the alley. I tried calling you like you asked, but you didn't pick up."

"We were being deprived of our phones at that precise moment," Grimm said.

"I feared as much," Brandt continued, "so I snuck down there to take a peek. That driver . . . he looked like a drug addict."

"He probably was," Krueger said. "The guys that jumped us all looked the same: sallow, thin, and a little high too. These Neo-Nazis have guns and they have numbers, but nothing else we should be worried about."

"They have the True Cross," Grimm cautioned.

"Not for much longer!" Brandt said with an iron-like voice.

The trio sped past a sign warning them that they were now on private property. Beyond, the storm clouds were turning the Pacific into a thunderous boil.

"This place is going to be crawling with guards," Grimm warned. "And killing them will only make our plight all the worse."

"I hope it doesn't come to that," Krueger insisted, turning on the windshield wipers. The scene before him became a streaky smear. "I figure we sneak in, find Sam and Dubchek, and then confront Dennilson."

Krueger carefully drove the car onto the promontory of rock. The surf below was white and churning. The outer fencing of the campus winked in the headlights.

"This is it," Brandt whispered.

But as they drew nearer, Krueger saw the guard box. It was empty. And the main gate was hanging open, the check-point clear.

"Something isn't right," Grimm whispered as the card slowed to a crawl.

"I don't care anymore," Krueger replied, his voice a slow rasp. He killed the car's engine and searched the guard post, finding nothing that could serve as a weapon. *I should have grabbed a gun from one of Hassler's thugs*, Krueger thought.

Unarmed, Krueger returned to the car and drove toward the silent, brooding tower before him. The windows were dark, the street empty.

"I'll get us as close to the entrance as possible," Krueger said. "Once we are in, we head to the subbasement."

Krueger left the smashed rental parked next to the wide, gleaming atrium. Holding Brandt's baseball bat, he led his two friends through the rain and into the vast, darkened entrance.

Brandt retrieved her cell phone and used the greenish light to guide their way forward. It wasn't much, but it was enough to see that the place was bereft of life. The main security desk was unmanned, the polished floors bare.

"I don't get it," Krueger said. "Where is Dennilson? Why would he leave his fortress unguarded?" Without answers, the trio edged forward.

The light from Brandt's phone caught a dark spot on the floor. Another, larger spot came into view further down the hall. Krueger crouched low and touched the dark marks.

It was blood. Fresh blood.

Krueger spun and ordered Brandt to play the feeble light across the walls. Still they found nothing. "Damn it all to Hell," Krueger hissed, turning haphazardly in all directions. He was desperate for another clue. Stumbling like a drunk, something struck him on his shoulders. He turned and saw a pair of brogues dangling in the dark air, like the footwear of ghosts.

Tired, confused, standing on the brink of utter emotional collapse, Krueger could not comprehend what he was seeing. He looked up, squinting, Brandt's light providing little illumination.

"Hey Krueger!" someone yelled from behind. Krueger turned to find Mac Hassler following him. He had a flashlight in his hand and two wounded men following him.

"They followed us!" Grimm said, bracing himself for another beating. But Hassler stopped when he saw that the atrium was empty and dark. The concern on his face revealed that this was not part of his plan.

Hassler caught sight of the dangling shoes and played his flashlight over the grisly scene. The shoes were attached to two legs, the legs of Curt Dennilson, who was hanging by his neck from a rope tied to the uppermost balcony in the atrium, one-hundred feet above.

Dr. Barnaby Grimm turned and vomited into the darkness.

"What in God's name have you done?" Hassler tried to shout. But the shock was too great, and his voice sounded like a plaintive squeak.

A gunshot, loud and terrible, answered Hassler's question. Krueger spun, straining to find the origin of the shot. He was so busy looking that he failed to notice his captain, Mac Hassler, falling to the ground, a red stain blossoming on the back of his sport coat like a crimson flower.

Tessa Brandt screamed and fell into Krueger arms. There was nowhere else to hide.

Suddenly, the lights of the campus turned on, flooding the murder scene with a buttery glow that revealed the extent of the carnage. Dennilson had been beaten before being hung; his face was a battlefield of wounds.

With the layout of the atrium now clear to see, Krueger pointed to the elevators and led his friends forward. But rank upon rank of black-shirted men suddenly came pouring forth from a dozen doors. They surrounded the glass entrance way.

"Who the Hell are you?" Krueger demanded, shielding Grimm and Brandt with his baseball bat held aloft.

"We are the future," someone replied, and Krueger looked at the serried, armed ranks at the front of the building. From amongst them emerged Preston Gates, wearing a smile as black as his trench coat.

- 18 -

THE TEMPEST OUTSIDE GREW WORSE, and so, too, did the mood of the mob.

With a frenzied yell, dozens of armed men surrounded Krueger and his friends. Some, he noticed, wore Nazi iconography on their uniforms, and more than a dozen wore swastikas. Enraged, Krueger swung his bat once, striking the hip of an aging biker, but it was not enough to scare away the crowd. Sustained by the strength of their leader, Preston Gates, they overcame Krueger's attacks and disarmed him.

"Search them!" Gates barked, and he discovered that he enjoyed giving orders with his newfound power. The way the minions before him leapt into action upon hearing his voice, the way they fought to curry favor with their new Fuhrer, gave him a feeling that no drug, drink, or woman ever had before.

A youth, with both the complexion and attitude of an Appalachian dope addict, licked his lips as he pawed over Brandt, winking at her as he squeezed her crotch. But Brandt could tell that this grimy adolescent was not experienced with women, and a swift hard kick between his legs was enough to send him away yelping. His friends, each wearing lank hair and pallid skin, laughed.

"Enough!" Gates said. "Bring them here." Gone were his yellowing t-shirt and cringing smile—the smile of a lackey. He was now donning a black shirt and tie, a Sam Browne belt affixed around his gut, and a pair of jodhpurs tucked into polished boots.

Gates' men hustled Krueger to the middle of the atrium, and he was forced to stand beneath Dennilson's hanging body. Mac Hassler was slouched on the floor, the blood from his fatal gunshot seeping onto the cream tile.

The sound of sudden commotion filtered from the elevator banks, and Krueger turned to see Sam O'Brian and Colin Dubchek being manhandled by a squad of neo-Nazis. He knew they'd both been beaten, but Krueger could not help feeling elated as they approached. Sure, they were captured, scared, and almost out of luck. But at least they were alive.

"It was you!" O'Brian screamed at Gates as he saw the bodies of both Dennilson and Hassler. Gates smirked. The pimples on his cheeks seemed to glow a brighter shade of red.

Shaking his head, Krueger turned to his old friend. "So you've been hanging around with some real charmers since I left, partner?" he asked. "Who is this joker?"

O'Brian and Dubchek were brought to a stop next to Krueger's group. At long last, they were all together, albeit with their enemies circling like sharks around them.

"This is Dennilson's crony," O'Brian spat. "Preston Gates. Well-credentialed but ill-educated. Guess he's trying to take over his boss's fascist operation."

"Dennilson!" Gates cried, before erupting in laughter so utterly without mirth that Brandt felt her skin crawl into chilled gooseflesh. Gates tugged at his black shirt as he did so, as if confirming to himself that he was still clad in the raiment of a dictator. "This wasn't Dennilson's work! He didn't have the vision. I alone shall lead the revolution."

O'Brian eyeballed the crowds of angry men who had swarmed the atrium. "Revolution? So you mean to overthrow the government with these dummies? Good luck!"

The guard standing nearest to O'Brian, a man who had the haircut of an ex-marine but the belly of a man who'd forgotten his training, kicked him in his gut. But O'Brian refused to give him the satisfaction of a whimper.

"These are patriots!" Gates declared, drawing closer to his prisoners. He was flanked on either side by large, well-armed sentries. "Well-bred heroes of the Aryan people! From Idaho, from Montana, from the parts of California that have not yet been surrendered to the hordes of lesser races. These fine men are the shock troops of the Revolution, which begins tonight!"

"You don't believe this shit, do you?" O'Brian asked.

In response, Gates flashed a smile of vulpine triumph, and O'Brian got his terrible answer. "Dennilson didn't give a damn about the future of our species," Gates said. "He only cared about hoarding art and hoarding wealth, nothing more. It was me who arranged the purchase of the Volcker-Blum facility. It was me who acquired General Krueger's body. And it was me who completed his search for the True Cross. Dennilson wanted it for his art collection! Ha! Only I understood its power."

"The power to resurrect the dead?" Krueger demanded, but his question only won a swift snarl from his captor.

"You'll see," Gates replied darkly.

"So Mr. Dennilson was your cat's paw?" Grimm asked. He found Gates looking at him with molten anger contorting the features of his face. Grimm paused, wondering why he, above the other four prisoners, would prompt such a display a hatred.

"Don't you dare look at me, scum!" Gates said, smashing his fist into Grimm's jaw. The academic fell to his knees as a ribbon of red dribbled from his nose. "Get that nigger up off my floor," Gates cried, drawing out the syllables of that vile slur and savoring them with savage delight.

Grimm rose to his feet, a chill blaze kindling in his heart as he heard the word; a silent fury at being dismissed with such a hateful term. He'd heard it before, of course, from irredeemable, ill-bred racists and degenerates drowning in booze and self-pity. But Grimm's unshakeable self-belief had given him the strength to ignore them.

Hearing that word spoken, however, by a man of such uncommon intelligence, a man who should have seen in Grimm a peer amid a world of mediocrity, proved to him that no matter how he excelled, there would forever be parts of the rarified world shut off from him.

"Dennilson," Gates continued, "thought this was just another of his expensive capers, a chance to find a priceless artifact and squirrel it away in his collection. He didn't know about the attacks General Krueger made on my orders, the signal to start our just war against the Semitic oppressors and the other inferior races. All he was worried about was keeping his common thievery hidden!"

Gates placed a gloved hand on Dennilson's shoe and swung the body from the rope, an act which Dubchek found strangely revolting. "If secrecy was so important," Dubchek asked, "why did you name those shell companies after the twins of Gemini? It was a big clue."

"Insurance!" Gates replied, before suffering a fit of giggles. "In case I failed to obtain the Cross, or worse, was denied its powers of resurrection! I needed to have someone ready to take the fall. So I left you a few breadcrumbs to follow. Naming his shell companies after the twins of Gemini? That was me. Registering their websites to a shadowy man with the same initials as Dennilson? Me too. I even put the proof of Dennilson's mother's notorious past online, taking care to make sure it looked like I wanted it hidden. It all pointed to that capitalist, Jew-loving swine!"

The crowd around Gates began to mutter curses. One of them even threw a shoe at Dennilson's bruised face.

"But I should not have feared. Our new Aryan Empire has been blessed with Holy sanction! God has gifted us the True Cross, and with it the power to forge a new chapter in human history!"

"If Dennilson was so important to your plans," Kruger asked, "why did you kill him?"

"Because he has served his purpose," Gates announced matter-of-factly. "Our weapon has been tested successfully in New York and Portland. We have no more need for secrecy in this war."

Using words like *war* and *revolution*, Krueger realized that Gates sounded more and more like the zealots he had faced in the Middle East. The comparison did not cheer him. "So that's what this was all about?" he demanded. "You racist kooks think the Cross is going to win you the war you're about to start?"

"It wasn't us that started this war!" Gates replied, jabbing his finger his Krueger's chest. "It was the Mexican hordes who came here with their Third World diseases. It was the Jews who are destroying the American Dream with their control over our banks and our media. All we want to do is defend ourselves against these assaults!"

Krueger turned his sullen gaze to the floor. Like Grimm, he'd heard such racist garbage before, but it had always come from the mouths of the unemployed or unemployable, the degenerates who refused to see that they themselves were the authors of their own suffering.

But now he saw that devious, cunning minds like Gates traded in race hate too.

"So why'd you do it, Gates?" Krueger screamed, realizing how desperate he sounded to his captor. "What turned you into this monster?"

Gates smiled and shook his head, enjoying the torment that was disfiguring the cop's already ugly face. "That doesn't concern you," he said at last, before turning to a lanky skinhead in sunglasses, who Krueger guessed was a captain of some sort. "Have these enemies of the Aryan people taken to the main hall. I want them to see the future of our mighty and measureless empire right before their execution."

CURT DENNILSON'S AUDITORIUM was a spacious, well-furnished room on the ground floor of the Gemini campus. He'd used it to flirt with the world's media, announce new product launches, and showcase the technologies of the twenty-first century.

But Preston Gates had turned it into a stage from which he would drag the world back to the miseries of the twentieth.

Before black drapes, Gates had erected a dais, flanked on either side by ugly icons. Confederate battle flags, Celtic and Sun crosses, and perched eagles holding fasces all stood erect, confirming the ideology that drove Gates and his men. On the dais, there stood a great oak table, all inlaid wood and intricate carving. The table was crowned with a series of big computers, which burped and chittered as the prisoners were led inside.

The scene was a combination of old and new, of science and faith, and as such, the perfect alter for Gates' new quasi-religion.

Krueger and his four friends were led to the dais and forced to kneel. Looking out into the auditorium, he saw ranks of soldiers, perhaps as many as two hundred, all whey-faced and hungry for violence. Krueger wondered what hatreds, ancient and modern, had driven these men from their homes and into the embrace of a pudgy, dime-store Hitler. Had lost jobs and lost wives put them on a road to fascism, or was it something more elemental: a simple anger toward those who looked different?

Two of the men pulled back the black drapes, revealing a Nazi banner. Some in the crowd brayed when they saw it; others gave the Nazi salute. But most, having convinced themselves that they were troops in a just war, simply stood at attention, waiting for their leader.

They did not have to wait long. Preston Gates strode onto the stage, surrounded by lab-coated assistants. The ranks of neo-Nazis applauded, then cheered as he approached and stood upon the dais in front of his captives.

Gates saluted, and when he had had his fill of the adulation, he silenced the audience with a wave of his hand. "Stormtroopers!" he said. "The moment we have planned for is almost upon us."

"Jeez," O'Brian said as Gates continued his speech. "Isn't this a little overripe?"

"Did you ever hear Hitler speak?" Grimm asked. "I mean, really sat and listened to an entire speech? It was nonsense delivered in a ridiculously high pitch. But people loved it. It gave them an enemy to blame for their misfortunes. And guessing by the look of this crowd, I think they've had a great many misfortunes, too. Addictions, criminal convictions, family breakups. One can only imagine."

"They're gonna have a few more misfortunes if I ever escape." O'Brian sniffed.

"When I went to college, do you know what I found there?" Gates asked his crowd. "Mongrel races, that's what! And I sat among those apes . . . those vermin . . . as our communist professors attacked our nation, our race . . . attacked YOU!"

The crowd of hopeless nullities cheered.

"And then, having been forced to listen to that drivel for years, I finally escaped. I graduated and tried to find a job and take my small slice of the American Dream. Isn't that what we all deserve?"

Gates raised his arms as his followers answered in the affirmative.

"But do you know what I found? Honest Americans like you and I don't have a shot at the American Dream anymore. We have to beg the Jews in our banks just so we can own a home. Asians are crossing the ocean to take jobs that should be reserved for real Americans. And we have a tidal wave of Mexicans crossing the border, bringing their diseases and idleness with them."

Gates shook his head and turned from the crowd as they simmered. He looked down at the prisoners kneeling behind him. Quietly, as if he meant these words only for Krueger, he spoke again.

"You have no idea how embarrassing it is to be smart and have to beg stupid people for the things you want. Jobs, dates, mortgages." Gates sighed, as if he were confessing. "It isn't right."

There was no hate in those words, no melodramatic rage, just the self-pitying wail of a man whose life had not been the success he had intended it to be.

At last Krueger understood his enemy. Kneeling on the stage, he imagined an old girlfriend of Gates' dumping him in favor of man with a darker skin color or a more exotic surname. Perhaps someone in New York had refused him a business loan. Perhaps he'd seen the job he wanted taken by a hungry, skilled immigrant from India. The specifics didn't matter; all that mattered to those killed in New York and Portland was that Gates had once been motivated to set upon the path to evil, and having taken that course, he hadn't turned away.

This moment of confession passed quickly between Krueger and Gates, and the aspiring dictator returned to his raging, fulminating speech that was, in its own strange way, utterly captivating. His young face, deeply expressive, was as red as the flag behind him, while his eyes shined with blazing hatred.

"But the revolution is now here, brother Aryans!' Gates screamed. Beside him, lab assistants in white coats began to type furiously into the computer keyboards. "We completed the mission as set forth by the Fuhrer. We finished what General Krueger could not. We discovered the True Cross!"

The crowds roared their approval as a team of four men pulled a black cart into the auditorium. Upon it stood the ancient timbers which had been pulled from the earth, their silence offering mute confirmation of their holy provenance.

The True Cross was just as Grimm had imagined it: the great vertical beam, which had once stood tall on the hills of Golgotha; the cross beam, from which mankind's savior had hung and died; and the titulus, which had proclaimed him an enemy of the Roman Empire. A small portion of the titulus was missing; the portion which, according to legend, Empress Helena had taken to Europe as proof of her discoveries.

From the dais, Krueger saw the magnificent relic as it was pulled into the room. It was splintered and dark with age. And yet those ancient timbers seemed to sparkle with soft radiance. It was, Krueger guessed, a trick of the stage lighting, but he couldn't escape the thought there was something unnatural, something divine about the way the Cross stood and shone.

Beside him, Tessa Brandt's mouth fall open in awe, and the light in her eyes gave only a hint of her feeling. In spite of her predicament, it was impossible for her to feel anything but joy as the relic drew closer. She wasn't particularly religious and couldn't have explained why she felt suddenly cheered by the site of the True Cross, but the feeling could not be denied. The sheer proximity of the Cross had, somehow, gladdened her heart.

"This," Gates said in somber tones, "will be not only be our totem, carried aloft by our victorious armies. It will be our weapon too."

Krueger found himself retching. He wondered what sort of mind could look upon the divine and then conspire to turn it into an implement of death.

"Yes, brother Aryans! The legends are true. The Cross enables those who wield it to extend life, to bring back those we have lost. And with such power, we shall grow the Aryan Nation, until at last we conquer the corners of this world which God set aside for us alone."

Most in the crowd cheered. Like automatons, they clapped whenever called upon to do so. But some, those who had not yet seen the resurrection of General Krueger, were more muted.

"You, Stormtroopers, you shall be joined on the front lines of this war by the warriors who marched before you. We will call them back to this world, to finish the job of cleansing it."

Krueger felt himself grow cold and still. He could sense that his grandfather, the man whose reappearance had forced him to start this sorry adventure, was close.

"And the first of them is here, restored to life thanks to the power of the Cross! It was he who fired the first shots in our righteous crusade, when he killed the Jews in New York and Portland. It is General Wolfgang Krueger!"

For a moment, Joe Krueger felt as though he would faint. The world started to swim before his eyes, and the bright rays of yellow light from above melted into a glossy sheen that obscured his vision.

But some small part of his brain commanded him to remain alert, and Krueger shook his head violently. When he opened his eyes again, they were clear, and his grandfather, his dead and disgraced grandfather, was slowly approaching the dais.

The crowds had stopped cheering now. They were silent, expectant, as the monster emerged from the shadows and stood before them. He wore a clean grey uniform, the uniform of the Wehrmacht, as if it had been bought recently, which it most probably had been. And his flesh, the flesh of a long-dead cancer sufferer, was smooth and pink, as if his lengthy confinement in a Berlin factory had rejuvenated him. Most terrifyingly of all, his blue eyes shone with life.

Brandt shuffled closer to Krueger, trying to comfort him in such a trying time. She stroked his shoulder, and together, they watched as General Krueger, his face serene, his expression passive, came to a stop next to Preston Gates.

And still the audience held back. They may have been stupid and drunk on their own self-importance, but they were wise enough to remain silent as Gates revealed his terrible power.

"General Krueger is just the first," Gates promised his followers. "Our fallen heroes will rise from their graves. They will take up arms again. Soon we will be detonating a hundred, perhaps even a thousand bombs a day! And when we do, you, my Stormtroopers, will have no fear."

"You're gonna trust your lives to this fruitcake?" someone shouted, and Krueger turned to find Colin Dubchek rising to his feet. The slender, wiry techie had righteous anger written over his young face. He was soon pummeled by two of the guards, who rushed the stage with clubs.

Gates paused and bit his lip, and he looked to O'Brian like the surly lackey once again. The cop was struck in that moment not by Gates' might or evil, though they were certainly in abundance, but by his smallness.

"Fool!" Gates responded finally. "I am the leader of the Aryan people! And I will deliver them to a new and better future." Gates nodded slyly to his audience. "And this," he said, "is how we are going to do it: with our Nazi brothers reclaimed from death." With a gloved hand, Gates pointed toward his prisoners on the dais. "General Krueger!" he screamed. "Kill these enemies of National Socialism!"

The air turned quiet and still. All Joe Krueger could hear was the feverish tapping of the white-coated assistants on their keyboards.

And then the General approached.

He drew forward slowly, carefully, with the same steady gait he'd shown when planting his deadly bombs. With each booted foot, he drew closer. His passive expression did not waver.

"Grandfather!" Krueger cried out suddenly and unexpectedly. He stared at the famed general in front of him, his eyes pleading for understanding. Krueger rose to his feet, but another of Gates' guards was upon him in an instant, and with a swift stroke of his club, the guard felled him.

General Kruger paused and watched the assault. With a sure, slow movement, he leaned down and stared at the young cop. His eyes were as blue as he remembered. But to Joe Kruger's surprise, he found no hint of malice in them. "I read your last letter to your wife and to your daughter, General Krueger," he said. "I am your daughter's son. I am your blood. And I know that you do not mean to do this."

"Stop begging and accept your fate like a man," Gates said with a dismissive air. "General Krueger is a hero of the Nazi war machine. He knows to obey orders."

And yet, General Krueger did not move forward. He remained standing, looking at the man who claimed to be his grandson, with curious eyes. It was as if he were pondering the claims made by the stricken cop.

"This is a monstrous deceit," Joe Kruger said, "and they've done terrible things to your body in the name of their hideous ideology. But I know your mind. And somewhere—somewhere inside of you, you know that this is wrong."

Can he hear me? Krueger wondered, as the guard looming over him punched the side of his head. *Can he comprehend that this disfigured New Yorker is his heir?*

General Krueger raised his hand.

"You see!" Gates cried. "He is a National Socialist! General Krueger does not wish to hear your prattle. He will help us forge a new Reich."

But as he spoke, something crept into General Krueger's eyes. Fear, cold and nagging, bit into his handsome Prussian features, and Joe Krueger began to see that his grandfather was not some demon, not some nightmare concocted in a diseased mind. He was something else—and something better.

General Krueger turned and pointed at Preston Gates.

"Silence the prisoners," Gates squeaked as he took an instinctive step backwards. He could not bear the General's gaze.

More guards rushed the dais, and Krueger was hoisted to his feet by the closest guard. He managed to choke the words, "Help me," before the guard closed his gloved hand around his throat. Another man kicked his legs, while a third used a club to ram his ribs with such force that more than a couple broke.

"Don't!" Brandt wailed, as she was seized by guards herself.

The sounds of the beating prompted the General to turn once more to the dais, and as he did so, Krueger discovered, to his relief, that the fear and confusion in his grandfather's eyes had been replaced by sudden understanding—and by rage.

The General reached his grandson with three mighty steps, and with a swift, remorseless punch, he felled the guard who was choking him. A second guard foolishly attacked, and in response, General Krueger grabbed both his arms and flung him to the floor.

"What?" Gates wailed. His lab assistants fled from the dais, leaving him alone to face the unfolding disaster. "Shoot them all!" he cried in a high-pitched wail.

The nearest guard to General Krueger raised his pistol and fired two rounds into his chest. The General paused to look down at the wounds, and finding them non-threatening, he bounded toward the gunman. With a swift and sickening twist of the man's neck, the

General left him dead on the ground. Another guard fired a round into General Krueger's leg and suffered a similar, gruesome fate as a consequence.

These two deaths were enough, finally, to break Gates' spell over his audience. Some of them, being nothing more than racist drug-peddlers and gang members, ran for the exits as panic wrapped its long and powerful tentacles over the crowd. A large number remained, however, for they were committed neo-Nazis and devoted to Gates' cause. Seeing the panic on their leader's face, they drew their guns and began firing.

As the air filled with smoke and gunfire, Krueger grabbed Brandt and jumped beneath the dais. His battered body was failing him, the pain growing too much to bear, but he succeeded in avoiding the bullets. He noted, gratefully, that each of his friends had done the same.

"We need some guns of our own!" O'Brian yelled over the din.

Slowly, trying to forget his bruises and agonies, Krueger raised his head to try and find his grandfather and a way to escape

What he saw defied all the known laws of science. General Krueger, struck by more than three-dozen bullets, was nonetheless attacking the remaining neo-Nazis. He grabbed one old, grungy gang member and flung him into the crowd, causing some of them to scatter. Another man fired and his bullet missed, striking the computers instead and sending up a shower of sparks. The sparks, floating like red angels, kissed the Nazi banner hanging beside the dais, and soon grew into a fire.

Seeing his banner destroyed, Gates gave up bellowing orders and instead reached for his own pistol. With imperfect hands, he fired rapidly, tearing away General Krueger's left epaulette. But the long-dead German would not fall. Five, and then six of Gates' men were seized and killed.

In the roiling chaos, Joe Krueger found an abandoned pistol lying uselessly by the dais. Ignoring the gun fire and forgetting his pain, he scrabbled crab-like the short distance to the weapon and tried to pick it up. But one of Gates' men suddenly loomed into view and smacked Krueger in his right temple, a blow that sent stars cascading down Krueger's field of vision. Krueger blindly launched a fist upwards, and by sheer chance, caught his opponent's chin. He hit it squarely, and the man fell to ground, unconscious and defeated. Krueger was free to reach for the pistol.

But when he rose, he found Preston Gates standing close by, with his own gun pointed toward him. "It is only fitting that my empire be conceived in flames," Gates said as the blaze crept slowly along the walls of the auditorium. Behind him, General Krueger was continuing to clash with those foolish enough to fight him.

As the air filled with smoke, Preston Gates smiled, savoring his enemy's imminent death. But his joy was short lived, for with a bellow, Colin Dubchek came running from behind the dais and struck Gates with his shoulder. They went tumbling to the ground together.

Joe Krueger was stunned. He'd been seconds from death and had been saved only by the heroic quick thinking of a man he'd never known until three weeks ago. It was only the sound of the gunshot that shook him out of his contemplation and urged him to action. As he rushed forward, so too did O'Brian and the rest of his friends.

Krueger leapt to where Dubchek and Gates were brawling. He pulled the young techie away from the dictator and saw, to his everlasting regret, a large gaping wound in his chest. Gates, animated now by an urge to survive the carnage he had caused, scrambled to his feet and backed away. He saw that his dream was being burned away around him, and the discovery brought fresh hatred to his features. Slowly, his eyes lost their steadiness.

"The Aryan race will never surrender to you mongrels!" Gates spat, before retreating into the fire and smoke. O'Brian raced after him yelling curses.

"I think you might have stopped them." Dubchek coughed weakly.

"*We* stopped them" Krueger said. He cradled Dubchek's head, and Brandt, suddenly weeping, wrapped his bloody body in her coat. "And you'll be remembered for it," Krueger added.

Joe Kruger never knew if Dubchek heard those last words, but the smile that curled in the corners of his mouth led him to believe that he did.

With his friend dead, Krueger looked up to see Gates' dreams collapse into nothingness. The last of his minions were fleeing, some barreling blindly into the flaming banners, others into doorways already crowded with men maddened by fear and confusion. A few lingered amid the flames, wandering like troubled ghosts, dismayed to find that their hopes for the future had been dashed.

For dashed they had been. There would be no Fourth Reich now, no return to the horrors of Nazi life. America, for all her imperfections, would endure as a land of liberty.

Amid this tumult was General Wolfgang Krueger, who now stood serene on the dais, as if admiring the view from a German mountain castle.

"Grandfather!" Krueger cried, in spite of the searing pain coming from his broken ribs. General Krueger looked down benignly. "Come with us!" Joe Krueger said.

General Krueger paused, as if seeing for the first time the roaring blaze that was growing and spewing around him. Slowly he shook his and head and turned.

"Come with us!" Krueger yelled a second time, and he had to be restrained by Grimm who feared he would follow his grandfather into the flames. General Krueger did not look back.

He continued to walk toward the flaming banner and the drapes, and was soon lost to those red, rising flames, leaving his grandson with a memory that would never vanish.

Joe Krueger sighed deeply, a signal to his body that it had done enough, that it had risen to the challenge and overcome it. With the danger receding, Krueger felt his legs grow heavy. He fell to his knees and dropped his gun. The weight was too heavy for his bloodied hands.

Grimm and Brandt took Krueger before he could hit the rubble-strewn floor. "We are gonna get you out of here!" Grimm said, but Krueger never heard him.

The two friends dragged Krueger toward the closest exit, passing the True Cross as they did so. Grimm winced and reached out as if to touch the sacred timbers. "We have to save it!" he wailed.

"There's no time," Brandt reminded him and tried to drag Krueger further to the exit. Blue smoke was beginning to fill her lungs. Her strength would soon be entirely spent.

"It is our last physical link to the Son of God," Grimm said, unmoving. Desire kindled in his eyes. "We have to save it. It's . . . it's God's gift."

Tessa Brandt, wise and defiant, shook her head. "Life is God's gift, Barnaby," she said. "That is what we must save."

Grimm silently nodded his head in solemn agreement and took Krueger's arm once again. They fled the blazing room, leaving the holy totem to the roaring flames.

WHEN DETECTIVE JOE KRUEGER awoke, he found himself outside the campus. He was lying on a gurney, surrounded by paramedics. Absently, Krueger raised a hand to his face and found his right eye swollen shut. But even in his weary, bloody state Krueger recognized the vivid red and blue light from the police sirens illuminating the walls of the burning building, and the footfalls of a black-clad SWAT team.

"Phone," he said weakly.

"Joe!" said Tessa Brandt, emerging suddenly into his view. She had not left his side since their escape from the fiery wreck of the Gemini campus.

O'Brian was next to her. "You're back, partner!" he said. "Listen, we couldn't find that SOB Gates, but don't worry. This city will be sealed up tight by the time you get to the hospital!"

But Krueger shook his head. He was done thinking about Gates and his evil. His thoughts lay now solely with his family. "Need to call Ma," Krueger said. "Tell her it's all over."

"Maybe later, pal," one of the paramedics said, engrossed in a clipboard. "Once we get you to the hospital."

Brandt hissed at the paramedic and handed Krueger her cell. He paused, then dialed the number from memory. No son, no matter his injury, no matter his pain, forgets how to reach his mother.

"Joseph," Trudy said expectantly on the other line.

Krueger chuckled, and realized he'd lost a tooth in the fight. "It's all ok, Ma," Krueger said. "Your father . . . my grandfather . . . he is at peace."

Closing his eyes, Krueger imagined seeing his mother grip the phone, tears rolling down her cheeks.

"He was not a bad man," she said. Krueger could hear relief—and defiance—in her voice.

"I know," he said. "He loved you."

"And I you," Trudy replied.

Krueger ended the call with a promise that he would come visit the moment he was able. He meant it. Handing back the phone to Brandt, and remembering that his dreams were far better than the reality around him, Krueger allowed himself to sleep once more.

JOE KRUEGER LEANED FORWARD, and his healing ribs roared in
protest. Despite the bandages and the bedrest and the pills, which
Krueger took less of than his doctor recommended, his wounded
body was still mighty sore. After five bored and restless days at
Laguna Honda Hospital, he'd been discharged that morning on the
solemn promise that he'd "take it easy," a promise Krueger had no
intention of keeping.

That's because Krueger had much to do. Not only was his
mother arriving the next day, but Colin Dubchek's funeral was
scheduled for the upcoming Sunday in New York. The young agent
had given all that could be asked of a man and had done it for
strangers he hardly knew. Remembering him in his last few
moments, when he'd fought an armed opponent with courage that
had terrified Gates' addled mind, Krueger was determined to pay
his last respects. In a world stained by the grime of crooks and
terrorists, ordinary people needed to know about the bravery of
men like Colin Dubchek. There was goodness out there, even if you
couldn't see it in the glare of the TV cameras that only seemed to
follow the bad guys.

A smartly attired waiter placed a cup of tea on Krueger's table.
He was seated at a Japanese eatery in San Francisco, an upmarket
joint with a pricey wine list and unpronounceable entrees, waiting
for his other friends to arrive. He was glad to have this moment of

peace. Freedom from the sterile hospital sure felt good. After all, that place had stifled his mind, smothering his fiery desire to discover the truth of what happened at Gemini. The hospital TV had proven a maddeningly poor source of information, and the online media, even the sources Krueger trusted, had only offered turgid tabloid fodder regarding the fire. Even the cops who had interviewed Krueger with callous indifference to his wounds offered only scraps of data to satiate his hunger for the truth.

"Damn it," Krueger whispered to the world.

Tessa Brandt bounded into the restaurant and sat next to Krueger with uneasy relief etched on her freckled face. This was the first time she had seen him outside of the ward since the fire. Brandt's eyes filled with concern when she saw Krueger struggling to retrieve his drink, so she brought the teacup closer to the edge of the table, smiling nervously as she did so.

Since the destruction of Gemini, Brandt had been striving with a huge conflict; she wanted both to forget, but also remember, the events of the last few weeks. She wanted to forget the violence and the rage . . . and yet she could not let it go until she knew the truth behind the magic they'd witnessed.

"I'm glad you're here," Brandt said and rested her head on Krueger's shoulder.

Dazed, perturbed, and lost amid all the confusion and distrust, Krueger and Brandt had found themselves drawing ever closer to each other. Brandt had even spurned the offer of a plush taxpayer-funded hotel suite downtown, preferring instead to sleep on the ratty couch next to Krueger's room in the hospital. She needed him, needed not only his strength but also his smile and confidence in the future. His very proximity was proof that everything, as they said in Hollywood, would be alright.

Krueger was no less grateful to the German doctor. Her tenderness was unlike anything he'd known in his harsh, war-weary life, and there were moments, tender and utterly unforgettable, when she stared into his vast grey eyes, stared past his deformity, and glimpsed into the naked soul of a man she cherished.

Krueger had realized, during those long nights laying on the starched sheets of his hospital bed, that he was falling in love, and the discovery had drawn little tears that ran joyfully down his bruised face.

Tessa broke Krueger's reverie by fiddling with the lapel on his sport coat, a crisp grey affair she'd bought at the thrift store that morning.

"They teach you how to be a nurse in those history classes of yours?" Krueger asked mockingly as he drank his tea.

"Oh, they teach you things that mere mortals like you would never understand," Tessa replied.

She leaned in and pecked Krueger's cheek, a kiss that suggested she would not be walking out of Krueger's life when she departed for Berlin the following day. The certainty of that fact stirred excitement in his heart, and he beamed as Tessa took his hand and squeezed it.

Sam O'Brian plopped himself down in the chair opposite, carrying a pitcher of beer in each hand and a whiskey chaser in his shirt pocket. The other diners looked at him as if they'd just scraped him off the bottom of their designer shoes.

"You were told Joe could have no alcohol!" Tessa protested.

"I know," O'Brian said. "I got these babies for myself." He meant it. Slurping on the foam, O'Brian sighed, stretched out, and put his hands behind his head like a retiree sitting on his sunny porch on a Sunday afternoon. "You're looking better," he said to Krueger. "That face fuzz is a good look on you."

Krueger tugged at the beard he'd been growing during his long days in the hospital and agreed that it masked his deformity well. "I think I'll keep it," he said.

Brandt nodded her hearty approval.

"Atta boy," O'Brian replied. The contents of half of the first pitcher was already in his belly.

"Easy on that, my good man," said Barnaby Grimm, as he settled his cashmere-clad legs under the table. "I've ordered a bottle of Japanese whiskey. Good stuff, too."

To his amazement, Krueger noticed that the dapper Dr. Grimm sat down with his white cheek and forehead fully exposed. He had not applied the makeup that obscured his illness.

"These last few days have taught me that life is too short to pretend to be anything other than what I really am," Grimm said stiffly, as if sensing Krueger's stares. Krueger, in turn, offered him a small smile and bowed his head, a gesture meant to convey his deepest respect.

Grimm's words conjured a vivid flashback before Brandt's eyes, and she saw once again the terrible tableau in which Colin Dubchek was slaughtered defending his newfound friends from harm. "I know what you mean," she said, shivering.

"So I suppose you're the one who made the reservation here?" O'Brian asked Grimm mockingly, changing the subject with the deft touch of an expert raconteur. He chuckled to himself as he stared at the bright pink handkerchief poking ostentatiously from the pocket of Grimm's Savile Row suit, wondering how on Earth he'd managed to become friends with such a peacock.

"Not I," Grimm answered, examining the menu languidly while O'Brian, wearing an old corduroy jacket with threadbare aplomb, ordered an assortment of fatty dishes.

"It was me," came a sharp, confident voice from the entrance. "And perhaps we should save those type of refreshments till after I've left." The fifth and last of the dinner guests had arrived: Special Agent Lucille Hawtrey of the FBI, newly restored to her position as head of the Counterterrorism Division. The President had made it known, publicly, that he'd personally asked her to remain in her post and had never had any doubts about her ability to bring down the culprits of the bombings. Not one.

Wearing a cream pant suit and matching heels, Hawtrey took her seat and ordered in accentless Japanese without glancing at the menu. She poured a cup of tea and let its steam hang over the table alongside the expectation.

"So is the FBI paying for this grub?" O'Brian asked. "I mean, you were the one who invited us here, after all, and I think I'd need a second mortgage just to sample to seaweed."

"Relax," Hawtrey said, waving her hand dismissively. "Uncle Sam is picking up the tab. It's the least we can do for you."

"So why did you bring us here?" Krueger asked, leaning forward and ignoring the burn in his ribs. "Hopefully you're gonna tell me more than the clowns you sent to interview me at Laguna Honda."

"Believe me, I'd have done the debrief myself, but the President ordered me back to Washington for a report on the situation."

"So what can you tell us?" Grimm asked.

"Preston Gates is missing, presumed still alive," she said curtly. "Of the three dozen bodies found in the blaze, dental records indicate that none of them are him."

"And what about my grandfather?" Krueger asked. His eyes were wide, wondering what new horror would be told.

"His body was found near the center of the blaze. Dental and DNA analysis prove that it's him."

"Dear God," Brandt whispered. She clutched Krueger's hand once more. "So it's true. He was resurrected by Gates and his neo-Nazis."

Grimm and Hawtrey shared a knowing glance. "I'm afraid not," Grimm said as tenderly as he could muster. "It's not that simple."

"Then how the Hell did a man with terminal cancer, a man who died decades ago in Germany, start walking around America planting bombs?" O'Brian shouted, before filling his mouth with a confection of items covered in tempura.

Hawtrey paused before answering as a waiter placed a small plate of raw squid before her. She thanked him and took the soy sauce.

"Look," she said, "you see this squid? It's dead right?" Her companions each nodded in agreement. "So how do you explain this?"

she asked, before dousing the squid in the sauce. Immediately, the flaccid tentacles began to writhe on the plate.

"So that's what health food looks like," O'Brian said. "Glad I'm sticking to the fried stuff."

"I knew the Japanese liked raw fish," Krueger added, "but I thought they at least killed it first. Guess I was wrong to say it was dead."

"Oh, it's quite dead," Hawtrey said, watching as the tentacles rhythmically rose and fell, as if waving to her. "What you are seeing here is an illusion, if you will. The salt in the soy sauce delivers ions into the cells, which in turn causes them to fire. Firing cells then move the squid's tentacles in a way which suggests it is still alive, though it died hours ago."

"Somehow I think this has something to do with my grandfather," Krueger said.

"You are perceptive," she replied. "My point is that science can trick the human mind into seeing life, when in fact, there is nothing but death. Joe, Preston Gates didn't resurrect your grandfather. He just created the illusion that he did so."

"How the Hell did he manage that?" O'Brian asked, suddenly not so interested in his tempura.

"Our engineers are still trying to discover the exact method by which he animated Krueger's dead body, but it appears he ran an electrical current through the dead tissue. In combination with a series of remote-controlled pistons, which he surgically grafted onto the General's joints, it created an utterly believable illusion. It is cutting-edge stuff; even my Ivy League nerd herd can barely comprehend it."

"This sounds like garbage to me," Krueger said. "I saw my grandfather's eyes. I saw life behind him. He saved me!" Krueger smashed his fist on to the table. The glassware jumped, and the maître d'hôtel raised an eyebrow.

"It's not as crazy as you think," Grimm said, taking Krueger's hand and putting a glass of expensive whiskey into it. "A man called

Giovanni Aldini pioneered the theory that electricity could move dead bodies back in nineteenth-century Italy. He made a small fortune selling tickets to his shows where he made dead animals move by applying electric shocks to them."

"And Indonesia provides another example," Hawtrey said, placing a crisp manila folder on the table and pulling the relevant documents.

Piles of food were being placed on the table by anxious waiters, but only Grimm's whiskey, it seemed, was being touched. It alone provided the fortitude the companions needed.

"The Toraja people are a tribe native to the mountains of South Sulawesi, and it seems they have a rather odd tradition regarding their dead relatives. Every few years, they will exhume their dead parents, siblings, even their departed children, and give them a wash and change of clothes before burying them again. But in the seventies, this tradition began to change. Western tourists reported that the dead would walk out of their graves, receive their ghastly make-over, and then return to their resting place. Locals suspected black magic, but western experts suggest these mountain people have found a way to hook generators up to these dead bodies."

"If you keep talking like this, I may have to arrest you on suspicion of drug abuse." O'Brian said, a quip that earned him a swift rebuke from Hawtrey's narrowing eyes.

She flung the huge Irish cop two glossy full-color photographs: high-quality images that suggested they were taken by a large, modern camera. The pictures showed eager-faced Indonesians standing next to their green-fleshed dead relative. Its nose had rotted away leaving a black maw; its eyes had sunk into the back of its skinless, dusty skull.

"Well, I'm about ready for the check," O'Brian said.

"That would explain all the computers Gates kept in the auditorium," Brandt said. "I always wondered what those guys in the white coats were doing when General Krueger made his entrance. They were controlling him like a puppet."

"But this can't be," Krueger replied in a small voice. He remembered the fear, the sorrow in his grandfather's eyes. Those were emotions that no one, not even a prince of Silicon Valley, could manufacture.

"The autopsy report is here," Hawtrey said softly, pushing the stapled pages across the table. "It proves everything O'Brian told you about the impossibility of cryogenic freezing. The ice that formed in your grandfather's body destroyed cells in every organ. His heart, brain, and lungs were all shredded."

Krueger turned away, unable to look at the text.

"But the Cross," Brandt said. "Gates got his hands on the True Cross. Why would he go to such lengths if it was just a charade?"

"On this matter, we are on much surer ground," Grimm said. "We found the Cross in the remains of the Gemini building."

"Destroyed behind all recognition, I suppose," Krueger said sullenly.

Grimm smiled and flashed another photograph. It showed the tall, wooden cross and the titulus hanging above it. It was surrounded by the blackened dreck of Gates' ruined Nazi temple. But the cross itself had been spared the wrath of the flames. It still stood proudly; the text on the titulus was as clear as the day Pilot's minions had carved it.

"A miracle," Brandt said breathlessly.

"Perhaps," said Hawtrey, "or perhaps the centuries spent buried in the damp earth surrounding Hattin left the Cross flame resistant."

"Just like the Vindolana Tablets," Grimm said, stirring his drink with his pinky finger. "Nearly 2,000 wooden writing tablets were discovered buried in 1973 amid the remains of a Roman fort in Northern England. They dated from AD 85 . . . and were preserved perfectly thanks to the layers of mud that had gathered over them. It's not impossible to believe that the Cross's long burial had a preservative effect."

"Well I find it hard to believe a wooden cross withstood a roaring fire thanks to being a little damp," O'Brian retorted.

"It is entirely a matter of faith what you chose to believe," Hawtrey said, and Krueger noticed for the first time that she was wearing a crucifix around her neck, something he hadn't seen her wear before.

"So we are certain that Gates found the True Cross?" Brandt asked.

"According to the expert hands at the California Institute of Technology," Grimm said, "the answer is an emphatic yes. The dendrochronological analysis proves two things: first, that the Cross is made from acacia, exactly the sort of wood the Romans used in their Middle Eastern domains to manufacture crosses. Second: the wood dates back to the first-century, the time when Jesus was crucified on the hill of Golgotha."

"Jesus," Krueger said. He was not cursing.

"And when you consider that the text on the titulus is written in the right languages and in the right order, I strongly suspect that your grandfather's research paid off: we have the True Cross upon which the Son of God was killed. We are still awaiting the results of a microbiological survey of the flora found in the crevices of the wood, but at this point, I suspect they will only confirm what we already know."

A terrible silence fell over the table. It seemed to Krueger that the whole restaurant was growing darker and more silent, until he realized that his very senses were recoiling from the enormity of the discovery.

"It must be sent to Rome," Brandt said in a hard voice.

"That is for our government to decide," Hawtrey replied. "But for what it's worth, I think the Basilica di Santa Croce in Gerusalemme, Rome would be a suitable resting place for this discovery, after our nation's men and women of science have had a further opportunity to investigate it."

"Haven't these last few weeks proven the danger of poking our arrogant, twenty-first century noses into the mysteries of the past?" Krueger demanded, and he saw with amazement that Hawtrey's eyes carried the unmistakable look of mortal dread.

She knew. Oh yes, she knew. But Hawtrey was, Krueger understood, now working on the orders of someone higher up the Federal Government's food chain.

"Okay, slow down, turbo," O'Brian said. He'd ploughed through both his pitchers and discovered, much to his chagrin, that he was not in the least bit drunk. "You're saying grandpa Krueger was a corpse when Gates busted him out of that pod, right? And that he stayed a corpse during the attacks? Your theory is that Mr. Silicon Valley just used him as a puppet?"

O'Brian coughed and loosened his tie. He was attacking the case with the reason and logic that made him such a formidable cop.

"So why did Gates spend a fortune getting himself the True Cross if he knew there was no way to resurrect Krueger? And why does he want the world to know that he had resurrected him in the first place?"

Hawtrey nodded and retrieved her smart phone. She cued up a video and showed it to the rest of the group with a grimace on her face. "This is why," she said. On the screen was Preston Gates. His thick glasses were gone, and his face was a ball of magnetic hatred. He spoke before a long table, an American flag hanging limply behind him. "He released this video the night you were captured," Hawtrey said. "It's already received over a million hits."

Krueger closed his ears to the hatred. He'd heard it before, and the live performance had been no better.

"So what does it matter?" O'Brian asked, waving his hand dismissively. "I can pull up videos of people claiming Elvis is still alive and living in San Juan with Jimmy Hoffa and Marylyn Munroe."

"It matters because Gates has managed to do something that no neo-Nazi leader in America has ever been able to accomplish,"

Hawtrey said. She paused, sighed, and shook her head. "There are 1400 far right groups in this country. Combined, they have several thousand adherents."

"Which could make them the biggest terror threat this country has ever faced," Krueger added. "If someone could unite them."

"And someone has," Brandt muttered. Her stomach revolted in protest when she looked at the sweat-stained ghoul on Hawtrey's phone. She turned her back on the footage with a shudder.

"Exactly," Hawtrey said. "Gates must have spent close to a billion of Dennilson's money on this caper, but to his warped mind, it's all worth it. You should see the junk spewing from neo-Nazi websites in the last few days: these guys truly believe Gates found the True Cross and will use it as a weapon to forge a new Aryan Empire."

"And he abused my grandfather's body because?" Krueger asked.

"Because Gates discovered it had been cryogenically frozen in Germany," Grimm answered. "Using his undoubted talents in mechanical and biological engineering, he used Krueger like a puppet to prove to his ignorant followers that the True Cross had granted him supernatural power. He was like a magician duping his audience."

Hawtrey removed the last of the items in her folder: it was a color photograph taken from a satellite. "These heat signatures," she said, "show militiamen from two neo-Nazi groups in Oregon meeting in the Umatilla National Forest. A month ago, these gangs were fighting each other in biker bars; now they are joining up and declaring themselves loyal followers of Gates.

"It's happening across the country. Montana, Idaho, the Deep South. Gates' giant lie worked: he's united the gangs. He's their new, all-American Fuhrer. And with the money they bring in from drug and gun sales, plus whatever millions he managed to swindle from Gemini, Preston Gates is now the wealthiest and deadliest terror leader we face."

"That's why he wanted us dead," Brandt said, her bright freckled face pained and drawn. "We were the ones who could expose him.

So he tried to kill us in Berlin . . . in Cairo . . . in Israel . . ." Brandt's speech died on her lips. Her jaw loosened in dismay as she recalled the violence unleashed upon her.

Krueger had heard enough. With bruised arms, he rose unsteadily to his feet. "Well," he said, "Gates may think of himself as a Fuhrer, but he's a Fuhrer who's on the run. We'll find him. And when we do, we'll parade him on every TV station in a jumpsuit and expose him as the weedy coward he is."

"Amen to that, brother!" O'Brian roared and joined him on his feet. He raised his glass. "A toast," he said, "to justice, and to those who fight for her."

"To Agent Colin Dubchek," Krueger said solemnly in response. At the mention of his name, each of his companions stood and raised their drinks. They drank in silence, remembering the lives Gates' evil pantomime had claimed.

THERE WAS A SOFT drizzle in the air when Krueger left the restaurant, but he didn't mind it. The water felt refreshing on his skin.

"So what do we tell the press?" Krueger asked as Hawtrey marched to the curb and hailed a cab.

"Whatever it is, it won't be the whole truth," Hawtrey confessed. "The less the American people know about this the better, at least until Gates is in custody. We'll explain how he got his dirty mitts on the True Cross by murdering Dennilson—and how you and your team retrieved it from him. But that's about it. We want the public to think Gates is a violent thug, not a brilliant engineer with the money and the intellect to wage a race war. It'll be better for the country that way. So, we'll probably claim that one of his minions dressed up as Krueger as part of their sick Nazi worship."

Hawtrey looked at Krueger and saw something hot and angry beneath his weariness: it was dismay at the thought his grandfather's name was being tossed around by people who didn't give a damn about his sacrifice or his accomplishment.

"This doesn't mean you aren't free to correct the record regarding General Krueger's actions in World War II," Hawtrey said soothingly, before adding the ominous phrase, "up to a point."

The Special Agent offered her hand to Krueger. After a long moment, Krueger enveloped it with both of his.

"Your grandfather was a fine man," Hawtrey said. "Go and tell the world. You have no need to walk the world in shame."

Krueger chewed on his lip and remained silent.

"Will it work?" Brandt asked. "Hiding the truth?"

Hawtrey's cab pulled up. "It will if people are wise enough to keep quiet," Hawtrey said, piercing Krueger and Brandt with her black gaze. "Are you two wise?"

"You can trust us," Krueger said, opening the door of the yellow Crown Victoria idling in the street.

Smiling, the FBI agent entered the cab. "I hope that you and I will be working together in the future," she said.

"We will," Krueger assured her, "until the day Gates is in handcuffs."

Hawtrey's small feminine mouth curled into a granite-like grimace as she nodded determinedly, and she closed the door. Soon the yellow cab was speeding down the greasy asphalt, taking the agent toward whichever new crisis demanded her expert attention.

O'Brian and Grimm came stumbling out of the restaurant just as Hawtrey's cab disappeared from view. "Damn it," O'Brian said, "I was hoping to split a cab!"

"Fear not, dear boy," Grimm replied, sliding a silver hip flask into the cop's hand. "I have our transport taken care of."

As if summoned by the power of Grimm's thoughts, a sleek limousine crept seductively up to the curb. A suited driver emerged, removed his cap, and opened the side door. All Krueger could see beyond were bright neon lights and a bucket of iced champagne.

"Hey, don't threaten me with a good time!" O'Brian joked before bundling himself into the limo. "You cats joining us?" he shouted from inside, having found himself a nice leather-back seat that he was unwilling to leave.

Brandt looked at Krueger, laughed, and then shook her head. "We are fine, thank you!"

"Suit yaself!" O'Brian said. "You guys did good. Real good. Go celebrate, and we'll meet up again in New York."

"Take care of yourself," Krueger replied, leaning into the limo and seeing his partner stretched out with the hip flash protruding from his mouth. "You're a good cop. We need guys like you, Sammy."

O'Brian smiled and pocketed the flask. He stretched out his hand, and Krueger took it. "It's an honor to serve with you, Detective Krueger," O'Brian said, his eyes dark and steady. They held each other's gaze, the diamond-hard bond of trust between them now utterly unbreakable. "Okay Jeeves!" bellowed O'Brian. "Let's get this spaceship on the road!"

Krueger chuckled and turned to shake Grimm's hand. He found him embracing Brandt with a tear tumbling down his cheek.

"You are . . . extraordinary," Krueger said, fumbling to find the right word to express the depth of amazement and respect he felt for his newfound friend.

"I shall never forget our adventures together," Grimm said, embracing Krueger. "I trust there will be more to come."

"Beware what you wish for," Brandt reminded her friend with a playful punch on his shoulder.

"Oh, I shall be prepared now," Grimm said. "I think I've about had my fill of adventures without purpose. They are, I now realize, thoroughly unsatisfying. Whatever I do next will serve some larger, better cause. Perhaps I'll keep a good watch over those Federal Government dullards meddling with the True Cross. Someone needs to make sure it isn't used in any more mischief."

With Grimm's defiant pledge hanging in the rainy air, he entered the limousine. It sped away into the summer night, toward whatever entertainments Grimm had planned and toward whatever future he wished to build for himself.

And so, at last, only Joe Krueger and Tessa Brandt remained. They stood together, holding hands, not caring for the rain nor the passage of time. Minutes passed, and still they stood, lost amid the revelations and half-revelations, which had at last been explained, safe in the fastness of their mutual affection. The nightmare, clad in the red and black of Nazism, was, for now, receding from view.

As this silence stretched out, a welcome summer wind cast aside the rainclouds above, revealing a velvety indigo sky. Krueger grew conscious of the silence and coughed to banish it.

"So what time is your flight tomorrow?" he asked, and he was answered by a sudden, irrepressible kiss. Brandt wrapped her arms around his chest, unmoored from her reservations, and Krueger was delighted and enlivened by the sudden intimacy.

The moment passed, but the feeling that had brought them so close endured. Smiling, Krueger took Brandt's hand and led her up the street. He didn't know the city; he didn't know where he was going. But if Tessa Brandt was with him, he didn't care.

"So do you believe everything Hawtrey said?" Brandt asked.

"She didn't lie," Krueger answered. "She was on the level."

"That wasn't my question," she reminded him.

Krueger sucked his teeth. The sight of the Cross, the sight of his own dead grandfather bearing down on him, had left Joe Krueger with questions to ponder that went beyond the equations on Hawtrey's crisp lab reports.

"General Krueger was alive, Tessa," Krueger said. "He saved me."

"So Gates used the Cross to breathe new life into him?" Brandt asked.

Krueger shook his head defiantly in response. The Cross was divine, but something hard and resolute within himself knew it was not a divine *weapon.* "No," Krueger said, "I don't think so. But even so, I think something is missing from Hawtrey's clinical analysis."

"Which is?"

Krueger paused and looked at the starlit sky, wondering what, if anything, lay beyond the infinite cosmos he saw above. "The power of the human soul," Krueger answered finally. "There's something inside us that endures, Tessa," he said. "And it endured inside my grandfather. Something lived inside of him—lived long enough to atone for what he did."

Brandt smiled, as if she were hearing poetry. "I hope that's true," she said. "I need something good to hold on to."

"We'll hold onto each other," Krueger answered, gripping Brandt's shoulder.

"My flight leaves early tomorrow!" Brandt giggled as she chewed her lip.

Krueger leaned down and kissed her. "How's about you cancel it?" he asked.

Joe Krueger and Tessa Brandt continued their long walk to nowhere in particular.

"Maybe," Brandt said.